The strength of A[illegible] *her, filled her with a torment she would never escape. . . .*

Buffy clung to him, but only for a moment, while she filtered out the lingering effects of the mirror and grounded herself in the bizarre reality. *Aztec temple. Black jaguar. Lucy and Dem. . . .* She pulled away to scan the cramped, humid chamber.

"Where's Willow?"

Angel lowered his gaze. "There wasn't time—" He lunged to stop her from racing back through the narrow doorway. "You can't go back!"

"I have to!"

"No!" Angel stood firm in the heated indignation of her glare. "You can't do anything to stop Tezcatlipoca if you're a prisoner . . . or dead."

"But . . ." Buffy heaved a resigned sigh. *Angel's right. Too many lives depend on us staying alive and free to fight.*

Willow was on her own.

Buffy the Vampire Slayer™

Child of the Hunt
Return to Chaos
The Gatekeeper Trilogy
  Book 1: Out of the Madhouse
  Book 2: Ghost Roads
  Book 3: Sons of Entropy
Obsidian Fate

The Watcher's Guide: The Official Companion to the Hit Show
The Postcards
The Essential Angel
The Sunnydale High Yearbook

Available from POCKET BOOKS

Buffy the Vampire Slayer young adult books

Buffy the Vampire Slayer (movie tie-in)
The Harvest
Halloween Rain
Coyote Moon
Night of the Living Rerun
The Angel Chronicles, Vol. 1
Blooded
The Angel Chronicles, Vol. 2
The Xander Years, Vol. 1
Visitors
Unnatural Selection
The Angel Chronicles, Vol. 3

Available from ARCHWAY Paperbacks

For orders other than by individual consumers, Pocket Books grants a discount on the purchase of **10 or more** copies of single titles for special markets or premium use. For further details, please write to the Vice President of Special Markets, Pocket Books, 1230 Avenue of the Americas, 9th Floor, New York, NY 10020-1586.

For information on how individual consumers can place orders, please write to Mail Order Department, Simon & Schuster Inc., 100 Front Street, Riverside, NJ 08075.

OBSIDIAN FATE

DIANA G. GALLAGHER

An original novel based on the hit TV series created by Joss Whedon

POCKET BOOKS
New York London Toronto Sydney Tokyo Singapore

This book is a work of fiction. Names, characters, places and incidents are products of the author's imagination or are used fictitiously. Any resemblance to actual events or locales or persons, living or dead, is entirely coincidental.

An *Original* Publication of POCKET BOOKS

POCKET BOOKS, a division of Simon & Schuster Inc.
1230 Avenue of the Americas, New York, NY 10020

ISBN: 0-671-03929-6

First Pocket Books printing September 1999

10 9 8 7 6 5 4 3 2 1

POCKET and colophon are registered trademarks of Simon & Schuster Inc.

Printed in the U.S.A.

For
Betsey and Demaree,
Friends forever.

Prologue

Captain Diego de Garcia groaned. Though his exhausted sleep was undisturbed by the bite of pebbles against his back and the rain pooling under the overhanging rock, it was tormented by the blood storm raging in his dreams. The hundreds of miles that separated him from Hernando Cortez's conquering force could not erase the haunting memories of ritual Aztec murder and brutal Spanish slaughter—or of his own narrow escape from death, beyond the tiered temples and gates of Tenochtitlan on July 1, 1520.

Run!

Sweat beaded on Diego's furrowed brow. His breathing became labored and his legs twitched, as he raced across the primitive causeway away from the Aztec island city and toward the safety of the hills on the distant shore. Even in the throes of nightmare, the tang of salt water and blood stung his nostrils. He ran, pursued by a frenzied horde dressed in the eagle feathers and jaguar pelts of their savage military orders. Around him fleeing Spaniards and native allies fell to wooden spears and knives or were pushed into the lake to drown, weighed down by pockets full of stolen gold. A league ahead, Cortez rode onto solid ground with his sword raised, while a flint knife pierced Diego's thigh—

"Uh!" Diego sat up, shivering and covered in mud. More than a year had passed since Cortez's army had been routed from the Aztec capital. Two weeks later, the Captain General had sent him north with a small exploratory expedition and a cache of native treasure. Yet his dream recollections were not fading with time and distance, but becoming more vivid and intense. A sudden uneasiness gripped him as the night pulsed, darkening by heartbeats. He scowled, refusing to accept the ominous portent of the dream, forcing the lingering images to retreat.

Wiping his nose with a wet sleeve, Diego crawled to the opening of the stone crevasse. The torrential rains of the past several days had stopped, and a sliver of moon shone through a break in the thick cloud cover. Cold and wet, he dragged himself upright on cramped legs to survey the dark encampment. His seven remaining men huddled under a ledge at the base of a gradual incline . . . the other eighteen had been lost to accident and attack on the long and treacherous journey across the desert. They had been neither warm nor dry for a week, nor would they be any time soon, for want of dry tinder. He could do nothing to alleviate their misery but let them rest.

And find a suitable place to hide the treasure so they could rejoin Cortez's army, the only enclave of civilization in this godforsaken land.

Diego cast a quick glance at the burros tethered in a

stand of scrub trees, their tails tucked and their heads lowered in bestial resignation and acceptance of rain and human whim. The packs they had carried more than a thousand miles were piled against a nearby boulder, containing beaded gold and turquoise jewelry, mosaic masks and shields inlaid with silver and precious stones, copper and obsidian idols depicting the bloodthirsty Aztec gods of light and dark hidden beneath layers of cracked leather and woven cloth. The fortune in artifacts entrusted to him would not be shared with the Crown but retrieved by Cortez at a more convenient time, after the vast territory had been tamed. Diego dared neither doubt Cortez's pledge to reward him for this service nor betray his trust. Only a fool would contemplate stealing from that obsessed and invincible champion of Spanish conquest. However, should Cortez fall in battle, Diego would have no misgivings about claiming the riches for himself. No one else would live to reveal the secret hiding place, which he had yet to choose.

Perhaps right here would do. Since they had not encountered any savage hunting bands or villages within the last hundred miles, the treasure would be safe from accidental discovery and theft by curious natives.

Diego nodded, as the cloud cover fragmented and his gaze brushed the moonlit terrain. At the crest of the incline above his men, concentrated streams of water flowed downward, skirting a solitary tower of rock and cutting gouges in the lower slope. The tall rock formation snagged his attention, commanding closer inspection at first light.

Diego shivered and stamped his feet, splattering more mud on his water sodden boots. It was unseasonably cold for mid-August; a fire would have heartened as well as warmed his weary men, but he had no hope of starting one. Everything within range of the camp was soaked, and the stench of damp rot hung heavy in the night air. Suddenly anxious, Diego limped toward the packs. The painful ache in his scarred thigh and the glint of burnished gold would take his mind off the stubborn sense of peril his dream had evoked.

He did not see the plume of smoke rising from one of the leather bags at first. He smelled it: pungent wood char laced with an acrid, metallic taint.

Kneeling before the pack, Diego stared at the gray wisps drifting upward in the wan moonlight. He ignored the vibration in his knees as he slipped a trembling hand under a wet leather flap. Logic deserted him with the hope of finding a charred bit of wood miraculously ignited by a flint left in a copper incense burner, a coal he might nurse into a fire with a handful of moldy packing straw. But there was no heat. His hand touched a cold, smooth surface.

Bewildered and curious, Diego flipped the leather flap back and pulled out a roughly circular, obsidian mirror framed with gold, silver, and turquoise and measuring two hands in diameter. Tendrils of smoke were rising from the inside edge of the frame and swirling within the depths of the black glass, drawing his gaze. Diego felt the ground shudder, but he was powerless to move. Neither his eyes nor his essence could resist the smoking mirror and the images within.

Diego's own bearded reflection looked out at him through the smoky haze. His long, wet, snarled dark hair framed a face lined and scarred by too many years of war and hardship. Narrowed brown eyes betrayed the decay of spirit that had seeped into his bones and aged him far too quickly. His pulse quickened as his face faded out and the swirling smoke irised open to reveal Templo Mayor, the heart of Tenochtitlan and the Aztec culture.

Diego cringed from the certainty that he had been driven mad by festering memories of Spanish massacre and barbaric atrocities. He had raised his sword to slay the helpless tribes that had defied conquest, but tens of thousands of human captives had died under an Aztec knife, sacrificed on altar stones at the pinnacle of the flattened pyramid. As though mocking his revulsion and fear, a river of blood began flowing from the upper sanctuaries and down the two long flights of stone steps. The blue-gray smoke rising from the mirror's outer edge reddened, as the image expanded to display the entire island. A battle raged through the narrow streets, but this was not a madman's hallucination of the retreat he had barely survived a year ago. A full Spanish assault had been launched against the Aztec city.

Or was about to be.

He did not question how he knew the events depicted in the mirror had not yet come to pass. Mesmerized, Diego watched as the brigantines patrolling the salt waters of Lake Texcoco easily capsized and destroyed the native canoes sent to repel them. Three Spanish divisions surged across the causeways to the island, then down the main boulevards toward Tlatelolco Square, forcing the defending Aztec warriors back—until they turned to make a stand. The unfortunate Spanish infantrymen in the front lines were seized and dragged to the temple steps. Diego shuddered but could not tear his gaze away, as the savages cut the soldiers' beating hearts from their chests and impaled their severed, helmeted heads by the temple, a gruesome, though ineffective, warning to the determined Cortez. Outraged by the spectacle, the invading army stormed through the city, a wave of destruction and death. A predatory roar pierced the night as the great temple collapsed into rubble under the fury of the human swarm.

Diego's men stirred, barking disgruntled curses that masked an ominous rumble deep within the earth. Curses became cries of alarm as the ground tremors intensified and the men stumbled to their feet. Fear rousing them from their lethargic dozing, the burros broke their tethers and stampeded up the rise.

Diego could not move or look away from the smoking, obsidian glass. Bound by the power of the mirror, he watched his face superimpose itself over the timeworn ruins of Tenochtitlan and whimpered when his reflected skin split open and peeled back. Muscle and blood dissolved in a swirl of red smoke. Terrified, he stared into the empty eye sockets of his own bleached skull, then into the glittering, golden eyes of a black jaguar.

Then the world exploded, and Captain Diego de Garcia drowned in a sea of mud and rock, a death grip on the mirror and his mouth open in a silent, eternal scream.

Chapter 1

Silence stalked the midnight streets of Sunnydale, pervasive and absolute, chilling the dreams of those who slept, sedating those who walked the moonlit shadows.

Buffy Summers listened, wary and waiting.

A heartbeat thundered.

A breath rasped.

A twig snapped.

Buffy whirled, stake drawn back. The quiet was getting on her nerves and she was ready for a fight, anything to relieve the tension that had her poised on the brink of a systems overload and breakdown.

Sitting cross-legged on the grass, Willow tensed. The petals she had picked off a dead daisy from the grave beside her fell from her hand.

"What?" Xander jumped up from his perch on a crumbling headstone. He swallowed hard and anxiously scanned the cemetery, looking for whatever abomination the Hellmouth had finally unleashed. Nothing moved.

Relaxing her stance, Buffy shrugged. "I thought I heard something."

"I didn't hear anything." An uncertain frown skimmed Willow's pixie face. "Did you, Xander?"

"No. Although, I was keenly aware of my toenails growing." Shoving his hands in his pockets, Xander flopped on the ground by Willow. "I hate to say it, but—I'm bored."

"It has been kind of dull around here lately." Palming her stake, Buffy peered into the night. *Too dull for too long.* The hypnotic effect was as dangerous as the vampires that had gone to ground. It bred complacency and smoothed the edges of vigilant readiness, an erosion of mental conditioning a Slayer could not afford. Buffy resisted the temptation to let down her guard. Her mom would never forgive her if she checked in at the morgue on her way home.

"I wonder why?" Willow drew up her legs, wrapped her arms around them, and rested her chin on her knees.

Buffy didn't know—and that's what bothered her. "It's like someone posted those circle signs all over town. With slashes over twin fangs."

"No vampires allowed?" Willow nodded. "Works for me, only . . . I don't think the vamps would take them seriously."

"Probably not." Shaking her head, Buffy moved closer. If anything threatening lurked nearby, she'd know. All was quiet on the graveyard front.

"Okay, so maybe the local chapter of the Marauding Monsters and Despicable Demons Union went on strike for a shorter work week." Xander's dark eyes narrowed when no one cracked a smile. "It could happen."

Willow laughed softly. "Monsters don't have a union—do they?"

"Do high school girls date werewolves?"

Point to Xander. Buffy absently followed the banter between her two best friends. Her enhanced Slayer senses were attuned to her surroundings, aware of every nuance. A soft rustle in the grass. A shadow shifting on a crypt. The musky scent of composting leaves. Nothing triggered the inexplicable sixth sense that warned a Slayer of imminent danger. Even so, Buffy could not dispel the feeling that something really bad was brewing underneath the calm.

"Only me. As far as I know," Willow said, answering Xander's question. "Except—I don't go out with Oz when he's a werewolf. I, uh—lock him in a cage."

"A technicality," Xander countered.

"Yeah, but—" Willow's pensive frown deepened. "That doesn't explain what's been happening."

"Nothing's been happening. No fresh graves to stake out. No newbie vampires making their debut." Xander shifted nervously. "So why am I worried?"

"Because it's creepy." Willow glanced at Buffy. Her large eyes reflected a genuine innocence, astonishing in an age of millenium madness and social disintegration, unbelievable considering the damning evils she had encountered and survived. Most relinquished their souls without a second thought.

"Definitely creepy." Buffy frowned. "Whenever the demons and walking dead guys take a break, it usually means all hell is gonna break loose. For real."

"Thanks for that reminder, Buff." Xander's sarcastic tone indicated that he was anything but grateful. "I almost forgot that the forces of evil lie low before a full-scale Armageddon assault."

"Maybe that's it and—maybe not," Willow said hopefully. "I mean, I think I'm just getting, you know . . . anxious about M.I.T."

"M.I.T.?" Xander asked without the veneer of a joke to disguise his dismay. "You're going to M.I.T.?"

"You've been accepted?" Buffy tried not to show her distress, either. She had consciously *not* been thinking about life after graduation. It wasn't written in stone that all her friends would leave for distant universities and colleges, opting for higher education and a daily routine that didn't include actively trying to stay alive. They might decide to stay in the most dismal, dangerous town on the face of the Earth. And so what if *that* wish reeked of denial and delusion? It cushioned a reality she couldn't conveniently ignore. As long as evil threatened the world from the Hellmouth in Sunnydale, she wasn't going anywhere.

"Nothing! Uh-uh. No, I—" Catching her lower lip in her teeth, Willow looked from Xander to Buffy and winced. "I, uh—just sent a query letter. That's all. Honest."

"That's all?" Xander sputtered. "We're talking a major mileage differential here, Will. The Massachusetts Institute of Technology isn't just around the corner."

"But I haven't been accepted," Willow protested. "I, uh—haven't even heard back!"

"Like there's any doubt?" Xander scoffed. "Every top university in the country is begging you to sign on the dotted line."

"Except M.I.T.," Willow clarified, pouting.

"Face it, Will. Unless you've been subjected to some irreversible brain drain, there is *no* question." Falling back on his elbows, Xander threw back his head and stared at the sky. "You'll be accepted."

"But that doesn't mean I have—" The rest of Willow's sentence dangled unspoken, when Buffy looked up suddenly.

"Who hit the mute button?" Xander asked.

Buffy held up a hand, silencing further comment while she honed in on the barely perceptible sound she *had* heard this time. Someone was moving through the brush along the fence enclosing the cemetery . . . or something. Whatever it was, it wasn't concerned with stealth. A solid *thud* brought Willow and Xander to their feet.

"Okay." Dusting dry grass off the seat of his pants, Xander whispered, "Did I say bored? I didn't mean bored, I—"

Willow nudged him and hissed at Buffy. "What is it?"

Buffy shrugged, and with a slight shake of her head adjusted her grip on the stake. She wasn't sensing anything that gave her a clue, which was a little disconcerting. Maybe there was nothing to be alarmed about, but that was no reason to toss caution aside. Especially given the recent lull in evil doings in and around town.

Motioning Willow and Xander to advance from the right, Buffy crept forward. Instinctively stepping over the flat stone grave markers hidden in the grass, she silently steered a course around the larger upright headstones, guided by a persistent rustling sound. She moved in, drawn to a park bench bathed in the glow of a nearby streetlight, nervously aware that no inexplicable rush of warning raised the fine hairs on the back of her neck. When she found and confronted the culprit, she realized that nothing in her Slayer experience could have prepared her.

A few seconds later, Xander and Willow paused just beyond the circle of light cast by the street lamp.

"Buffy?" Willow asked tentatively. "What's in there?"

Buffy stared at the captive in the metal trash container. "Well, it's got fangs and it's wearing a black mask."

"What?" Xander gasped. "Some creep turned the Lone Ranger into a vamp?"

"I don't think so, but I'm open to a second opinion." Suppressing a grin, Buffy stepped aside as Xander and Willow cautiously came forward.

"Hey!" Willow jumped when the trapped creature snarled.

"Oh, look. It's a warm fuzzy varmint vamp." Xander snarled back at the frightened raccoon.

Daniel Coltrane parked by a battery-powered camp light sitting on a sawhorse, doused the headlights, and turned off the engine. The motor in his old Dodge Colt hatchback sputtered, clunked, then rumbled before falling silent. Grabbing a flashlight and reference book off the passenger seat, he opened the door to slide out.

"Who's there!"

Through the windshield, Dan saw Lucille Frank at the top of the path leading to the dig site. Shielding her eyes with one hand, she held a camp lantern high with the other. "It's just me, Lucy! Dan Coltrane!"

"Kind of late to be dropping by, isn't it, Dan? Don't you have school tomorrow?"

"Yeah, but I'm the teacher!" Dan stepped out and slammed the car door. Bits of rust and flakes of red paint dislodged from the door panel and floated to the ground. "No one's gonna complain if I fall asleep in class. It'll just reinforce the teenage perception that history really *is* boring."

Lucy's laugh rippled through the stillness. "Well, can't say I'll mind the company. Get your butt on over here. I'll start another pot of coffee."

"Be right there!" As Lucy left for the large tent that served as dig headquarters, Dan reached through the back window of the Colt for his jacket. He had been warm in the heated car, but needed protection against the midnight chill at the archaeological site, especially since he intended to do a bit of digging on his own. If his theory proved correct, he had no intention of letting Lucy's boss, the pompous and much-published university professor Dr. Garret Baine, identify or remove it.

Tucking the book under his arm, Dan snapped on the flashlight to guide him up the path, around equipment, and along the edge of a deep gully. Baine wasn't the only one who'd fly into a rage if he slipped and fell into the dig area, crushing a rusted metal shield or splintering a brittle bone. Lucy would send him packing with no arguments and no hope of return.

The existence of the buried Spanish expedition on the outskirts of Sunnydale had remained the earth's secret for almost five hundred years. A recent extended period of heavy rain had eroded the gorge through a level stretch of terrain at the base of Coyote Rock Hill. Hikers had discovered the protruding tip of a sword scabbard at the bottom of the wash. They had reported the find when they realized the scabbard was belted around a human skeleton. Dr. Baine had immediately been appointed to supervise the excavation.

Dan glanced up the incline on his left. Standing three quarters of the way up the gradual slope, Coyote Rock stood in solitary vigil. The towering rock formation had been spared when a natural disaster, presumed to be a flash flood, had taken the Spanish soldiers by surprise. The sedimentary nature of their tomb had preserved everything that was not subject to deterioration from rot. Baine's crew of university students and Sunnydale Historical Society volunteers like himself had only begun to uncover the artifacts that had lain undisturbed for centuries. Most of them were Spanish in origin—swords, shields, buckles, coins, field kits, and armor. However, despite Lucy's opinion to the contrary, the piece that had attracted his attention that afternoon was not Spanish.

It was Aztec.

And tonight he was going to prove it to her.

Slim, with dark brown eyes and dark hair blunt-cut just below her ears, Lucy Frank had a confident, fiery nature that was in direct opposition to his quiet, easy-going personality. Which was probably why he found her so fascinating. Dan grinned, feeling foolish about his infatuation with a graduate student ten years younger than his thirty-five. But not so foolish he would pass up an opportunity to take her out to dinner, if such an opportunity ever presented itself. So far, none had. Although Lucy hadn't said or done anything to make him think she might be interested beyond their mutual love of the past, she hadn't done anything to discourage his hope for a more personal relationship, either.

A low rumbling sound impacted the primal centers of Dan's brain, jarring him from his thoughts. A jolt of instinctive fear brought him up short. The flashlight beam shimmied in his shaking hand as he targeted the rock shelf that undercut the slope. The light glinted off boulder and brush and a stand of scrub trees where the stone shelf burrowed back into the ground. Nothing stirred—except the tent flap Lucy flipped aside.

"Just because I have all night doesn't mean you *have* to keep me waiting."

Dan's uneasiness dissolved in the warmth of Lucy's impish smile and teasing demeanor. Shrugging off the ominous sound, he ducked into the warm tent and pulled up a folding chair. He set the flashlight and pre-Columbian reference book aside. They had another matter to settle before he confronted Lucy with his incredible theory and findings.

"Okay, I give." Letting the flap fall closed, Lucy picked up two mugs from a metal shelving unit and eased past Dan to the propane camp stove. "What brings you all the way out here in the middle of the night?"

"I suddenly had this uncontrollable craving for a cup of camp coffee." Dan took the mug she held out and inhaled deeply. "Perfect."

"Right." Eyeing him curiously, Lucy swung a long leg over another folding chair and sat with a heavy sigh. "Actually, I don't care why you came, Dan. I'm glad to see you."

"You are?" Dan looked up too quickly, startled by the sincerity in her low, husky voice. Cursing himself for acting like a love-sick teenager, he raised an eyebrow to cover his pleased discomfort.

"Absolutely." Lucy leaned forward, gripping her coffee mug in both hands. "Do you have any idea how boring all-night guard duty is?"

"Let me guess." Dan frowned thoughtfully. Fearing theft and vandalism, Baine had delegated the overnight watch responsibility to Lucy and two undergraduates on a rotating basis. Occasionally, the professor took a turn, but not with any regularity. "It's so tedious you don't mind having coffee with a short, stocky, hopelessly dull guy, huh?"

I didn't just say that. Yes, I did. Inwardly, Dan groaned. He would have rolled his blue eyes if Lucy hadn't been staring directly into them.

"Who said you were dull?" Lucy asked indignantly, not expecting an answer. "I *wish* I had had high school teachers as enthusiastic about their subjects as you are, Dan. My American history teacher, Mr. Chapman? He was so dull he collected cobwebs in his beard during class, time slowed to such a crawl."

"I can't imagine."

"I know." Sitting back, Lucy blew on her steaming coffee. "So what's so important it couldn't wait until tomorrow?"

Dan hesitated, smoothing back his blond hair and shifting into a more serious tone and manner. "For one thing, the History Club field trip is on for this weekend. I'll be here with my students and their gear Friday after school."

"Oh, boy." Lucy sagged and shook her head. "You know how Dr. Baine feels about that. He'll be furious."

"How the good professor feels about it isn't a factor, Lucy—unless he makes trouble. If Baine refuses to cooperate or prevents my kids' from working on the dig, Mayor Wilkens has assured me he'll be replaced."

Lucy sensed he wasn't kidding and just nodded. No one knew the identity of the person or persons funding the excavation, with the exception of Richard Wilkens III. The site was on undeveloped city property, and the mayor had had no trouble convincing the City Council to approve the project, since the expenses wouldn't be coming out of municipal coffers. Consequently, whatever conditions the anonymous benefactor chose to impose were accepted without question. And he, she, or they had chosen to encourage local participation, especially that of Sunnydale's student population.

"Maybe I'd better tell him, Dan. I've had a lot more practice weathering his lordship's tirades."

"You sure you want to go out on that limb?" Dan's concern for Lucy was not unfounded. Baine perceived her—and anyone else with a potential for brilliance—as a threat to his undisputed reputation as the foremost authority on southwestern U.S. and Central and South American cultural anthropology. She was writing her doctoral thesis on pre-Columbian myth and prophecy as they related to the coming of the Conquistadors. Being part of the Coyote Rock dig could be extremely beneficial to her career. Baine, however, could dismiss her at any time—for any reason.

"Not a problem." A sly smile enhanced the sparkle in Lucy's dark eyes. "I'll just hint that if he's removed, I'm the most likely candidate to take charge of the project."

Dan started to laugh, then caught the subtle shift in Lucy's expression. Her jaw clenched and the sparkle in her eyes hardened to a glint. She would, he realized, like nothing better than to supervise the excavation in Baine's place.

"What's the second thing?"

"Hmmm?" Dan drew a momentary blank, then remembered the primary reason for his midnight visit. He picked up the reference book, flipped it open to a bookmarked page, and held it out to her. "I found something I think will interest you."

Lucy frowned, puzzled by the photo of a beaded cloak. "This was probably worn by someone in the

Aztec aristocracy, but I don't understand the significance."

Dan pointed to a pattern in the center of the cloak, a black circle framed in turquoise and gold. "I think that's a representation of Tezcatlipoca's smoking mirror. Look familiar?"

"I don't recognize—" Lucy's head snapped up. "You don't think—"

"That the mirror is buried roughly a hundred feet from where we're sitting?" Dan nodded. "And if I'm right, it's got to be buried again. Some place where it will *never* be found."

Lucy stared at him as though he'd completely lost his mind. "No way. Dr. Baine knows we've found something unusual. He won't stand by doing nothing if it suddenly turns up missing."

"I think preserving the world as we know it is a little more important than the potential repercussions, don't you?"

"Come on, Dan!" Lucy laughed. "Tezcatlipoca's smoking mirror is a myth! And even if it isn't, there's no chance it's *that* artifact out there. We're fifteen hundred miles north of any Aztec Empire territory—"

A clatter of rocks cascading down the nearby slope aborted Lucy's argument. Hushing Dan with a finger to her lips, she gave the book back, stood, and picked up the camp lantern.

"Where are you going?" Dan hissed as Lucy moved by him toward the opening in the tent.

"It's probably nothing, but I've got to check it out. Don't worry. I'm loaded with mace." Lucy patted a small aerosol spray can stuffed in the back pocket of her jeans.

"I'm coming with you." Dan picked up his flashlight.

Lucy hesitated, then shrugged. "You take the front. I'll circle around back. Can't hurt to be cautious, I guess." Then she disappeared into the night.

Dan paused to grab a trowel off the metal shelves and ducked out after her with an expanded agenda. Sunnydale at night was not midnight-stroller-friendly. People had mysteriously vanished or died at an alarming rate, a fact that didn't seem to bother the local police and residents of the town as much as it did him. He wasn't worried about the History Club camp-out that weekend. He and four Historical Society members would be supervising the students at night, and there was safety in numbers. However, although it was probably the rain-soaked, settling ground or a prowling coyote that had dislodged the rocks, he wanted to be on hand should teenaged vandals or someone with more malicious intent be on the property tonight.

Secondly, it had become clear during Lucy's argument that he couldn't ask her to help dispose of the artifact. Even if she believed him and was willing, her reputation and career aspirations would be ruined with a felony accusation on her record. He was prepared to risk his job and imprisonment for grand larceny to insure that the obsidian mirror of Aztec legend was lost forever.

A quick scan of the area between the tent and his car revealed nothing usual. Behind the tent, Dan could see the glow from Lucy's lantern. She was moving at an unhurried pace in a systematic patrol pattern and obviously didn't sense any danger. Still, he held his breath when the light disappeared behind the large water tank that stood to one side behind the tent, and breathed easier when it emerged again. Satisfied that Lucy was safe and the site secure, Dan headed toward the gully.

The crevasse carved by floodwaters rushing through the original shallow wash measured six to ten feet across, from three to ten feet deep and ran for several hundred yards along the base of the slope. The excavation had been confined to the area in front of the protruding rock shelf, where skeletal remains and equipment seemed concentrated. The golden edge of the unique artifact had been uncovered a short distance from the initial find.

Scrambling down a short metal ladder, Dan quickly made his way over the drying mud with the flashlight beam aimed low. He had to remove and hide the mirror before Lucy wondered where he had gone. He expected her to tell Baine and the police of his intentions when the theft was discovered tomorrow, to prove her innocence—and because she might feel betrayed. He just didn't want anything to interfere right now. Besides, his suspicions might very well be wrong, and it would be tragic to spoil his slim chances of a dinner date for nothing.

When Dan had counted eighteen paces, he shined the flashlight on the mud wall to his right and quickly found the edge of the gold object. He carefully dug a hole in the opposite bank, shoved the end of the flashlight inside and adjusted the beam to light the work area. Oddly, more of the object was exposed than he remembered from when they had shut down the dig at dusk. Only a crescent of black glass was visible below the etched gold frame with inlaid turquoise, but it was enough to confirm his theory. The object was identical—down to the last beaded detail—to the image in the book.

Tezcatlipoca's smoking mirror.

"Dan! Where are you?"

Thrilled and anxious, Dan ignored Lucy's call and brushed more of the dirt away with his fingers. He started when a large chunk of dried mud fell off and the loosened sediment gave way beneath the mirror. Reacting on reflex, he squatted with his hands out to catch the obsidian-and-gold treasure, but it didn't fall. It dangled, clutched in the death grip of a white, skeletal hand.

Sitting down, Dan struggled to catch his breath and calm his pounding heart. His pulse was still racing when he heard a low, predatory growl above him. On the edge of the gully, silhouetted in moonlight, a black jaguar with glittering gold eyes stared back at him.

Dan Coltrane's terrified shriek froze in his throat and the mud wall collapsed as the huge cat sprang.

Chapter 2

Buffy awakened with a distinct uneasiness, the lingering residue of the uneventful night. Sunnydale, however, was living up to its name in the early hours of this Wednesday morning.

At least on the surface.

Outside her bedroom window, the sun shone in a cloudless sky. A robin chirped as it settled onto a nest shaded by a canopy of emerald green. The leaves whispered in a light breeze that promised to take the edge off the heat later in the day. A dog barked. At the corner bus stop, elementary school kids laughed at an old joke making the rounds of yet another generation. Telephones rang and car motors hummed as moms and dads went about their daily business, unaware that daylight only obscured the town's dark and evil heart.

The Hellmouth.

Cancel that! It was a gorgeous day and Buffy opted to spend it in blissful oblivion like almost everyone else in Sunnydale. Grabbing her books and bag, she bounded down the stairs and into the kitchen. "Good morning, Mom." Emphasis on the good.

Joyce Summers looked up from her newspaper and coffee with a bewildered frown. "Is it?"

"In my line of work, *every* morning is a good one." Buffy smiled as she perched on the other stool. The aroma of buttered toast with raspberry jam and freshly brewed coffee enhanced the illusion that her life was a five on a one-to-ten scale of teenage normal.

Already dressed for the gallery in pleated slacks and a tailored blouse, Joyce smiled back, sadly. A permanent record of her constant worry was written in tiny creases around her eyes and punctuated by a slight twitch in her tightened jaw. In the Summers's household, breakfast meant Buffy had survived another night as the Slayer, the world's first and foremost line of defense against the vampires and miscellaneous demons that staked their claim on Sunnydale at night.

Until she staked them, which she so didn't want to talk about right now. Apparently, her mother didn't want to spoil a perfectly good morning discussing her dangerous duties as the Chosen One either.

"Are you hungry?" Joyce asked.

Buffy shook her head. "If I'm not totally famished at lunch, I can't swallow the cafeteria's featured gunk of the day. Is there any O.J.?"

"I think so." Waving Buffy to stay put, Joyce took a glass from the cupboard and pulled a juice carton from the refrigerator. "I'm way behind schedule arranging things for Juan's show this weekend, so I might be late getting home."

"Juan—he's that hot new Mexican artist you've been babbling about for a month, right?"

"Right. Juan Hernandez." The tension in Joyce's face

eased when she smiled, pleased that Buffy hadn't completely spaced on the event that was so crucial to the gallery's success. Her eyes sparkled as she handed Buffy the glass. "*Definitely* hot and *totally* unknown."

"That hot, huh? As in artistic or romantic?"

"Strictly artistic." Joyce turned away.

"Uh-huh. Well, he won't be unknown after this weekend." Buffy had seen slides of the young man's work and knew he was a find. Juan's attention to detail, combined with a vibrant primitive style, infused excitement and drama into his paintings of life in ancient Mexico.

"I certainly hope not!" Joyce laughed as she rummaged through her bag for her car keys. "This show is costing a bundle, but if—" She hesitated, then charged into troubled territory in spite of her second thoughts. "If Juan's work takes off like I think it will, paying for college won't be a problem."

Buffy stiffened. The subject of her future, and college in particular, had become another source of contention after she received her S.A.T. test results. Her scores had been high, Himalayan compared to everyone's expectations, including her own. However, being thrust into the ranks of the brainy elite had just complicated everything.

"Have you, uh, sent out any query letters yet?" Joyce asked, cautiously hopeful.

"Not yet." Buffy's high spirits plummeted. She had thought about it, had flipped through the college catalogs her mom had gotten for her. Even Giles, her so annoyingly intense, duty-above-all Watcher, had encouraged her. But the facts, like her predetermined destiny, couldn't be ignored or changed. College and a career just didn't factor into the average life expectancy of Slayers throughout history, which was short. As in pushing the survival envelope—especially since she had already died once.

Which had created a major glitch in the scheme of Slayer succession.

Kendra had assumed the duty the instant Buffy had died; but her call had not been cancelled just because Buffy had had the unprecedented audacity to come back to life. So there had been two Slayers—until the insane lady vamp, Drusilla, killed Kendra.

And left Buffy to carry the torch of entrenched Slayer tradition in spite of her own independent attitude and typical teen approach.

Consequently, higher education seemed pointless. Unfortunately, her mother didn't get the point.

"Well, if you need help, let me know. I'm not trying to push you," Joyce added quickly. "It's just that—"

"What?" Bristling, Buffy met her mother's concerned gaze with a challenging stare.

Sighing, Joyce fisted her keys and headed out the door. "Even Slayers need day jobs."

Xander looked at his watch, scanned the Sunnydale High campus, and slid deeper into brooding mode. Make that fuming-heavily-spiked-with-irritation-and-anxiety mode. Okay, so that wasn't the ever-witty, always-on Xander everyone expected to take the sting out of harsh reality with a sarcastic quip here and a joke there. But what the hell! Even the stand-up pros had bad days. Time to take five for a little depressed self-indulgence.

Cordelia was notably absent, as in not returning his calls last night as usual and being nowhere to be seen this morning.

If the evil element in Sunnydale hadn't been on vacation the past week or so, he'd be worried. Truth was, the town's underground contingent—literally, guys who unlive in graves and other equally dark and disgusting places—was as notably absent as Cordy. He filed his anxiety about *that* under "not a problem 'til sundown," which brought him back to the number-one problem of the day.

Was Cordy late or still avoiding him?

Yesterday on her way off campus, she had definitely said she'd see him before school today. Why, he dared not imagine. Could be good. Most likely wasn't. Then again . . . Xander glanced at his watch. Ten minutes to the bell. So where was she? He could deal with late, even if the always-punctual Cordelia had an excuse so lame it limped, but he so didn't want to address an avoiding issue. Avoiding could only mean that she didn't even care enough to verbally abuse him anymore. He didn't expect her to get over a stolen kiss with Willow and almost dying because of it after a few miserable months. Still, insulting him meant talking to him, and where there was talking, there was hope. Which proved that a guy with questionable cool status could justify just about anything.

"Hi, Xander." Willow's smile faded as she bounced to a halt in front of him. "Are you mad or . . . just practicing your beware-I'm-bad look? Not that it's any of my business, of course . . . unless you're mad at me. Are you? Mad at me?"

Xander glanced at Willow's wide, worried eyes and smiled. She was only a fledgling witch, but she had the perky spell nailed and the charm was irresistible. Warning!

"Mad at you?" Xander slid off the wall and looked

away before his heart and hormones jumped directly to critical mass and total meltdown of his love-life—again. Fall back. Regroup. Lock and load. Xander turned and fired off a snappy Harris comeback in self-defense. "Not unless you whipped up a Cordy repellent spell you forgot to mention."

"Spell? On you?" Willow's eyes got impossibly wider. "No. No spell. Uh-uh." She shook her head emphathically, then paused, puzzled. "Why?"

"You look like I feel, Xander." Buffy walked up behind Willow. "Somewhere between totally bummed and why bother."

Xander smiled tightly. Buffy looked way too alluring in that short black skirt and snug green top with those provocatively thin straps. And he didn't mean dangerous in the Slayer sense. Fortunately, he had deliberately cultivated an immunity to Buffy-lust and had settled for appreciative affection and admiration.

"That good, huh?" Xander tore his eyes away from the thin straps. Since Buffy had an annoying knack for keeping them firmly on her shoulders, idle ogling was a futile exercise. He had more than enough female-related problems on his plate at the moment. Speaking of which—

"Well—" Willow brightened with relief as she followed Xander's gaze toward the school building. Cordelia rushed out the main entrance, waving a paper and grinning broadly. "It looks like Cordelia's in a good mood today."

"I'm in a good mood," Oz quipped as he joined the circle of Sunnydale High's Most Unwanted.

Xander tensed as Cordy paused to compose herself. Cordelia Chase was the only exception to the freaky, weird loser reputation that separated the Slayer and

Slayerettes from the mainstream of student society. Which wasn't necessarily a bad thing. However, whatever had made Cordy so happy she had momentarily forgotten to *act* like she was too above it all to care, he was sure it couldn't bode well for him.

"You're always in a good mood, Oz," Willow said. "Almost always anyway."

"What's your secret, Oz?" Buffy asked.

Good question. Feigning indifference when Cordy resumed walking, Xander focused on Oz. Like Buffy, who had been born programmed to battle vampires and whatever other nasty demons the Hellmouth deposited on Sunnydale's doorstep, Oz had the unenviable distinction of being a werewolf. And there was nothing either one of them could do but accept their extraordinary fates.

"I play in a band." Oz shrugged. "And I don't sweat the small stuff."

"Or the big stuff, either," Xander said. "Like graduating, *really* bad hair three nights a month, and rabies shots."

"Who's got rabies?" Cordelia stopped abruptly.

"Oz doesn't. I mean . . . nobody." Willow's voice shook slightly, as it always did when she was nervous.

Oz held up his hands, palms out. "No. I'm clean."

"Good." Cordy eyed Oz narrowly. "Because I don't want anybody's problems spoiling my incredible news."

Xander charged through the opening. "Which is obviously not that you woke up with the realization that you are not the center of the universe."

"Read this." Cordelia shoved the paper into Xander's hand. Her smile was chilling.

"What is it, Cordy?" Willow craned her neck to see.

Forgetting herself again, Cordy jiggled with excitement. "It's—"

"An interview at *Stanford?*" Xander interrupted, appalled. "You got an interview at *Stanford?*"

"Whoa!" Willow rocked back on her heels, suitably impressed. "I still haven't heard back from M.I.T."

"Stanford is good." Oz nodded, not quite as impressed as Willow, then pointedly drew her gaze. "M.I.T. is in Massachusetts."

"Oh. Well, yeah . . . but I haven't decided to actually *go* to M.I.T. I just, you know, wanted to see if I could get in . . . if I wanted to." Willow wilted under Oz's alarmed scrutiny. "But then . . . I've also given serious thought to being a Dingoes groupie for a while, too."

"There you go." Oz smiled.

Buffy frowned pensively.

"Stanford?" Xander stared at the university letterhead. The Hellmouth would start spewing out cute cartoon characters before he'd be admitted to that illustrious institution of higher learning. Or any institution of higher learning. "This is why you wanted to see me? To rub it in?"

"Of course. And don't act so surprised because Stanford wants to talk to me, Xander." Cordelia snatched the letter back before his closing fist crumpled it. "Although I don't go around advertising it, I have excellent grades. Not to mention S.A.T. scores that were through the roof."

"Buffy scored higher." Oz's deadpan expression didn't change when Cordy smugly parried that observation without batting a big green eye.

"*And* a wide range of extracurricular credits that *don't* include monster mashing and survival skills." Cordy folded the letter and slipped it into her purse.

Xander winced as the insensitive slings and arrows struck their intended target, and Buffy shifted uncomfortably. There were times, like right this second, when hanging out with Cordy made him want to crawl into a hole. And he would have, except in Sunnydale chances were better than even that the holes were not occupied by harmless little fluffy furry things.

Buffy quickly excused herself. "I'll catch you all later, okay? I have to see Giles about . . . something."

"Wait. I'll go with you." Xander reached for his books. He needed a few minutes away to digest the implications of Cordelia's Stanford interview and to devise a strategy for dealing with it that didn't involve saying or doing something he'd regret. But he wouldn't *know* what he'd regret until he could figure out how he really felt about life with or without Cordelia Chase around to remind him that he was a reprehensible jerk. With no cool.

Willow glanced at Buffy anxiously. "Did something happen after Xander and I left last night?"

"Boy, I hope not!" Cordy started. "It's been so quiet so long around here, I've totally readjusted to a non-life-threatening lifestyle."

"Relax, Cordelia. Rescuing a raccoon from a trash can was the only adrenaline rush of the evening." Buffy apologized to Xander with large hazel eyes he would have happily drowned himself in a few months ago. "It's, uh—Slayer stuff, Xander. Private . . . you know?"

"No problem. I can do two rejections in less than five minutes without permanent trauma."

"Later." Shaking her head, Buffy walked away.

"Something's bothering her," Oz said.

"Yeah," Willow agreed. "She was kind of quiet, huh?"

"No kidding." Xander frowned.

"Maybe she's suffering from Slayer withdrawal." Cordy huffed indignantly when everyone turned to stare. "What? The vamps haven't exactly been coming out of the woodwork begging to be turned into dust bunnies lately."

Xander's frown deepened. "You think?"

Buffy trudged toward the library—a.k.a. the Office of Demon Discovery and Dispatch. Since she had left the Slayerettes outside, no one would be in the hallowed halls but Rupert Giles, librarian, historian, and keeper of the Watch—watching her and taking notes. One of his not-so-thrilling duties was to chronicle her life for future reference—Watcher eyes only. She shuddered. Knowing her ultimate destiny lay in the pages of a musty old book gave her the creeps.

Shelved but not forgotten.

Shaking off that abysmal thought, Buffy slipped through the library door. Destiny of a more immediate nature was the designated topic of the day.

As expected, no students wandered the aisles looking for a reference or something interesting to read. No one ever questioned the library's lack of activity, which was a definite plus. The Slayer and company needed privacy and access to Giles's extensive collection of rare volumes, most of which would be banned and condemned to the bonfire at other schools—almost had been at Sunnydale High thanks to her mom, who'd fallen under a demon's influence and become delusional. She had recovered, fortunately, with regrets.

At the moment, Buffy's trusted adviser was sitting at the center table with his back to her, so engrossed in one of his ancient tomes that he didn't realize anyone had entered.

She hesitated just inside the door, overwhelmed by a surge of fondness that she didn't want him to see. A façade of stubborn denial and indifference was all that stood between her and a more grueling schedule of training and patrolling than she already had. Not that Giles had it easy. Aside from being born into a family of Watchers and given no choice in his career path either, he had had to improvise and adjust his no-nonsense British approach considerably since being assigned to her. Unlike Kendra and Faith, who had both lived to slay—Kendra from a profound sense of duty and Faith because she liked offing vamps—Buffy refused to totally relinquish her life as an ordinary, confused, and tortured teenager, which compounded Giles's difficult task of keeping her functional and alive.

"Is there something on your mind, Buffy?" Turning in his chair, Giles impaled her with his probing gaze.

Although startled, Buffy didn't flinch. "Eyes in the back of your head, Giles? You've been holding out on me." Shifting her bag to her shoulder, she sauntered to the table and pulled up a chair. "Although I suspected."

"A sixth sense." Giles removed his glasses and rubbed his eyes. "Quite necessary when one must be ever aware of potential danger lurking behind one's back."

"I wasn't lurking."

"Yes, well—" Replacing the glasses, Giles resumed his intense scrutiny. "But you are troubled."

"Me? Troubled?" Buffy scoffed with a short laugh. "Hardly. It's a beautiful day and I'm still breathing. What more could the Chosen One ask for?"

"Very well, then." Giles sighed wearily, then glanced at the time. "Class starts in five minutes."

Buffy blinked. Giles knew she used flippancy to mask uncertainty, to make her feel less vulnerable to things beyond her control. So why wasn't he needling her to spit it out as usual? Crushed by the abrupt dismissal, she didn't move.

"You were saying?" Giles didn't look up, daring her to try his patience. Which, she noted, seemed to be at a lower ebb than normal today.

Buffy surrendered without a fight, matching his sigh and adding a dejected slump. How to begin? Dread momentarily rendered her mute.

Prompted by her silence, Giles leaned forward. "Did you encounter any vampires on patrol last night?"

"No. Only a twenty-pound creature with a black mask, sharp teeth, and claws." Giles squinted, puzzled, and Buffy quickly qualified the remark. "A raccoon I freed from a trash can. Not that it was particularly grateful."

"I see. . . ." Giles sat back, the librarian's version of the Buffy slump. Rather than dispel his concern, her report made his worry quotient shoot up a few degrees. "It's been—what? Six nights now with no sign of a vampire?"

"Seven." Resting her chin on her clasped hands, Buffy glanced at him hopefully. "I don't suppose that means the Hellmouth closed up shop and the vamps left town for darker pastures."

"I hardly think so." Giles rose and began pacing. "To be honest, I find the absence of attacks unsettling in the extreme."

"Ditto that. Makes me wonder what's simmering on the back burner, you know? Like something totally massive and *really* ugly is in the works."

"Yes, quite. My thoughts exactly." Giles waved at the

dusty book lying open on the table as he passed. "I've been reading up on other instances of prolonged, reduced activity. Hoping for some insight on what to expect, I suppose."

"Find anything?"

"Nothing relevant." Giles paused, then turned abruptly. "Is that what's bothering you, then? Are you anticipating something more ghastly than normal?"

Buffy smiled, amused because what they considered "normal" in Sunnydale was beyond the scope of imagined horror anywhere else. Compared to demons like the Judge, who could turn humans into char with his touch, and Acathla, who had sucked Angel into hell, the ordinary, run-of-the-mill vampire wasn't much of a threat. Not to her anyway. Still, ghastlier demonic dangers were not on her list of things to worry about today.

"You could say that. Mom brought up the college thing again this morning."

"Did she?" Giles exhaled slowly, crossed his arms and stared at the floor. "Yes, well—the college thing." He hesitated, then looked up cautiously. "You're aware of my feelings on that subject."

Buffy nodded. "Not a secret. You want me to go. And I've been thinking about it. Seriously thinking about it."

Giles perked up. She could tell by the raised eyebrow. "It's just that—"

"Yes?" Giles took a tentative step toward her.

"Okay. So let's say I actually get into a college. I don't have a clue what I want to do with my life . . . assuming I still have one when the time comes."

"Let's assume that, yes." Nodding, Giles sat back down. "I do understand the problem, Buffy. Since you're the Slayer, choosing an appropriate career is not a simple matter, is it?"

"No. For one thing, I can't work the graveyard shift." Buffy held up a hand. "Strike that. Seriously . . . any suggestions?"

"Well, actually . . . I have given this some thought." Pulling his chair closer, Giles cleared his throat. "There, uh—are courses of study that could be quite beneficial to a Slayer."

"Oh, right. There's Stake Sharpening One-Oh-One and—"

"Buffy!" Giles whipped off his glasses to glare. "Forgive the pun, but your life *is* at stake here. And, as you so appropriately pointed out, what to do about your future will hardly be an issue if you're dead."

"Okay. I'm sorry." Buffy took a deep breath. "I'm thinking seriously now. Really."

"I do hope so." Calming down, Giles continued more aggressively. "I would recommend liberal arts with a major in history—"

"I get D's in history!"

Giles ignored her. "—augmented by courses in cultural anthropology and archaeology, perhaps. As you know, most Slayers do not have the kind of research resources and personnel that have contributed to your success and, if I might add, your continued existence. I'll be here for you, of course, but your friends will be getting on with their own lives."

"You have an incredible knack of making people with problems feel worse, Giles." Annoyed, Buffy pouted. But he was right—She couldn't and didn't expect her friends to sacrifice their futures for her sake. Being a Slayerette left a lot to be desired as a hobby. "Guess I'll have to learn to use a computer."

"That would be helpful, since I have no intention of dabbling in the technological." Giles smiled, breaking the tension.

"History, huh?" Buffy winced, then shrugged. "Okay. *If* I get accepted somewhere, which is doubtful considering my grades and transcript. I mean, let's face it. Pyrotechnics, inciting students to riot, and creating general mayhem aren't exactly acceptable extracurricular activities."

"Well, no . . . I suppose not." Giles frowned, thoughtfully. "You still have time to remedy that, though. You could join one of the school's clubs. The History Club, for instance."

"Insert knife and twist."

Giles pressed. "Mr. Coltrane is the faculty adviser, I believe."

"This is where I run into the proverbial brick wall. I had him for American History last year and barely passed. I don't think he likes me much."

"I've had some fascinating discussions with Mr. Coltrane in the faculty lounge," Giles said wistfully. "He's quite knowledgeable about American myth and archaeology. I'll ask him to overlook your past performance as a personal favor—"

"I'm afraid Mr. Coltrane is no longer with us." Principal Snyder barged through the door.

Buffy stiffened. Dealing with the short, scrawny, balding dictator of Sunnydale High rated lower than demon demolition on her list of favorite things to do.

"I beg your pardon?" Stunned, Giles snapped his head around. "Is he—"

"Dead? Hardly." Snyder halted by the table and clasped his hands behind his back. "He stole a valuable artifact from that archaeological dig over by Coyote Rock and disappeared."

"So much for the History Club," Buffy quipped.

Mr. Snyder turned his beady gaze on her. "The History Club will be meeting as usual this afternoon. So will Coltrane's classes. Skipping is not an option. In case anyone asks."

Still dazed, Giles shook his head slightly. "I simply do not believe Daniel Coltrane would do anything—"

The bell rang.

"You're late for first period, Summers," Snyder growled.

"I'm out of here." Buffy grabbed her books and ran.

Snyder waited until Buffy was out the door before sitting down to relate the circumstances surrounding the history teacher's disappearance.

"Lucy Frank called this morning to tell me Coltrane wouldn't be coming in. He was at the dig last night and she left him alone for a few minutes to patrol the grounds. She gets back and he's gone. And so is the artifact the excavation team uncovered yesterday afternoon. Not hard to figure out what happened, is it? There's a huge black market demand for rare antiquities."

As he listened, Giles curbed his desire to grab the smug, little man by the lapels. He had done so once before, while trying to convince the principal to readmit Buffy back into school. The experience had given him a decided rush, as his young associates so aptly put it. At the moment, however, the need for additional information made prudence more advisable.

"I always knew Coltrane couldn't be trusted." Snyder snorted. "He actually *likes* teenagers."

"Yes, well . . . some of us do." Giles didn't give Snyder an opportunity to comment. "There is one thing I find rather curious about this unfortunate incident."

"What's that?" The glint of perpetual suspicion in Snyder's close-set eyes flared brighter.

"This artifact Mr. Coltrane is alleged to have stolen—"

"Artifact Mr. Coltrane *stole,*" Snyder rudely interjected.

Giles looked at him askance. "Am I mistaken or does the United States have a justice system based on a suspect being innocent until proven guilty?"

"What about the artifact?" Snyder prodded impatiently.

"Yes, the artifact." Giles paused, annoyed at having allowed himself to be sidetracked. "What was it?"

"I don't know," Snyder whined, his expression pained. "Some Aztec thing. Does it matter?"

"Perhaps not," Giles said evenly. "Aztec, you say? Odd."

"Why?" Snyder asked warily.

"The Aztec Empire was located in central Mexico. I'm just curious as to how an Aztec artifact wound up so far north."

Giles had a plausible theory and was only hoping to coax more details about the theft from Snyder. The archaeological site appeared to be the ruins of a Spanish encampment from the period of Cortez's initial explorations in the New World, almost five hundred years ago. He had been meaning to stop by and have a look, but hadn't found the time. Snyder's reasoning, if not his tone and attitude, agreed with his hypothesis.

"The Spaniards probably stole it from the Aztecs. Now, if you don't mind—" Snyder rose and adjusted his jacket. "I've got teachers to harass and students to intimidate."

"Yes, of course. Whatever." Focused on the scant information the principal had provided, Giles had already dismissed the man. Rising, he pulled a pen from his pocket and turned toward his office.

"Oh, and by the way—"

Giles glanced over his shoulder.

"You're the new faculty adviser for the History Club until I hire a permanent replacement for Coltrane." With a curt wave, Snyder headed for the door.

"Me? But I—"

Snyder continued without breaking stride or looking back. "The meeting is in Coltrane's classroom at three-thirty. Don't be late. Lucy Frank is coming over to brief you on the overnight field trip to the Coyote Rock dig this weekend."

"Overnight? This weekend? But—" Giles stared as the door swung closed and Snyder disappeared down the hall. Apparently, the issue was closed to debate.

Giles saw no way out of the unexpected and inconvenient assignment. He was a school employee and subject to Snyder's reasonable demands. However, after a moment's reflection, he realized there were positive aspects that made the situation tolerable. Buffy wouldn't have any difficulty joining the History Club, and he would have all weekend to poke about the Spanish ruins.

Sighing, Giles found a notebook and jotted down the scant information he had regarding the missing Aztec artifact and Dan Coltrane's mysterious vanishing act.

Chapter 3

Professor Garret Baine glared at his assistant. The archaeological site had been violated on Lucy Frank's watch, and the impudent young woman had not uttered one word of apology or remorse since he had arrived an hour earlier. She didn't seem to care that Dan Coltrane had desecrated the dig and absconded with a priceless Aztec artifact!

Baine's chest constricted with a sharp pain. Heeding the warning sign, he took a deep breath. His traitorous heart was a damned nuisance, more so because he was only fifty-two and looked robust. His determination to conceal his cardiac condition aside, having an attack in the midst of this crisis would not help recover the mirror or bring Coltrane to justice. And now that he had vented his initial explosive outrage, the situation, his health, and his professional purposes would be better served by dignified restraint.

"I should fire you this instant. For incompetence, insolence—"

"The police are here." Lucy leaned forward on the folding chair and motioned toward the outside. Her tone bore no hint of apprehension. "I imagine they'll want to talk to me."

"No doubt," Baine said coldly. "We'll finish this discussion later." Turning his back on her, he left the tent.

A Sunnydale Police Department squad car and an unmarked black car had parked in the designated area well beyond the flat terrain the gully cut through. The half-dozen Historical Society workers munching doughnuts and drinking coffee at a table outside the tent fell silent as all heads turned to watch. Ordinarily, Baine would have had them busily dusting and picking in their assigned areas by now. Today, the excavation was a crime scene and out of bounds until the police finished their investigation.

Baine paused at the far end of the wash and waited as two uniformed officers and a thin detective in an ill-fitting brown suit walked up the path. He did not acknowledge Lucy when she came up beside him.

"Dr. Baine?" The young man in the suit extended his hand. The officers stopped a few feet behind him, their critical gazes surveying the dig area. "Detective Dwayne Thomas, sir."

Baine introduced himself and Lucy, then led the detective to the rim of the gully overlooking the area Coltrane had ripped apart. Thomas started at the sight of the skeletal arm protruding from the wall of the trench. A mound of dirt had fallen on the floor below it, evidence of Coltrane's greed and unforgivable indifference to the delicacy of proper excavation.

"We haven't touched anything, Detective, although there's no question about who's responsible for this sacrilege." Baine cast an accusatory glance at Lucy, who matched it with an equally cold, unflustered stare.

The hostile undercurrent in the exchange did not escape Thomas. "You know who did this?"

"Yes," Baine answered without hesitation. "Dan Coltrane, a teacher at Sunnydale High. He told Lucy he was going to steal the artifact."

Surprised, Thomas pulled a notebook and pen from his pocket. "Care to elaborate, Ms. Frank?"

Baine paid only passing attention as Lucy explained what had transpired the night before. His thoughts and gaze were concentrated on the gully. He had been so livid when he had first seen the damaged dig site he hadn't looked for smaller, perhaps telling details. Three distinct sets of boot prints were visible in the soft ground leading to within a few feet of the skeleton: Coltrane's when he had entered the gully to steal the mirror and Lucy's when she had gone in to look for him. Only Lucy's prints led out of the wash. The prints in the immediate vicinity around the skeleton had been hopelessly mangled together. Coltrane had probably fled up the bank. The level ground on the far side of the gully was wet with scattered puddles, which seemed odd since it hadn't rained in the weeks since the site had been found. *Seepage or runoff?* Baine dismissed the anomaly as unimportant within the context of the theft. The water would have obliterated Coltrane's tracks. However, when the police apprehended him, his boot soles would match the prints *in* the wash, providing conclusive evidence of his guilt.

"If the artifact was still mostly buried before Mr. Coltrane allegedly dug it up, and then he drove off with it before you realized he was gone . . ." Thomas hesitated with a bewildered frown. "How can you be so sure what it was?"

Thomas asked Lucy casually, but the question jarred Baine. The detective's guarded implication hadn't occurred to him. Thomas had not ruled out Lucy as a possible suspect, perhaps an accomplice. In retrospect, Baine realized that Coltrane's amorous feelings for his assistant had been obvious for some time. It was unlikely but not impossible that Lucy shared his affection. Or maybe she had simply taken advantage of it.

Either way, Baine decided it might be more beneficial to keep her on the project—at least until the mirror was recovered. He was not about to let a graduate student and a high school teacher get the best of him. If Lucy was working with Coltrane, sooner or later he would contact her.

"Dan showed me a picture of a similar item in a book," Lucy said evenly. "And I saw the artifact myself before we stopped working for the day. Enough of the piece was exposed to conclude that the patterns and craftsmanship were Aztec and that it appeared to be a mirror."

"Anything else special about it? Besides its obvious gold market and historical value?"

"No, Detective. Nothing."

Nodding, Detective Thomas glanced into the gully, then turned back to Baine. "I'd like to take a closer look down there. Doesn't look like there's much to find, but you never know."

"Yes, of course. Look all you want, but do not *touch* anything." Baine eyed the young man pointedly and gestured at the half-buried skeleton. "Coltrane may have already done irreparable harm to that poor fellow's remains and who knows what else."

"If you don't need me anymore, I'll put the crew to work on some exploratory probes along the rock shelf." Excusing herself with a nod, Lucy turned to leave.

"No!" Baine called out sharply, vexed by Lucy's assumption that she still had a job and that he would approve of having the Historical Society volunteers blundering about. Locating additional areas likely to yield more remnants of the old Spanish camp was best left to the archaeological students. "Those people are amateurs. I'd rather wait until Rolf and Carrie arrive before anyone starts poking around."

"Fine." Lucy shrugged, turned, then looked back again. "And before I forget—Mayor Wilkens has given the okay for the student field trip this weekend. I'm going to the school this afternoon to discuss the ground rules with the new faculty advisor."

Baine stared at her retreating back, seething with indignation. He had told Wilkens he would not tolerate a disruptive and potentially destructive bunch of teenagers tramping around the site. The mayor, who was supposed to be working on behalf of the project's anonymous benefactor, obviously had no appreciation of the dig's value or any regard for scientific method and expertise. He saw no reason to postpone making the call to tell him so.

Shadows danced in the light of the blazing fire, adding a note of macabre merriment to the somber décor of the darkened house. Laying the morning newspaper aside, Mr. Trick turned the horseshoe-shaped upholstered chair to face the stone fireplace, then sat back and steepled his fingers. He closed his eyes for a moment to subdue a flutter of agitation. Patience was as essential to a vampire's continued existence as the black paint and heavy drapes that kept the murderous sun from breaching the windows. The darkness that was his sanctuary suited the antique furnishings and centuries-old art he had collected to remind himself that some things endured through the ages.

As would he.

He, however, left nothing to mere chance.

Over the years, while the other undead indiscriminately hunted and fed on human prey, leaving themselves open to destruction by a Slayer's stake or by mobs who discovered their lairs, he had killed with a calculated cunning that did not endanger him. Possessed of a greater intelligence than most of his kind, he had also acquired the wealth and knowledge that would insure his continued existence. This he had accomplished with both careful planning and careful execution of plans.

He had a plan now.

The pieces were in place.

He just had to be patient.

The muted tone of the French phone on the table by the door invaded his meditation. The interruption was annoying, but not one he chose to disregard. Only his most trusted or powerful associates called him on the secure line. He rose and crossed the room with a fluid, unhurried grace and picked up the ornate receiver with a languid hand.

"Yes."

"There's news from the Coyote Rock dig."

The hint of excitement in Mayor Wilkens's voice evoked a twinge of anticipation that Mr. Trick adeptly concealed. He despised the arrogant, obsessive little red-haired man, and would have gladly had him for lunch if not for his netherworld connections. Sunnydale's mayor had proven himself extremely useful when properly managed. At the moment, he was the ideal liaison between Trick's financial support and the renowned professor in charge of the Spanish excavation.

"And that would be?" Excitement threatened to stir Trick's silent heart as he listened to the Mayor's report. An Aztec mirror framed in gold and turquoise had been stolen. The legendary smoking mirror had vanished shortly before Cortez had razed Tenochtitlan and conquered the Aztec Empire. Trick had investigated every archaeological dig with even a remote connection to the Spanish Conquistadors and nothing fitting the mirror's description had been found in almost five hundred years. Until now.

"Detective Thomas has instructions to report directly to me regarding the investigation," the mayor said. "Coltrane drives an old wreck that should be easy to spot, so we're not anticipating any difficulty tracking him down quickly."

"That would be advisable," Trick said calmly.

"Don't worry. If what he stole *was* Tezcatlipoca's mirror, I want it back. Being able to see the future and manipulate destiny could be most helpful with regard to my other associates."

Trick did not know the details of the bargain Wilkens had struck with the Hellmouth's other demonic elements, nor did he care. "If it was the smoking mirror, Mayor, it will be found. Should your detective fail, I assure you that my associates will see to it."

"I'm counting on it, Mr. Trick," the mayor said. "I've given permission for the student excursion to the dig this weekend. However, I'm not sure we can trust Dr. Baine to cooperate."

"If he does not, I'll see that he's taken care of, too." Teased by the thought of a kill, Trick's facial features fluctuated, were briefly transformed into the heavy ridges and fangs of the vampire within. "Personally."

Trick returned to his chair by the fire and sat down with a profound sense of satisfaction. What the mayor or his troublesome mentors wanted was of no consequence, nor was he concerned with the teacher's theft. If Tezcatlipoca's obsidian mirror had been unearthed near Coyote Rock, the god of darkness would not allow it to be removed from the vicinity.

Tezcatlipoca needed the power emanating from the Hellmouth, and—although the Aztec deity wasn't aware of it yet—he needed Trick to achieve his ancient and ultimate goal.

Buffy stirred the glop *du jour* the cafeteria was passing off as chili, then dropped her spoon. Since she had skipped breakfast, she was hungry. She just wasn't *that* hungry. Apparently, Xander didn't have an appetite either. He'd been staring at his jelly doughnut for ten minutes. "Now that you've stared that pastry into complete submission, Xander, are you going to eat it or let it go?"

"Somebody better eat it," Willow said seriously. "Before Giles finds out there's still a jelly loose on campus."

"Yeah." Buffy nodded. "Lately the snack bar runs out of jellies before I get here in the morning."

"That's because Giles hoards them." Oz brushed sandwich crumbs off his jeans.

"That's a little manic, isn't it? Should we worry?" Buffy shoved her plate aside. Prolonged exposure to the inedible chili could not possibly be beneficial to her digestive system.

"About what?" Xander looked up.

"About Giles." Willow sighed. "The Silas Marner of jelly doughnuts."

"Silas who?" Xander and Buffy asked in unison.

"*Silas Marner.*" Oz looked back and forth between them. "The novel by George Eliot about a miser? It's required reading in sophomore English."

"I didn't read it." Xander glanced at Buffy. "Which explains why *we're* not waiting to hear from M.I.T. or getting interviews at Stanford."

"Among other things." Cordy slid into the empty chair at the table. "You do know that the Community College *has* to take anyone that graduates from Sunnydale High, don't you? Not that you'd both be home free. If you're not making the grade after six months, they can kick you out."

"Forget the doughnut, Xander," Buffy said. "I'm not hungry anymore."

"Cordelia has that effect on people." Xander smiled tightly. "Sickening."

"So—who wants to hang out in Oz's garage after school?" Willow asked brightly, hoping to dull the verbal knives. "That's okay, isn't it, Oz? If we all come?"

"Fill me in," Xander said. "I missed the reason why Oz's garage is suddenly happening."

"Don't tell me the Dingoes are *still* rehearsing in your garage, Oz." Cordy shook her head. "What's wrong with the Bronze?"

"We're not playing the Bronze this week." Oz looked back at Willow. "It's okay with me. Might be kind of crowded with the whole band there, but we'll adjust."

"A rehearsal is cool." Xander stabbed the jelly doughnut with a fork. "You in, Buff?"

Buffy grimaced as red raspberry goo spurted out of

the punctures in the glazed dough. "Sorry. I can't. I've, uh—got other plans."

"What?" Cordy asked, then scoffed. "Oh, I forgot. You're the Slayer. Deadly weapons, hand-to-hand combat, and sweating are so much more fun than hanging with cool musicians who're still breathing."

Buffy sheathed her verbal claws. Cordelia was immune to insult, making any effort to dent her self-esteem futile and frustrating. "Actually, I'm joining the History Club."

Xander almost choked on a mouthful of doughnut. "Why?"

"Giles's orders." Buffy sighed. "Let's face it. Being the dauntless destroyer of the undead isn't exactly an acceptable college credential."

"That's what I said." Cordy frowned.

"The History Club? You're serious?" Willow's eyes lit up. "I've always wanted to join the History Club, but . . . I didn't because, well . . . we're always so busy tracking down the bad guys and stuff."

Xander nodded. "But now that the Hellmouth is on hold—"

"We can all join the History Club!" Willow looked at each of them uncertainly. "If we want to."

Cordelia objected. "Watch that 'we' stuff. I'm not part of this 'we' anymore, remember?"

"I'm not wild about doing the geek thing, either, but—" Xander cast another sidelong glance at Buffy. "College credential, huh?"

Buffy shrugged. "It might not help, but it can't hurt."

"And Mr. Coltrane is so nice . . . for a teacher." Now that Willow had latched onto the idea of pursuing an activity outside the parameters of demon containment, she wasn't about to let go. "Like Giles."

"About Mr. Coltrane—" Buffy hated to deflate Willow's enthusiasm, but the unsettling news would be ripping through the school halls before the day ended. "As of this morning, he's no longer in charge of the History Club." She had everyone's attention as she related Principal Snyder's account of the teacher's theft and flight.

"But Mr. Coltrane wouldn't—I mean, he couldn't—" Willow deflated.

"Apparently, he did." Buffy smiled sympathetically. "I'm sorry, Will."

Xander shook his head. "Just when you think you know a guy, he robs a mass grave and takes off."

"Well, this is certainly juicy grist for the rumor mill." Cordelia's eyes narrowed as she calculated how to use the inside info to her advantage.

"So I guess that means the overnight field trip is off," Oz said.

"*Overnight* field trip?" Xander interest level rose several degrees. "What field trip might that be, Oz?"

"The History Club was supposed to spend the weekend at the archaeological site. A combination camp-out and down-and-dirty learning experience." Oz cocked his head. "Might be fun. For anyone who's into digging up old bones and sleeping in a tent."

"And the dead guys out at Coyote Rock really *are* dead," Xander said. "That's a definite plus."

Willow eyed Oz expectantly. "Do you want to go? Because I would. I mean, how often do you get a chance to dig up old bones . . . and things? For fun, that is."

"Sure." Oz nodded slowly, a gesture of near giddy excitement within his narrow scope of emotional displays. "The band's not playing this weekend, and there won't be a full moon for another two weeks."

"There's just one problem." Xander leaned back. "Mr. Coltrane opted out of teaching to pursue a life of crime."

"Not a problem." Buffy didn't want to appear overly eager, but her own enthusiasm for joining the academic ranks had increased in direct proportion to her friends' interest. "Mr. Snyder said the club was meeting as usual this afternoon. He'll probably just assign another teacher to take over."

"Then I'm in," Xander said. "Staying out all night for fun instead of demon damage control has a certain appeal."

"What about you, Cordy?" Willow asked.

"Sorry. I don't do roughing it."

"Of course not." Xander nodded with feigned understanding. "Stanford and dirt under the fingernails just don't mix."

"Speaking of Stanford—" Cordy eased out of her chair with an unruffled smile. "I've got an appointment with my guidance counselor to discuss my interview. Have fun playing together in your super sandbox this weekend."

"You know?" Xander sighed as he watched Cordelia pause to flirt with a basketball player. "A day without a Cordy put-down is like a day without rain."

"Rare," Oz said.

Buffy couldn't disagree with that. "I hope Stanford has flood insurance."

Willow welcomed the musty isolation of the library, even though the dismal atmosphere amplified Xander's dismal mood. He had hardly said a word on the walk over from the cafeteria. Probably because Cordy still hadn't forgiven and forgotten. And maybe never would.

Giles locked the rare-book cage and glanced over as they entered. "Willow. Xander." A flicker of concern passed over his face. "Has something happened?"

"Not unless you count the insidious cafeteria conspiracy to poison the student body with rotten chili." Sighing, Xander sank into a chair.

"Or Mr. Coltrane and, well—you know." Matching Xander's sigh, Willow slipped behind the book counter and into the chair by the computer. She didn't turn it on.

"Yes, Mr. Coltrane." Giles hung his head a moment. "I must say I'm most distressed about his alleged role in the theft at the Coyote Rock site. Did Buffy tell you? Or has this nasty business become a matter of school gossip?"

"It's zooming through the grapevine as we speak," Xander said. "Cordelia knows."

"Alleged?" Willow perked up. "Does that mean Mr. Coltrane might not be guilty?"

"I don't have enough information to form an educated opinion regarding his guilt or innocence, Willow." Giles rubbed the back of his neck, then paced slowly to organize his troubled thoughts. "Based on what I know of the man, I'd venture to say Daniel Coltrane is not capable of such a despicable act."

"That's what I think, too. He wouldn't. Uh-uh." Willow shook her head emphatically. "Unless—some weird Hellmouth thingie, you know—got to him?"

"Hellmouth activity is suspiciously lacking of late, also." Giles slammed his fist into the wall by his office door. He looked back apologetically. "Both situations have me rather frustrated, I'm afraid."

"Because?" Xander asked. "Aside from the obvious."

"The obvious being the absence of vampires combined with a dedicated teacher's inexplicable decision to act contrary to his nature and reputation?" Giles sighed. "To begin with, I can't establish whether there might be a connection between the two situations since I know nothing about the missing object. Beyond the fact that it's Aztec in origin."

"But the police would know . . . wouldn't they?" Willow frowned, puzzled and worried.

"If they do," Giles said dryly, "they're—not talking, as you Americans like to say."

"Uh, well—" An impish smile softened Willow's mouth. "I could hack into the police files . . . probably."

Giles stared at her levelly. "Yes, you probably could, Willow. However, as a responsible authority figure, I couldn't allow you to undertake an illegal procedure on a school computer."

"But—"

Xander turned to Willow. "Don't you have an English paper to research or something?"

"Yes, but this is more—" Willow's eyes widened. She hadn't been born with a capacity for deception, which made her a little slow on the uptake when devious measures were required. "Oh! Yes. I do . . . have an English paper. And, uh—I'm going to do it. Right now." Willow turned on the computer.

"Yes, well—" Giles smiled. "If you need anything, I'll be in my office."

Xander stood up. "I'll just go sharpen the crossbow arrows or polish the mace. Maybe check the garlic supply. I'll find something."

Willow just nodded as she connected to the web and began a systematic search for a back door into the Sunnydale Police Department's computer by a path that couldn't be traced. The operation was routine and she found her gaze and her mind wandering back to Xander. He was totally bummed.

Cordelia's fault? Or hers?

That whole situation was too bizarre considering that Xander and Cordelia had been bickering since they were six years old and she and Xander had been friends for just as long. Well, not quite *just* friends. She had loved him most of that time, but she had kept it a secret. From everyone including Xander—until Buffy arrived in Sunnydale.

The Police Department menu suddenly appeared on the computer screen. Willow automatically typed in key words relevant to the Coyote Rock theft to access the investigation report. Her thoughts were still on the awkward romantic circumstances.

Buffy had picked up on Willow's feelings about Xander right away and had rejected his infatuated and fumbling advances. Buffy had even tried—in a discreet kind of way—to get Xander to wake up and see *her* for something other than good old dependable Willow. Neither one of them had *dreamed* that Xander and Cordelia would discover a mutual attraction and start going together . . . or that Xander would finally realize that his best friend since kindergarten wasn't a little girl with band-aids on her knees anymore. She had been totally blindsided when he kissed her before the Homecoming dance and stupid for returning his belated interest. And in the end—luckier. She and Oz had patched things up again.

"That's odd." Willow scowled at the results of her file search.

"What is?" Xander wandered past Giles's office swinging a sword.

Giles stepped out of his office door and clamped his

fist over Xander's wrist. "I'd rather you didn't accidentally decapitate yourself in here, Xander. If you don't mind."

Xander let Giles have the blade and folded his arms over his chest. "What'd you find, Will?"

"Not much." Willow looked up. "Lucy Frank called the police from the site at 6:34 this morning, but . . . no one on the force filed a follow-up report."

"How's that, Lucy?" Henry Stemp carefully peeled damp flakes of sediment away from an unidentified metal object buried under the rock shelf. The mysterious seepage had washed away more compacted mud, revealing another concentration of remains on the site.

"Excellent." Lucy smiled at the earnest man. A retired hardware store clerk in his early sixties, Henry had been an active member of the Sunnydale Historical Society for thirty years. Like the other volunteers—among them several retirees, bored housewives, and a bank teller on leave from his job—he had no practical experience with archaeological excavation but was eager to learn. "It's tedious work, I know, but the results are worth it, Henry."

Henry nodded and tugged on the brim of his baseball cap. "I just don't want to chip too hard and break something."

"You'll be fine, Henry. Just take it slow. I'll be right back."

Rising, Lucy headed toward the main tent. Baine was still in the gully where he had fled to lick his wounds after the mayor refused to change his mind about the student overnight. Engrossed in his examination of the skeleton Dan Coltrane had sabotaged, the professor didn't notice her retreat, which was a relief.

Exhausted and worried, she couldn't handle another confrontation with him right now. She desperately needed a few minutes alone to think.

After pouring herself a glass of water, Lucy pulled a stool into the narrow strip of shade on the western side of the tent. She sat down, shielded from Baine's view, and gave herself over to thoughts of the disturbing and frightening events of the past twelve hours.

She was a scientist, observant and trained to think logically. Therefore she wasn't shocked or outraged that Detective Dwayne Thomas suspected she had helped Dan Coltrane steal the artifact. Thomas hadn't said as much, but the implication was clear in his questions and manner. Conversely, Garret Baine's failure to dismiss her had come as a complete surprise, especially since his suspicions, like the detective's, were not unwarranted given the circumstances and her reticent attitude. She hadn't offered any information beyond her sparse account or tried to defend herself, nor had she mentioned Dan's misguided mission to save the world from a mythical threat.

As much as she wanted to hold onto her job and protect herself, there were too many things she couldn't explain.

She did not know why she had felt compelled to call the police and the high school that morning—*before* she had checked the gully and discovered that the Aztec mirror was gone.

Or how she knew Dan Coltrane had stolen it and was not expected to return.

Or why she had volunteered to help with the student outing to the site that weekend.

The disturbing truth was—she didn't remember *anything* from the moment she had returned to the tent after her quick midnight patrol to when she had awakened at dawn.

Nothing except flashes of that dream . . . red blood and black fur, water and stone. . . . The significance of the vague, haunting images still eluded her.

Lucy closed her eyes against the glare of the sun. She felt as though she hadn't slept at all the night before. Fatigue made it difficult to think clearly and augmented the need to be more wary of her volatile boss than normal. Dr. Garret Baine could ruin everything she had worked so hard to attain—her doctorate, her career, the darkness in the rocks, the power of blood—

Lucy's eyes snapped open, her gaze drawn to the tower of stone that dominated the hill—that had dominated her dream.

Coyote Rock.

Stone called to her, silent and commanding. Suddenly anxious, Lucy started up the slope taking cover behind boulders and scrub trees so she would not be seen from the dig. As she climbed, more dream images surfaced to torment her.

Water flowed around her, soaking her boots and flooding the terrain above the wash.

She stopped short, her breathing ragged. The vivid image was not a strange, incomprehensible distortion of her subconscious. It was a memory disguised as a dream. Neither runoff nor seepage had been responsible for the flood. She was. She had used the hose connected to the water storage container to drench the soft ground between the rock shelf and the gully, almost depleting the camp's water supply. The realization was startling, yet she made a mental note to have more trucked in before Baine realized what had happened.

Baine was a threat.

Driven by an urgency she could not define, Lucy scrambled over a low mound of rocks and plunged through a dense thicket of brush. Her knotted shirt snagged on a twisted branch. She pulled loose, tearing the fabric and scratching her arm. She stumbled over a buried slab of rock and bruised her knee when she fell, but she did not slow down. She surged upward, spurred by the surreal nightmare unraveling in her mind.

A trail of large, blood-soaked feline paw prints vanished in a stream of forced water, and a predatory roar split the night.

A black shadow flashed through Lucy's field of vision, blurred by the tears of exertion filling her eyes. Sweat ran down her neck. Her legs ached, but she was not in control of them now. Another, more powerful force drove her to the base of the natural stone formation just below the summit.

Lucy collapsed when the power released her. Eyes closed, she sat in an exhausted heap on the rough ground until her labored breathing eased.

A black jaguar streaked across the crest of the moonlit hill.

Disoriented and confused, Lucy opened her eyes slowly this time. She frowned when she saw Dan Coltrane's pre-Colombian reference book lying in the grass a few feet away. The upper half of the cover had been darkened by mud. Or was it blood? Swallowing hard, she shifted her gaze to the boulders lying in scattered disarray around the wide base of the tapering rock tower, which rose forty feet into the air above her.

Headlights consumed brush and rock as she drove off the dirt track . . .

Getting to her knees, Lucy patted the front pockets of her loose-fitting jeans. Each one contained a set of keys. She did not pull them out. Her eye settled on the arm wedged into a break in the massive rock. Physically taxed and mentally numbed, the unthinkable meaning of the scene failed to register. She crawled closer on hands and knees and froze when she saw Dan Coltrane's mangled body. He had been torn apart by savage fang and claw.

Too horrified to scream, she turned away and saw her own face reflected in obsidian glass. Propped against a rock behind her, the gold frame on the Aztec mirror gleamed under the midday sun. Transfixed, she picked up the precious artifact in trembling hands and stared into the blue-gray smoke swirling within its infinite black depths.

The glittering eyes of the jaguar stared back.

Chapter 4

Buffy walked down the deserted corridor toward Mr. Coltrane's classroom feeling like a beached whale—totally out of her element and in macro trouble. Hunting vampires in the cemetery was a Sunday picnic compared to exposing herself to the study-smart kids in the History Club. Although she was more than adequately equipped in the I.Q. department, she was entering the fray unarmed. She could read mystical rocks—at least on a fundamental level—and had a working knowledge of weapons ranging from archaic to state-of-the-art, but she was out in the cold when it came to history that didn't relate to demons, curses, vampires, and other diabolical villains. Not that she was a whiz there, either. As a rule, she had to rely on Giles and Willow to do the research and help her cram for the final exams. Live or die. Pass or fail.

Holding her chin high, Buffy breezed through the door as though she actually belonged there and came to an abrupt halt as five students and Principal Snyder turned to stare at her. She could handle peers questioning her audacious intrusion, but she wasn't going to beg Snyder for admittance to this inner sanctum of historical hotshots. The awkwardness of the situation was heightened because Willow, Xander, and Oz were all no-shows. She could have understood Xander and Oz having second thoughts about volunteering for academic enlightenment masquerading as a camping trip, but she had counted on Will's support.

"You're late, Ms. Summers, but then so is the new faculty advisor. Sit down or leave." Snyder handed a black marker to a blonde girl who looked like she had just stepped off a heavy-metal CD cover. The girl proceeded to write her name on a folded piece of paper, stood the name card upright, then gave the marker back. Snyder stopped to eye Buffy with sneering contempt on his way out the door. "You're out of here at the first hint of destruction or mayhem."

"No destruction. No mayhem. Got it." Tensing under Snyder's warning glare, Buffy exhaled softly when he left and braced herself for the next round.

The five students were still staring. Buffy recognized Chance Greyson, blond hunk and super-jock with a GPA significantly lower than his phenomenal basketball scoring average. He was leaning over to whisper to the dark-haired girl beside him. Her name card identified her as Sienna Patterson. She gasped softly and giggled. Bart Laughlin, slightly overweight and with straight brown hair that fell over his eyes, shook his head disdainfully and turned his attention back to a book on nuclear physics.

"You heard the man. Sit." Kilya Stodard's unwavering gaze, black leather, mane of shaggy blond hair, and multiple ear piercings exuded defiance.

Dem Inglese smiled shyly, then quickly averted his gaze as Buffy took the seat beside him. Still whispering with Chance, Sienna cast an occasional curious glance in her direction. They obviously weren't discussing the missing teacher, an observation that bordered on paranoid but was not an unfamiliar development. Her reputation and exploits invited gossip and speculation. Engrossed in his book, Bart apparently had no interest in idle small talk. Bored, Kilya propped her chin on her hand and closed her eyes. Buffy shifted in the unsettling silence and caught Dem watching her.

"So—who is the new faculty advisor?" Buffy asked.

Dem blinked and hesitated, either stymied by the question or surprised that she had spoken to him. Buffy suspected the latter. He was cute in a bookish sort of way, with short dark hair, a square jaw and brown eyes that shifted nervously behind wire-rimmed glasses. He looked and acted the way she had pictured Giles as a teenager before she found out the staid librarian had been a young scoundrel dabbling in the black arts.

Dem cleared his throat self-consciously. "I, uh—don't know. I'm new."

"Been there. Two years ago. It's not easy . . . being new." Buffy nodded.

"Yeah, well—" Dem pushed his glasses back into place. He was so Giles—like it was eerie. "I moved here three months ago. Roughly."

"That's, uh—really new." Buffy looked away, wishing the club advisor or Willow would arrive to extricate her from this pathetic dialogue. Dem was shy, but not easily put off either.

"So—you like history, too. Maybe we could, uh—go to that Bronze place to talk some time. Maybe."

Buffy winced inwardly when she glanced back and

saw the spark of hopeful interest in his gentle eyes. He seemed nice enough, but the last thing she needed right now was a smitten puppy dog panting at her heels. Aside from the fact that junior Giles wasn't her type, she couldn't ignore the greater truth. Scott had dropped her without warning or hesitation because she was "distracted," which translated as "still in love with Angel." She instinctively recognized that Dem was lonely and desperate, and she couldn't take the chance that he'd misinterpret a friendly overture as a prelude to romance. He'd only end up with a broken heart or dead, and she didn't want either potential tragedy on her conscience.

"I don't think so. I've got a pretty full schedule. But thanks."

"Sure." Dem nodded again, trying not to show his disappointment.

"Sorry I'm late." Giles strode into the room, nodding at Buffy as he passed.

Buffy smiled back, lamely. One of the few attractions of the History Club had been the occasional escape from her life as the Slayer. Hard to do if Giles was the faculty advisor. No matter what other duties occupied him, he never stopped being a Watcher.

Willow, Xander, and Oz trooped in after him and took seats behind and to Buffy's right.

"Hey, Buff!" Xander winked. "It's a Cordy-free zone. I couldn't resist."

Willow looked passed Buffy. "How come everyone else has name card thingies?"

"Uh—so the new teacher knows who we are." Dem spoke spontaneously, then shrank back as though he expected some serious backlash. Buffy felt sorry for him—just not sorry enough to risk getting mired in another traumatic situation.

"Oh." Willow shrugged. "Then it's okay if we don't because, well—Giles already knows us. Which isn't always such a good thing, huh, Buffy?"

"It could be worse," Buffy muttered. "Snyder was here when I arrived."

"Don't look now—" Oz said softly. "—but it just got worse."

Cordy froze in the doorway. "Oh, no. You're all here!"

"Yes, we are." Xander cocked an annoyed eyebrow. "And we all wish *you* weren't."

"Too bad, Xander." Tossing her head, Cordy entered and paused to glower at him. "My guidance counselor says I need another academic extracurricular activity and this is the only campus club that's doing anything remotely cool."

"I thought you didn't like to camp out, Cordy," Willow said, surprised.

"I don't, but participating in a real archaeological dig will look great on my transcript. Mrs. Makem said Stanford would love it." Cordy looked at Dem quizzically when she realized he was staring.

"Hi, I'm, uh—Dem Inglese. I just moved here."

"Like I care?" Huffing scornfully, Cordy moved to the back of the room to sit by herself.

Willow jumped in to soothe the wound inflicted by Cordelia's cutting tongue. "Welcome to Sunnydale, Dem."

"Where everyday is doomsday," Xander added.

"Mr. Giles?" A slim, attractive woman with short dark hair paused in the doorway and smiled as the librarian turned. "I'm Lucy Frank."

For one staggering moment Giles thought he was seeing a ghost—Jenny Calendar's ghost. Although she was dressed casually in jeans, boots, and a fitted green shirt, the young woman poised at the door bore an uncomfortable resemblance to the woman he had loved and lost. Provoked by Lucy Frank's unexpected appearance, the image that haunted his sleep rose unbidden now.

Jenny lying on his bed, her neck broken by Angeles—the evil incarnation of Buffy's vampire love, Angel.

Angeles, whom Jenny's gypsy ancestors had cursed with the restoration of his soul.

Angel, who had forfeited his tormented salvation in a moment of pure rapture.

Angeles, who had savagely murdered so many before Willow reinstated the curse and Buffy sent him to hell.

Angel, who had mysteriously returned to walk among them again.

Jenny was dead.

The intensity of Giles's lingering grief was captured in a split second of shock. Despair deepened the lines on his face and dimmed the brightness in his eyes. The effect of being confronted by Jenny's lookalike did not escape Buffy. The Slayer's worried gaze caught him for an agonizing instant before she looked away.

"Perhaps I don't have the right room," Lucy said, misunderstanding Giles's hesitation. "I'm looking for the History Club meeting."

"You found it, lady." Kilya's abrupt and disrespectful tone jolted Giles from the daze.

"Civility would be appreciated, Kilya." Having accepted the temporary extracurricular duty, Giles felt obligated to pursue the endeavor to the best of his ability. Composing himself, he stepped toward the visiting archaeologist. "Yes, this is the, uh—right room. Won't you come in, Ms. Frank?"

"Just Lucy, please."

"As you wish—Lucy." With a curt nod, Giles gestured for her to take the chair behind Dan Coltrane's desk. He sensed a restless tension in the students and simply wanted to get on with what had suddenly become a more unpleasant task than anticipated.

"Thank you, Mr. Giles." Lucy exuded a disturbing self-assurance and grace as she walked by him to settle in the chair. She set a briefcase on the floor.

"Just—Giles will do." Disarmed by her smile, Giles turned his attention to the curious and not entirely friendly audience. He had not expected to see Willow, Xander, Oz, and Cordelia in attendance with Buffy, but their familiar presences helped him regain his shaken sense of control. They also took the edge off the undercurrent of animosity emanating from the other students, who apparently felt a certain loyalty to the errant Dan Coltrane. He appreciated the sentiment, but would not be intimidated by it.

"As some of you know—" Giles glanced at the Slayerette contingent. "—I'll be standing in as the History Club's faculty advisor until a new history teacher is hired to, uh—replace Mr. Coltrane."

"Did they catch him yet?" Kilya asked boldly.

"Yeah, Giles, what's the scoop?" Cordelia leaned forward.

"Well, I feel right at home. Blunt and rude rules." Xander draped his arm over the back of his chair.

Inured to Cordelia's outspoken, tactless indiscretions and Xander's defensive quips, Giles focused on the blond girl in black leather. Her jacket sleeves creaked as she folded her arms on the desk and glared at him.

He wondered if the punctures in various parts of her facial anatomy hurt, while he concluded that her outrageous appearance and brusque manner cloaked a personality rife with insecurities. Which was probably best ignored for now.

"Not that I'm aware of, no. Mr. Coltrane is still missing. However—" Giles's attempt to continue was interrupted by an annoying jangle. A rather vacant-looking dark-haired girl anxiously was waving an arm adorned with numerous thin metal bracelets. He glanced at her scrawled name card. "Yes, uh—Sienna. What is it? Do you have to—" Giles nodded toward the door.

"Not! I just, like, don't think he did it, you know?" Sienna bounced when she talked, which was somewhat distracting. "Because I mean, Mr. Coltrane was just, like, too cool to steal some old fossil. You know?"

"Yes. I quite concur." Giles nodded, aware that his opinion had drawn Lucy Frank's studied scrutiny.

"Ditto that." Chance Greyson, a basketball player if he remembered correctly, gave him a thumbs up.

"Anyone else have something to add?" Giles asked.

Bart Laughlin—a certified genius—still had his nose buried in an advanced physics book that would have probably taxed Giles's comprehension. Dem, the boy sitting beside Buffy, lowered his gaze, then fumbled with his glasses when they almost fell off. As a result, he slouched in a manner that suggested he'd rather be anywhere else. Buffy and crew didn't seem inclined to contribute their views on Mr. Coltrane's plight, perhaps because they were the newcomers. The group as a whole seemed hopelessly mismatched, but since the Slayerettes managed to work together in spite of their contrasting personalities, it wasn't a matter of concern. Except insofar as prolonged association could well strain the limits of his adult tolerance.

"As I was saying, or trying to say—" No one interrupted, and Giles forged ahead. "Recent events will not affect the field trip to the Coyote Rock archaeological dig this weekend. We'll be leaving Friday after school as planned."

"Are there, like—creepy-crawly thingies out there?" An exaggerated grimace twisted Sienna's pretty face.

"That depends on your definition of creepy-crawly." Xander didn't crack a smile.

"By our definition, probably not." Oz glanced at Willow with a lopsided grin.

"Duh! I mean, like snakes and spiders. Stuff like that."

"That's a good question for our guest, I believe." Anxious to hand over the reins, Giles introduced Lucy. "Ms. Frank is hear to tell us something about the findings at the site, but more importantly, to explain the rules. One does not dig up a five-hundred-year-old campsite with a pickaxe."

"You've had some excavation experience, have you, Giles?" Lucy flashed a brilliant smile as she rose and came to stand beside him.

"A smattering. In Egypt and, uh—the Congo. I believe nowadays it's just called Congo, isn't it? But, yes, I've spent some time digging into the past, you might say." Appalled because he was babbling, Giles stopped before he made a complete fool of himself. "Do carry on, Ms. Frank."

"Lucy." She whispered as he moved behind her toward the chair and grinned as she turned toward the class. "You are all about to embark on an incredible journey into the past. . . ."

When it became clear the group was being relatively cooperative, and that Lucy was quite capable of fielding pointed questions and comments, Giles split his attention between her presentation and Dan Coltrane's troubling disappearance. He had been delayed after the last bell waiting for Willow to finish another unauthorized incursion into the Sunnydale Police Department computer. There was still no follow-up report regarding the archaeological theft. He was aware that there could be a rational explanation—an ongoing investigation, a breakdown in communications, or a problem with the city computer system, perhaps. However, in Sunnydale, it wasn't prudent to assume that anything happened for ordinary reasons. Coyote Rock was located within range of the Hellmouth's influence, and the extraordinary couldn't be discounted.

"Consequently, we have reason to believe the site contains more than the common equipment worn and carried by Spanish soldiers of that era. We're hoping to uncover treasures stolen from the Aztecs."

The mention of the ancient Central American empire snapped Giles's wandering thoughts back to the discussion.

"Ohmigod! Really?" Sienna bounced and jangled with excitement. "So can we, like, keep what we find?"

Lucy laughed. "No, I'm afraid not. All the artifacts will be donated to museums, either here in the States or in Mexico."

"Mexico can argue that the Aztec things belong to them, right?" Willow asked. "I mean, if you find any—"

"Yes." Lucy nodded. "Although conflicting claims are usually worked out amicably between governments.

We may end up putting together an exhibit at the university, then arranging for it to tour museums throughout both countries."

The atmosphere of academic camaraderie and curiosity in the classroom infused Giles with a rare sense of normalcy. He set his misgivings aside to enjoy it. Lucy Frank's genuine interest in sharing her expertise and enthusiasm with a bunch of kids was impressive. More impressive was the student interest she generated in return. Even Buffy was paying attention and looked more relaxed than usual.

"Do you have any idea what *kind* of Aztec artifacts might be buried there?" Willow posed the question casually, but Giles recognized it for what it really was—a fishing expedition to identify the item that was missing along with Dan Coltrane.

Lucy shrugged. "That's difficult to say. The Aztecs were marvelous craftsman and much of their art could have survived. If we're lucky, we might find some carved stone or jade pieces, gold and silver jewelry—pottery, perhaps. Did you know that they had a primitive democratic society?"

The abrupt change of subject struck Giles as odd. Given the absence of a police report, it was possible Lucy was deliberately evading any references to the missing artifact.

"The Aztec ruler, or Great Speaker," Lucy went on, "did not achieve the position by right of heredity but was selected by a Council of Wise Men, who were also selected based on their accomplishments as warriors and priests."

Kilya frowned. "Didn't those Aztec guys slaughter people to appease their gods or something?"

Giles glanced at the girl, surprised by her reference

to the Aztec's practice of ritual human sacrifice and disturbed that he might have misjudged her intellect based on her crude manner and appearance.

"Yes." Lucy smiled tightly. "Although the underlying reasons are more complex."

"Ewww. Gross much!" Sienna wrinkled her nose.

Chance shook his head. "How could anyone willingly kill one of their friends or kids for some stupid religious ceremony?"

"Actually, certain sacrificial positions were an honor." Bart looked up from his book. He was, Giles observed, obviously adept at maintaining two separate trains of thought simultaneously. "For the daily mass sacrifices, they waged war against other tribes and used their captives for god fodder."

"Aztec takeout, huh?" Xander shuddered. "Not my idea of a fun weekend."

"Yes, the weekend—" Lucy reached into her briefcase, then held up the papers she pulled out. "You'll need to bring your own camping equipment and supplies."

"Kilya and I can do the grocery thing," Sienna said. "Okay, Kilya?"

"Whatever." Kilya looked at Giles. "Who's gonna pay for it?"

Giles hesitated. School clubs usually held fundraisers to finance their activities.

Lucy answered. "That's already been arranged. Just see Principal Snyder, Kilya."

Chance raised his hand. "I've got a garage full of tents and stuff. If everyone brings their own sleeping bags and Bart can drive his dad's van, I can cover the other equipment."

"I'll get the van." Bart closed his book and stuffed it into his backpack.

"I've, uh—got a camp stove and a couple of lanterns," Dem offered tentatively.

Buffy bristled when none of the original members of the group acknowledged the shy boy. "Good. We might need them, Dem."

Oz nodded. "We can take them in my van."

After instructing everyone to meet in the school parking lot Friday afternoon, Giles adjourned the meeting. The four supply volunteers stayed behind to discuss the lists Lucy gave them. Cordelia left without a word to anyone, while Buffy and her entourage trooped out en masse. Dem lingered at his desk, waiting hopefully for an invitation that wouldn't come. The boy didn't know that associating with Buffy was a definitive health hazard, and she couldn't tell him.

Willow stepped back into the doorway. "We'll be at Oz's, Giles. Just in case, you know—anything comes up . . . or anything."

"Thank you, Willow." Giles waited patiently until all the students were gone, then walked out with Lucy. "Is there anything else I should know about this outing. Aside from making sure the dig isn't compromised by treasure-happy students."

"Such as?"

Giles thought he detected a defensive flutter in Lucy's demeanor, but didn't react. "Nothing in particular. As the faculty advisor, I feel obligated to make sure everything goes smoothly."

"Don't worry. I'm sure everything will be fine." As Lucy turned to leave, Giles called after her.

"There is one other thing—"

"Yes?" Lucy turned to regard him narrowly.

"This artifact Mr. Coltrane is said to have stolen—" Hoping his motives weren't too transparent, Giles feigned a historical interest. "What was it? I don't mean to question your expertise, but since this, uh, site is over fifteen hundred miles from Mexico City, the discovery of Aztec relics so far north is a bit difficult to accept."

Lucy deftly deflected his implied challenge. "I assure you, the missing object definitely reflects Aztec art and craftsmanship."

"Fascinating." Her answer was too ambiguous to be of any help, but Giles refrained from pressing her further. She obviously wasn't open to a discussion, perhaps from a disproportionate sense of professional caution.

"Isn't it? I'll see you Friday, then."

"I'll look forward to it." Which, he realized as Lucy waved and walked away, was true. He found that surprising, unsettling, and rather an odd relief. He would always love Jenny, but perhaps, he was finally starting to recover from the loss.

Chapter 5

Buffy turned off the TV and pushed a half-eaten frozen dinner aside when her mother trudged in the front door. "Hi, Mom. You're late."

"Didn't you get my message?" Joyce set down her briefcase and dropped a pile of promotional fliers for the Hernandez show on the coffee table. She sank onto the couch and exhaled wearily.

"Yeah, but how often do I get a chance to say that?"

"True." Joyce smiled. "Did you eat?"

"Freezer gourmet *a la* microwave. I'm all set." Buffy picked up one of the fliers that announced the times and dates of the gallery exhibition. "A reception on Friday. Sounds like fun. Am I invited?"

Joyce's eyes widened. "You mean you'd take an evening off from Slaying?"

"It's been a little slow the past week." Buffy took a sip from her soda can.

"Is that good or bad?" Joyce asked.

"Good question and I don't know." Buffy's unusual

calling was harder on her mom than it was on her in many ways. Every night Joyce had to sit, wait, worry, and wonder whether or not dawn would find her childless. And on too many occasions, her own life had been endangered because her daughter was the Slayer. Even so, her mother was supportive and accepted the perilous circumstances with admirable calm—most of the time. She deserved respect and an honest answer. "But I can't shake the feeling that something's up. I just don't know what."

"Doesn't Giles know?"

Buffy shook her head. "Not a clue. Although . . . Mr. Coltrane running off with an Aztec antique is pretty weird."

"I heard. Everyone's talking about it—which is pretty weird, too, when you think about it. Is there any more soda?"

Nodding, Buffy picked up her dish and followed Joyce into the kitchen. "What do you mean?"

"Well, look at all the strange things that happen in this town that nobody *ever* talks about. Or even *knows* about." Joyce pulled a can from the refrigerator and sat at the counter.

"And the point?" Buffy dumped the remains of the dinner in the trash and rinsed the plate.

"That just makes me believe there's nothing sinister about Mr. Coltrane other than an underpaid history teacher wanting to score big on the antique black market and retire." Joyce popped the tab and held the can up in salute. "Cheers."

"Down the hatch." Buffy drained her can and tossed it.

"Juan's reception is at seven Friday. You're friends are welcome, too, if they want to come."

"Oh, no!" Buffy slapped her forehead. "I can't go."

"What?" Joyce sat back.

"It's not a terrible reason," Buffy quickly explained. "It's good. Really. In fact, you'll probably approve. I think."

"Approve of what?" Cocking her head, Joyce instantly reverted to suspicious-for-your-own-good-mom mode.

"Well, I was talking to Giles about college this morning, and how I don't exactly have a great school record. I mean, high SAT scores aren't enough, if that's all there is."

"Um-hmmm. Go on."

"So he suggested I join the History Club."

Joyce nodded. "And?"

"So I did, but there's an overnight field trip to the archaeological dig at Coyote Rock this weekend." Buffy shrugged. "We're all going. Willow and Xander and everyone else in the club."

Shaking her head, Joyce covered her mouth and lowered her gaze.

"It's a school thing, Mom. Chaperoned. Lots of adults. Including Giles. Honest."

"Oh, God, Buffy—" Joyce looked up and brushed her hair back. "I'm sorry. I'm, uh—just—" She started to laugh.

"Finally having a nervous breakdown?"

"No." Joyce breathed in deeply. "No, it's just that—there was a time when I would have had severe reservations about letting you go on an overnight co-ed field trip. Now it's a relief."

"So you're not too upset because I can't make the reception."

"No." Still struggling to control her giggles, Joyce

waved away Buffy's concern. "Not at all. I think it's terrific you're going to spend Friday doing something for fun. That's normal."

Buffy nodded. "Right. Like digging in dirt and sleeping on the hard, cold ground without a real bathroom for forty-eight hours is every teenaged girl's idea of a cool getaway weekend."

"You'll have fun."

"My hair may never recover," Buffy shot back playfully.

"You'll survive."

"Yeah, I will." Grinning, Buffy grabbed her jacket and Slayer bag off the back door knob and slung them over her shoulder. "Don't wait up."

Joyce immediately sobered. "Patrol?"

"Duty calls." Buffy opened the door and glanced back. "Do we have a sleeping bag?"

"I'll find one."

"Thanks." Buffy blew a kiss and fled into the dark, a sanctuary from the worry her mom couldn't erase from her eyes.

Buffy walked along the packed dirt jogging path, alert and anxious. The park was not deathly quiet tonight. The dark that usually drove everyone indoors had lured an alarming number of people outside. A couple necked on a bench by the fountain. An old man walked his dog. A group of teenagers played hoops with squashed soda cans on the basketball court, disrupting the quiet with laughter and the clank of aluminum hitting asphalt. Two more boys shoved bikes into a rack, then walked toward the court tossing a ball. Following the trail into a wooded section, Buffy wondered how many would be around to have breakfast and rejected an impulse to chase them all home. She had to stay focused on whatever crept through the shadows, choosing its foolish prey.

Except nothing crept through the shadows. Not that she sensed. Squirrels didn't count. Or joggers.

Buffy stepped to the side of the path as the steady thud of running footsteps behind her drew nearer. She listened, assessing the runner from the sound. *Human, not too heavy, not in a hurry.* She turned slowly, reaching for the stake stuck in her back pocket as a precaution. Her vision adjusted to the pale glow of a nearby park light. *Male, gray sweats, tiring.* He ran with his head down, watching the path.

A movement in the trees diverted Buffy's gaze and brought the jogger to a halt a few feet away.

"Buffy?"

Stake in hand, Buffy tensed, her attention divided between the woods and the jogger. The breathless voice was familiar, but she couldn't place it. "Who are you?"

"Dem Inglese. From the, uh—History Club meeting this afternoon." He doubled over to catch his breath, then stretched and shifted nervously. His glasses were secured to his head by a band attached to the ear hooks. "Do you do this a lot? Jog at night, I mean."

"No. I, uh—walk mostly," Buffy said.

Dem laughed. "I haven't run this path before. It's, uh—longer than I thought. I've only gone halfway and I'm already winded." His words trailed off when he realized she was paying more attention to the woods.

"A word of advice, Dem." A shiver tickled the back of Buffy's neck. She didn't sense a vamp, but she heard the stealthy tread of something moving closer. "It's not safe to be out and about in Sunnydale after dark. Go home."

"It's a free park." Dem bristled, more hurt than angry.

"And the fav hangout of all the local—muggers." Buffy cursed under her breath when Dem made no move to leave. Apparently, he was so desperate for company he'd rather endure an abusive exchange than be alone. She didn't want to pound on his already bottomed-out ego, but his presence was an annoying and dangerous distraction. "I'm not kidding."

"Uh-huh. Seems safe enough to me." Dem's face twitched as he scanned the dense woods on both sides of the path. He couldn't hear or see the threat that she felt. He covered his shy uncertainty with a burst of bravado. "Except for what? Killer chipmunks? You gonna skewer and roast them over an open fire?"

"What?" Buffy followed his gaze to the stake in her hand. She didn't try to explain. He wouldn't believe her unless he saw a vamp up close and personal, an introduction he probably wouldn't survive. "Dem, please—"

"All right. I can take a hint." Shaking his head, he turned back down the trail. "I know when to get lost—"

A savage roar shattered the tranquility as a black shadow sprang toward the helpless boy from the brush.

The Slayer responded instinctively, running, jumping and thrusting both feet against the massive form to kick it off course. The force of her flying body knocked Dem off his feet. He staggered and fell, striking his head against a tree trunk. Buffy hit dirt and was back on her feet as a huge black cat whirled and sprang again—toward her. Its claws raked her arm as she ducked and rolled, then quickly regained her footing and spun. The cat landed cleanly and whipped around to stare with glowing, golden eyes.

Panther? Jaguar? She didn't know and at the moment that hardly seemed important. The beast easily measured five feet from its head to the base of its swishing tail and probably weighed over two hundred pounds. It roared again, displaying long gleaming fangs a vampire would envy. Buffy braced herself when the sleek, muscular cat crouched. When it leaped, she raised the stake as she fell back, hoping the animal would impale itself under its falling weight.

The cat twisted in midair. The wooden stake glanced off thick black hide and flew out of Buffy's hand as she brought her knees up and flipped the beast over her head. The cat screeched and landed hard, but was unfazed by the jolt. Scrambling to all fours, the cat turned toward her without pause and crept forward. Barely back on her feet, Buffy prepared to duck and roll rather than take the full force of another hit. None of her vamp weapons would take out a crazed four-legged predator. Unless Giles showed up with the crossbow or tranquilizer gun—not likely—her only hope was a defense utilizing her wits and Slayer agility.

She glared into the intent, feline eyes, but the beast was not intimidated into retreat.

It charged.

Buffy waited, poised on the balls of her feet, timing her evasive maneuver to maximum advantage.

As the cat sprang, a roaring blur burst from the trees and sent the cat flying down the path with a broadside kick.

"Angel!"

The vampire turned his ghastly eyes on her, but the fanged snarl and demonic ridges that marred his face were a welcome sight. Buffy assumed a fighting stance beside him.

The cat landed on its massive paws ten feet away and

hesitated, glaring at the unlikely pair. It growled, then silently melted back into the dark forest.

Buffy stepped back and waited until Angel's features softened to normal before she relaxed. Even then, she was painfully aware that the danger he presented in his dark and brooding human form was more threatening than the vampire cravings he struggled to control. They had crossed the forbidden line once, not knowing that the price of consummating their love was Angel's soul. They could not cross it again. Ever.

"You're hurt." Angel's hand moved toward the bleeding gouges the cat's claws had torn in her arm.

"Just a couple of scratches." Buffy's heart ached as she flinched from his touch. She had not seen him for several days, but suspected he had been keeping her under surveillance on her uneventful patrols.

Angel's jaw flexed and he nodded curtly, fighting his own war between desire for her and rejection of Angeles. He looked away into the night that had swallowed the cat.

"Any idea who that was?" Buffy heard Dem moan and glanced back. The boy's eyes were still closed, but he would be regaining consciousness soon. "Or what it was?"

"No." Angel shook his head, "but I don't think it escaped from the zoo."

Framed by dark hair, Angel's pale, bloodless face shone with an ethereal aura in the dim light. The dichotomy he had had to live with, the good and evil that had alternately possessed him during the two hundred and fifty years of his undead existence, had left invisible scars. Only Buffy could see them in his tortured eyes.

Shivering, Buffy forced her thoughts back to the cat,

recalling the calculated cunning in the golden eyes. Those *glowing* golden eyes. Like Angel, she sensed more than predatory instinct behind the feline stare.

"You better make sure your friend is okay. I'm going to follow it, see where it goes, what I can find out." Angel hesitated, then started to turn.

Buffy clamped onto his arm, staying him just long enough to bestow a quick, sweetly terrified kiss on his cold mouth. "Thanks. For the rescue."

"I'll catch up with you later."

"At the library." Buffy eased back before she threw herself into his arms, an ever-present impulse that could overpower her resolve. "Giles will probably want a report."

His fingers traced her cheek, a fleeting caress that burned with the chill of his lifeless touch. "Wait for me."

"Always," Buffy whispered. She stood quietly after he vanished into the shadows, indulging herself in a moment of futile wishful thinking.

As much as Angel despised the monstrous nature of his vampire being, the primal instincts inherent in the beast served him well. He flowed like liquid through the trees, silent and swift, tracking the predator by scent and a savage knowledge of the hunt. The cat would not give up because it had lost the Slayer. The park was full of easier prey.

The image of Buffy's face faded as Angel homed in on the dark shadow crouched behind a hedge on the far side of the basketball court. Two boys were playing one-on-one for a cheering audience of teens gathered around a nearby picnic table. The crowd would scatter when the cat attacked and it would single out whoever had the misfortune to be last in the terrified stampede. Or it would go for the old man sitting on the bench with a small terrier under a shade tree several yards away.

Young blood was sweeter, more psychologically satisfying to a vampire, but the cat was not one of them.

The beast would try for the old man.

As determined now to preserve life as he once was to take it, Angel moved out of the trees onto the grass. Turning up his collar, he cut across the far end of the asphalt court toward the old man. A rage born of blood lust simmered within him, tempting and explosive. He took conscious control of the killer instinct. Holding the power in check, he channeled his savage thirst for human blood toward the cat waiting patiently to strike.

Another presence teased his acute senses.

Vampire.

A female . . . behind the shade tree.

And a male by a park shed . . . down the slope on the left. A third in the woods. Another near the cat. . . .

The intrusions momentarily disrupted Angel's concentration and he was caught by surprise when one of the ball players dashed toward the hedge chasing the ball. The cat bounded from cover, bringing the boy down instantly with a powerful slash of its paw. The boy's scream was aborted when massive feline jaws closed over his neck, snapping it.

The other player slowly backed off the court, his gaze fastened on the huge cat. Shock held everyone else in a paralyzing grip for several seconds. Chaos erupted when the cat roared, then ripped into its kill to feed. The teens raced for the parking lot, screaming.

Too late to save the boy, Angel turned his attention to the old man who sat frozen on the bench. The dog strained against its leash, yapping frantically. Behind them, the female vampire hugged the tree, watching the snarling cat. By the time Angel crossed the intervening space, she was gone.

"Hey! Old man." Angel stood back a pace, just beyond reach of the frantic dog. "Time to go."

"Huh?" The old man turned his head slowly. He blinked, then suddenly came to his senses. "Go away! Don't—"

Angel held up a hand. "I'm not going to hurt you. Just take your dog and go home. Now."

The man jumped up and scurried away, dragging the furious little terrier.

A police siren sounded in the distance.

Angel glanced at the cat, then looked away, repelled and drawn to the fleshy gore clamped in its teeth.

Even though the other vamps had vanished from the park, Angel followed the old man at a discreet distance to make sure he got home safely. As the quiet settled around him, Buffy invaded his thoughts. The longing to be with her, to hold her without fear, was almost more than he could bear. He wondered how long he could resist the dangerous passion that would damn him and destroy her. Must resist. He would suffer with that bittersweet pain for all eternity, but he could end the torment for Buffy. He could simply disappear into the night. . . .

"Wha—what happened?" Dem rubbed the sore spot on the back of his head and squinted at the three blurred faces looking down on him. "Where're my glasses!"

"Right here. The band broke when you fell."

Buffy Summers. Dem took the glasses she placed in

his hand and put them on. Two of her friends were with her: the ditzy redheaded girl who was named after a tree—he couldn't remember which one—and the clown. Xanadu or something.

"You pushed me!" Dem tried to glare at the pretty girl who had stolen, then crushed his heart. She stared right back, making him nervous and forcing him to look away.

"You were in the way." There was no hint of apology in Buffy's tone, which really rankled. She was just like everyone else who couldn't wait to ditch the dweeb, except she wasn't as brutal about it as most. At least Buffy had talked to him, even if she was just politely killing time until her friends arrived and she had an excuse to ignore him.

"In the way of what? Dare I ask?" The tall boy asked insolently.

"Cat." Buffy smiled at the lanky comedian and held up her arm, which was bleeding from long gashes. "A really big cat. Very black."

The tree girl's eyes widened. "A cat? And we weren't even a little bit worried, were we, Xander? 'Cause it's been so, you know—peaceful lately. It's all my fault."

"How do you figure that?" Buffy asked.

"Well, because the Dingoes decided to rehearse tonight instead of this afternoon . . . so Oz wouldn't miss it. And I wanted to, uh—listen for awhile . . . which is why we weren't here to help. And look what happened! You're wounded!"

"It's a long way from my heart, Willow."

"How big is really big?" Xander scowled. "Exactly."

Dem's fuzzy recollection of events cleared as the others talked. He vaguely remembered hearing a horrific roar right before Buffy shoved him into the tree—

"Like a panther, maybe. Or possibly a jaguar. Angel went after it." Buffy shrugged, then peered at Dem. "You might have a concussion. Maybe we should get you to the emergency room—"

"No, I'm okay." Ignoring the hand Xander offered, Dem wobbled to his feet. A wild cat *had* attacked and Buffy had saved him. He was grateful, embarrassed, and furious. No way Buffy could ever look at him again without seeing a helpless, bumbling nerd. Which he was, but now he wouldn't get the chance to prove otherwise. Too curious for his own good, he blurted out the next question that came to mind. "How'd you manage to fight off a jaguar, Buffy?"

"Not very well." Buffy elaborated when Xander and Willow looked at her quizzically. "If Angel hadn't shown up that critter might be helping himself to Buffy buffet right now."

"Who's Angel?" Dem asked, although he wasn't sure he wanted to know that Buffy was seriously involved with someone else. His chances of becoming a close friend were slim and hope for anything beyond that was almost nonexistent, but slim and almost were better than zero.

"Just a friend." Buffy glanced down the dark path.

Dem's heart flip-flopped, but he just nodded as though that news wasn't vital to his desire to wake up tomorrow. "You'd think the authorities would warn people when a dangerous animal escapes from the zoo or circus or whatever."

Xander nodded. "You'd think."

"I think we should get out of here while we're all still in one piece." Buffy eased Willow and Xander aside. "I'll meet you two at the library after I walk Dem home. Giles should know—"

"I don't need an escort." Dem regretted the words the minute they passed his lips, but it was too late to take them back and save face, too.

"I didn't mean—" Buffy's words were cut short by the sound of screaming deeper into the park.

Dem paled when he heard the roar.

"New plan." Xander took Willow's arm. "We'll all walk Dem home and then hit the library. Safety in numbers and all that."

"Angel's out there. Maybe I should—" Buffy grunted as Xander grabbed her hand.

"Angel can take care of himself. Come on."

Dem couldn't stop shaking as they raced back down the trail. The tremors weren't simply a delayed reaction to almost being torn apart by a ferocious beast. He had seen the look in Buffy's eyes when she thought Angel was in danger. Whoever he was, he wasn't *just* a friend.

Cordelia swept through the library doors, ignoring Xander, Buffy, and Giles as she marched toward Willow waving a credit card. Nothing horrible was happening in town, so she wasn't interrupting an emergency meeting or anything. Not that she cared anymore—much. Keeping the world safe from fiendish Hellmouth visitors had gotten old fast. Every time they did in one demon a worse one popped up to take its place. Not that she couldn't cope with being on the losing side of worthy-but-hopeless causes. She could have—if Xander hadn't betrayed her and brought her within knocking range of death's door. The sooner she left him and Sunnydale behind for a university the better.

"I'm glad you're here, Willow. Is that computer fired up and ready to rock? I need a huge favor. Like right now."

Willow blinked, her hands poised over the keyboard. "Uh, yeah, but—"

"Is there a problem, Cordelia?" Giles peered at her over the open book in his hands. He was the only person she had ever met who could pace and read at the same time.

"I'll say." Exhausted after tramping through almost every store in the mall, Cordelia flopped in a chair at the table.

"What's the matter?" Xander lounged on the steps leading up to the raised floor at the back of the library. "Afraid to tell your parents you maxed out that card?"

"Hardly." Cordelia huffed. "I found these great hiking boots at Shoes Plus and some dynamite shirts at The Outlet, but nobody in this stupid town carries pith helmets!"

"Pith helmets?" Baffled, Buffy sat back with a slight shake of her head. The Slayer's arm was bandaged, but Cordelia didn't ask. She didn't want to know.

"Right. Pith helmets. Those hard hats with round brims and little holes all over them?" Cordelia returned the blank stares leveled at her with unabashed disdain. "If I have to spend a weekend crawling around an archaeological dig, *I'm* doing it in style."

"And we'd expect nothing less." Xander rolled his eyes.

Cordelia turned her back on him and put the credit card on the keyboard in front of Willow. "Someone on that web thingie you're always hacking into must sell pith helmets, Willow. I want it shipped overnight tomorrow so I have it Friday."

"I'll, uh—check into it. As soon as I'm done with . . . this." Willow grimaced apologetically. " 'Cause this is sort of more important . . . sort of."

"What *this?"* Taking a good look at the serious faces around her, Cordelia wilted. Something was wrong, and whatever it was—it was probably gross and awful. "No, don't tell me. Unless it involves me in some disgusting way I can't possibly avoid. And it better not! I'm retired, remember?"

"Well, yes, but you might want to refrain from purchasing a pith helmet just yet," Giles said.

" 'Cause the camp-out might be cancelled," Willow added.

"Why?" Cordelia couldn't believe it. She had finally gotten psyched up about the outing and a totally cool notation on her transcript and now the field trip was *off?*

Giles sighed. "I haven't made a definite decision, Cordelia, but given tonight's events—"

"Who got killed by what?" Cordelia asked, annoyed.

"Nobody by a big, black cat . . . but that new guy, Dem, and Buffy almost—" Willow faltered when Angel strode through the doors. "—got killed."

"Angel—" Buffy's eyes lit up as he approached the table. "Did you find out anything?"

Cordelia shuddered. Angel was hot for a dead guy, but she preferred boyfriends who didn't have someone else's blood running through their veins. At least Angel got his fix from the blood bank . . . didn't he?

"Not much." Angel paused off to the side, away from Giles. "The cat killed a kid playing basketball and someone else near the cemetery. I heard a police call on my way over here."

"A little kid or, uh—a big kid?" Willow asked, stricken by the news. "Not that it makes a difference, but—"

"Teenager," Angel clarified.

"Anyone we know? Not that that makes a difference, either," Xander added hastily.

Angel shrugged. "No one I recognized."

"The attack—" Buffy paused uneasily. "In the park?" She stiffened when Angel nodded. "Maybe if I had stayed—"

Angel shook his head. "It happened too fast, Buffy."

Xander looked at Angel askance. "So death goes on as usual in Sunnydale."

"Excuse me, but I don't see the problem." Cordelia often wondered if she was the only one in the bunch who wasn't prone to overlooking the obvious. "A big *gun* should take care of a big *cat,* shouldn't it? Or better yet! Call the zoo it escaped from and let them handle it."

"That would work—" Xander nodded. "—except nobody's misplaced a wild cat lately."

"No reports in the whole state." Willow shook her head. "Nothing. *Nada.*"

"Which means—" Cordelia prompted.

"That it might not be just a big black cat." Buffy looked at Angel for confirmation of her assessment and continued when he nodded. "I sensed something—sinister."

"Yes, well, I can see why a man-eating kitty could give that impression." Cordelia shook her head.

"There were other vampires in the park," Angel said, "but they didn't interfere with the cat or attack anyone."

"Curious, to say the least, and does suggest the animal may be supernatural. And quite powerful." Giles started pacing again. "This is far-fetched, but it's possible there's a connection to the archaeological site. The jaguar was worshipped as a god in several of the pre-Columbian cultures in Central and South America."

"And we've a got a missing *Aztec*—something," Willow said.

"But we still don't know what that something is." Buffy frowned.

"Except that it 'reflects' Aztec art—" Giles shrugged. "—According to Lucy Frank, who seemed to take perverse pleasure in toying with my curiosity."

"Maybe that's a hint!" Willow looked up beaming.

"A pretty obscure hint, if you ask me," Xander said.

"No, actually, I think Willow may be right." Giles took off his glasses and stared at the ceiling. "Something that reflects—"

"Like a mirror?" Cordelia flinched when Giles looked at her sharply. "Sorry. It was the first thing that—"

"No apology is necessary, Cordelia. That was quite possibly a brilliant deduction. I'm quite certain there's a legend involving a mirror—" Giles put his glasses back on and dropped the book he was holding. He was totally lost in his own thoughts by the time he crossed the room to the book cage.

"Well, now that I've saved you all hours of guesswork, I'll be going." Cordelia rose to leave. "I still want that pith helmet, Willow. If I don't use it this weekend, it'll look great hanging on my dormitory room wall—" She turned to glare at Xander. "At Stanford."

"Better get an extra large, Willow," Xander said. "To accommodate Cordy's swelled head."

Mr. Trick walked into Richard Wilkens's office without knocking, knowing it would annoy the meticulous mayor. It did.

"I do wish you wouldn't barge in like that, Mr. Trick." A stickler for propriety, Richard Wilkens III looked up from his desk. "It completely unbalances my sense of order in the universe."

"Really?" Perching on the corner of the desk, Trick smiled enigmatically.

The mayor leaned back in his leather chair and folded his hands in his lap. "You must have good news."

"I do. Our friend is on the prowl."

"Yes, I know." The mayor rocked slightly, pleased. "I've dispatched a cleanup team to dispose of the scraps when he's finished. Too bad there were witnesses, but I've muzzled the media. I'll be informed in the event anyone talks."

"Excellent. And my people have reported back from the site. The mirror is still there."

Wilkens eyed him pointedly. "Then why didn't you bring it to me?"

Trick cocked an eyebrow. "That can be arranged—if you're prepared to deal with an angry Aztec god with a taste for human hearts."

"I'd rather not." A petulant scowl creased Wilkens's face. "When?"

"When Tezcatlipoca no longer needs it to survive. If everything on your end is under control, he'll be free of it this weekend."

Grinning, the mayor sat forward abruptly. "The field trip is going forward as planned—with a bonus."

"Such as?" Trick asked curiously.

"The Slayer has joined the History Club."

Trick laughed. How appropriate that the Slayer's blood would be shed to herald the dawn of perpetual darkness.

Chapter 6

Dr. Garret Baine woke up with a start and fumbled for the switch on the battery-powered lantern. He hadn't meant to fall asleep when he had stretched out on the camp cot a little after 2:00 A.M. If one of his students had slept through the overnight shift, he'd be furious. It was still dark, however. Perhaps he had only dozed off for a few minutes. Turning the lamp up to full illumination, he swung his feet to the floor and glanced at his watch.

6:07! Sunrise was less than an hour away.

"Damn!" Standing up, Baine rubbed the stiffness out of his neck and shoulders. Yesterday's distressing events had taken a greater toll on his stamina than he had realized. Between the theft, dealing with the police, and assessing the damage to the site, he had spent the entire day in a maelstrom of frustration and anger. Lucy's insolent attitude hadn't helped, and as of last evening Detective Thomas had made no progress tracking down Coltrane or the artifact. On top of that, the mayor had threatened to remove *him* from the project if he didn't cooperate with the student field trip! As though he had nothing better to do than babysit teenagers who in all likelihood didn't give a damn about the past and were just using the excursion as an excuse to party. He was caught in a conspiracy of fools determined to ruin the most valuable archaeological find in southern California in decades.

Today wasn't getting off to a much better start. There was no water in the tent for coffee.

Grabbing a large, plastic container and a flashlight, Baine stomped outside to the large, water storage unit. Placing the container under the spigot, he scanned the lamp-lit site. Everything looked secure. However, when he turned the storage unit's tap on, no water came out. Scowling, he pounded the metal drum with his fist. Hollow. Empty. Impossible! The tank had been filled with a two-week supply last Saturday, only five days ago.

No coffee. Not until later when he could send a volunteer into town for takeout. His cardiologist would approve, but being denied his morning caffeine only drove him deeper into an already dark mood. Fuming, Baine turned toward the table beside the tent, hoping to find a water pitcher left from the day before. He didn't need much. Just enough to brew a couple of cups. . . .

A flickering glow near the towering rock formation on the hill jarred him.

Fire!

Baine's faulty heart palpitated wildly. The site and its partially unearthed treasures would be irrevocably damaged by a brush fire. Fright gave way to anger when he realized the glow was not spreading. The flames were contained, but the dry brush covering the hill could too easily be set ablaze by a stray spark.

"Blasted kids." Muttering, Baine fisted his flashlight

and set off up the slope. He didn't question his assumption that a bunch of teenagers was responsible for the predawn bonfire on his hill. Sunnydale reputedly had a higher-than-average crime rate and an extraordinary amount of teenage violence. Who else would be so bold?

Lucy Frank.

Taken by surprise when he cleared the large boulders downhill from the tower, Baine glared at the young woman. She stood between two lit torches at the base of the tall stone formation, wearing a crude crown fashioned of feathers and a white bed sheet knotted over her left shoulder. A loincloth underneath the sheet was her only concession to modesty.

"You fell asleep, Doctor."

"Have you been up here all night? Spying on me?" Baine shifted uneasily. Given the glazed look in her eyes and the ridiculous costume, she had, apparently, suffered some kind of breakdown.

"Waiting for you. As usual, your timing is impeccable." Lucy glanced to the east. "It's almost dawn."

"I'm well aware of the time." He was also aware that showing his outrage might push his unhinged assistant completely over the edge. A single reckless reflex could topple one of her primitive torches, touching off a dreaded brush fire. He took a cautious step toward the nearest torch. "I have a flashlight. Let's douse the fires, shall we?"

Lucy snapped her head around, her brown eyes blazing with madness. "No. Let's not."

Holding up his palms, Baine backed off. "I assume you have a reason for this—demonstration."

"I do." Lucy stepped aside. The missing gold-framed mirror was propped on a rock outcropping behind her.

"*You* took it?" Sputtering, Baine lunged toward her, but stopped when she raised a large hunting knife. The polished blade shimmered in the light of the cavorting flames. Calming himself with difficulty, he opted for reason rather than direct confrontation. "I'm glad you found the mirror, Lucy, but—it's not yours to keep."

"No. It belongs to Tezcatlipoca and has only been entrusted to me."

"Tezcatlipoca?" Baine swallowed hard. The smoking obsidian mirror that the Aztec god of darkness used to defeat his enemies and foresee the future was a myth. Sadly, Lucy was convinced this valuable but quite ordinary object *was* that legendary mirror. What could have driven such a promising and brilliant student so completely insane? Ambition? More upsetting was the now unexplained disappearance of the history teacher.

"Where's Dan Coltrane, then, Lucy? Do you know?"

Lucy nodded and pointed down the slope. A pile of bloody bones, shredded clothing and rotting flesh was barely visible in the glow cast by the torches. A skull covered with dried blood and gore hung on a pike driven into the ground beside the grotesque remains.

Baine choked back the bile rising in his throat and fought the nausea that threatened to bring him to his knees. Coyotes had surely gorged themselves on Coltrane's corpse, and Lucy had put the skull on display in the tradition of the ancient Aztecs. Another question was of more immediate concern, however. Had Coltrane died accidentally or had Lucy killed him?

Although Lucy had a knife and he was unarmed, Baine thought he could win in a physical struggle with the slim woman. She did not have the element of surprise on her side this time, as must have been the case with Coltrane. Still, considering his heart condition, escape without exertion was the wiser option if possible.

"Perhaps I should take the mirror back to camp." He

hesitated to quell the tremor in his voice. "To make sure nothing happens to it."

"By all means." Bowing her head in acquiescence, Lucy dropped her arm and motioned him to approach. "Take it."

Baine licked his parched lips and moved forward, keeping his eye on the knife. She made no move to stop him. When he was within reach of the mirror, he shifted his gaze to the black glass and his own strangely captivating reflection.

His graying hair was still tousled and matted from being slept on, and the lines around his eyes had deepened and multiplied. Stress and fatigue. And age, he admitted ruefully. Still, time had been kinder to him than to most of his colleagues. His wife, Ruth, often made a point of saying so at university social gatherings. He had to remember to call her as soon as he got back to camp. She hated being left alone all night—

Baine frowned as his face began to recede. Neither he nor the mirror had moved, yet he saw himself growing smaller as the image expanded to include the rocks, Lucy and the torches, and the surrounding terrain accented by the blush of approaching dawn on the eastern horizon. Odd. And unnerving. He tried to look away and could not. He was forced to watch a series of terrifying images strobe in the depths of the mirror.

He saw Lucy step up behind him. His image looked back, eyes wide with fear as she raised the knife. A savage, primal roar echoed off the rocks as the knife plunged into his chest and Lucy reached into the wound to rip out his heart with her bare hand—

"No, no, no—" Baine shook his head, refusing to accept that the black glass might actually be the mythical vessel of Tezcatlipoca's enormous power. The image shifted again, as though to mock his disbelief. He saw his face and moaned as flesh dissolved into an obsidian skull mask inlaid with gold and turquoise, the Aztec symbol of death.

He heard Lucy breathe behind him.

Mr. Trick's vampire chauffeur parked the car as close to the Spanish dig site as possible and kept the motor running. Trick powered down the window, then adjusted the magnification on his binoculars and followed Baine's progress up the slope. Not knowing what to expect from the ancient Aztec entity, Tezcatlipoca, he had heeded his instincts and driven to Coyote Rock when his watchdogs reported that the jaguar was returning. His less powerful minions were not thrilled about relinquishing their hunting grounds to another predator, but the ultimate reward offset the temporary sacrifice.

Trick chuckled at the irony in his choice of words. Sacrifice was the key to success and he certainly hadn't expected to be treated to a preview of the main event this morning. Or to find that Tezcatlipoca had appointed Baine's attractive assistant as his High Priestess.

"Charming." Trick grinned when Lucy brandished the knife, bringing the haughty professor to a startled halt. She was really getting into the part, which added a delightful flare to the unfolding drama. The head on the pole was a macabre touch that lent an amusing authenticity to the scene. Baine didn't seem to think so. The man looked away in disgust to focus on the mirror.

Trick stole a glance toward the east and quickly averted his gaze from the dim light heralding dawn. The sun was scheduled to rise at 6:35. The time was now 6:27.

The V8 engine in the luxury car hummed. Assured the power windows would close when necessary, he turned his curious attention back to the hill as Lucy stepped behind Baine and raised the knife. The professor looked back as a blue-gray smoke plume emerged from the mirror and transformed into the black jaguar. The animal leaped onto a stone ledge on the tower and roared, then crouched, waiting.

If he had a pulse, Trick mused, it would be racing with anticipation right now. Even from a distance, he experienced a vicarious thrill from human terror in the face of death. Baine's eyes widened in shock. He shook his head in denial. A scream hesitated, then surged forth as the woman pushed her victim backward against the rock and drove the blade home with a downward slash that ripped open his chest. The jaguar leaped to the ground as Lucy reached into the cavity and extracted Baine's heart. The man lived long enough to see the jaguar catch the pulsing organ in eager jaws and swallow it.

Trick nodded in approval. The ritual was not nearly as elegant as a vampire's bite, but certainly worth the price of admission. Especially since it wasn't over yet.

The clock on the dash flashed 6:32.

Three minutes and counting. Fascinated, Trick leaned forward as the black cat leaped toward the mirror, changing back into a plume of smoke that was absorbed by the dark glass.

The eastern sky glowed brighter with the imminent appearance of the rising sun.

Although he would have liked to watch Lucy decapitate Baine's corpse and skewer the head, Trick dropped his binoculars and pulled a stopwatch from his pocket with his left hand. He kept his right index finger on the power window button. The instant the dash clock turned to 6:35, he started the stopwatch and kept his eyes on the horizon to the east.

Two minutes later he was certain the sun had stalled.

It did not resume its ascent until nine minutes and forty-seven seconds past scheduled sunrise.

Disoriented by a hundred flickering torches, Buffy ascended stone steps that rose toward the pinnacle of a flattened pyramid. She paused on a step inlaid with mosaics of gold, silver, jade and turquoise and looked back to see Giles, her mother, and her friends staring up at her.

Their faces morphed into hideous black masks with empty eye sockets.

Her mother screamed as a knife flashed on the periphery of Buffy's vision.

The wild cat roared.

Buffy turned toward Angel on the steps above her. A river of blood flowed downward to pool at his feet.

Then he was gone in a flash of brilliant light—

Buffy opened her eyes and sat up suddenly, drenched in a cold sweat. The vivid nightmare would have left anyone shaken and alarmed. For her the implications woven into the lingering images were far worse.

The Slayer's dreams foretold the future.

"—No chance of rain."

Willow woke up to the blare of the local radio announcer's voice.

"And for all the concerned citizens that called in this morning, an explanation after this commercial break."

Another, more mellow but louder voice replaced the upbeat announcer's patter. "Are you fed up with fad diets that don't work?"

Groaning, Willow covered her head with her pillow to muffle the volume. She didn't dare turn the radio off.

She hadn't gotten home from the library until after midnight and she was sure she'd just go right back to sleep. Then she'd probably oversleep and be late for school. And she really didn't want to start the day with a lecture from Principal Snyder. Besides, she wanted to get back to the library early in case Giles's research had turned up something important.

The commercial ended and the announcer launched back into the morning newscast. "The sun did *not* rise late today—"

She hoped Giles' time and energy hadn't been as wasted as hers. She had checked every police and city computer program she could think of looking for some mention of Mr. Coltrane. Or the mysterious missing Aztec treasure that Giles thought might be a mirror. There was no reference to the teacher or the artifact anywhere.

"—glitch in the National Weather Bureau's computer system caused a miscalculation," the announcer said.

She hadn't found any reports about an escaped jaguar, either. Not in the police files or on the state and local news web sites. Which wasn't exactly reassuring, since Angel knew the police had been called to the scenes of the cat killings.

"The predicted time for sunrise this A.M. was off by almost ten minutes—"

Which meant that something weird probably *was* going on and their vacation from demon duty was over.

"So rise and shine, folks! It's another beautiful morning in Sunnydale—"

Tossing her pillow aside and throwing off the covers, Willow hit the off button. She was going to need a really long shower this morning to clear the cobwebs out of her sleep-fogged brain.

Chapter 7

Dem fretted all the way to school, running last night's humiliating events over and over in his mind, wondering what he could have done differently. He finally decided that nothing would have had a positive impact on Buffy. Except maybe taking the brunt of the cat's attack, which would have gotten him maimed or killed, thus making the whole issue null and void. His attempts to get Buffy and her friends to talk about the wild cat on the walk home had been a total washout, too. They had been so withdrawn he might as well have been mute and invisible. The only good thing that had come out of the encounter was Buffy's denial of a romantic relationship with the mysterious Angel, and there was only one logical conclusion to be drawn from that. Buffy was smitten, but Angel did not return her affections. Why, Dem couldn't imagine.

However, he was sure her elusive hero didn't hang around school. No guy with a dorky name like Angel could escape being the topic of either ridicule or respect, and until last night he had never heard anyone mention him. So Angel was probably older, in college or something, unattainable even for a gorgeous girl like Buffy.

As he mounted the stone steps onto the school grounds, Dem searched the scattered knots of students, looking for her. He couldn't believe his luck when he saw her walking across the lawn. Hip-hugging blue jeans and a denim vest over a white T-shirt emphasized the aura of no-nonsense purpose in her bearing and stride as she headed toward the front doors. She was alone and accessible, without the friends who seemed so intent on keeping interlopers out.

Dem despised the unwritten clique law that applied to everyone between the ages of thirteen and nineteen: jocks, punks, nerds, the socially cool, and the socially outcast. Stick with your own kind and no misfits allowed. He had joined the History Club hoping to remedy his isolation, but there was no bonding agent at work among the other members. Sienna had joined to be close to Chance, who needed an academic activity that wouldn't put undue pressure on his jock mentality. Bart needed a humanities credit to balance his predominantly scientific transcript. For Kilya, it had been no contest with her only other option—indefinite detention. He had been on the verge of quitting when Buffy and her friends had shown up. Wheedling his way into that circle had seemed like a feasible goal since nothing obvious linked them together and they had made an effort to include him. Last night he had realized he was wrong. They were bound by something that wasn't outwardly apparent; whatever it was—he didn't have it.

Unless Buffy was the nucleus. She had cared enough to make sure he got home safely. That wasn't much, but it was more encouragement than he had gotten from anyone else at Sunnydale High. Dem broke into a jog to intercept her.

"Hey, Buffy."

Buffy paused as she was about to push through the door. She covered her dismay with an awkward smile. "Dem. Hi. How's the head?"

"Fine." He rubbed the sore spot, then shrugged. "A little tender, but I'll live."

"Which is more than Luke Wellstone and a couple of others can say this morning."

"That cat killed him?" Dem's voice cracked. He had been so consumed with thoughts of Buffy he had mentally evaded the reality of his close call with the predator. People had actually died! The news was sobering.

Buffy nodded and looked him squarely in the eye. "You really do have to stay off the streets at night, Dem. After dark in Sunnydale is extremely harmful to human health."

"Until they catch that cat anyway."

"Always." Buffy sighed. "Just take my word for it, Dem. Sunnydale has a really ugly underworld problem."

"I'll certainly keep that in mind." Dem scowled, recalling that she had used almost the identical words last night.

"A word of advice . . . not safe to be out and about in Sunnydale in the dark. . . ."

At the time, he had thought she was trying to soften the brushoff. Now he didn't know what to think. Was she crazy or telling the truth? Either way, he was intrigued. "Can I walk you to class?"

"Uh—no. Sorry, but I've, uh, got a student-teacher meeting thing. Gotta go." She shoved the door open and hurried away leaving no opening for argument.

And in way too much of a rush to be going to a student-teacher meeting. Dem followed her and was surprised when she went into the library.

He had only been in the school library once, shortly after he had first arrived at Sunnydale High. He hadn't been able to concentrate in the musty, dismal atmosphere, and the stiff, British librarian gave him the creeps. Mr. Giles had seemed oddly distracted and frazzled at the time. Since then Dem had used the public library, but he still wondered about the school librarian, and whether he knew more than he'd let on about the vandalism that had closed the library for repairs, or about the defused bomb found in the boiler room.

And yesterday Dem had hidden his distress when he realized the creepy Mr. Giles was taking over as the History Club advisor, especially since Buffy and company seemed comfortable with him. Maybe he'd just caught the guy on a bad day that time before.

Dem opened the library doors a crack, then quietly slipped inside when Buffy disappeared into the office. The librarian's voice drifted through the open door.

"Are you ill, Buffy? You look pale."

"Bad dream, Giles. Really bad dream. I think it's connected to the dig, but I'm not sure. There was a temple, I think, and black masks and blood—lots of blood. No vampires."

"Interesting considering what I've discovered. Let's wait for the others, shall we? They should be here soon. Would you care for some tea?"

Black masks and blood? Vampires? Connected to the archaeological site? What kind of student-teacher meeting was this?

Hearing voices in the hallway, Dem dashed into an open cage room opposite the office and ducked behind a stack of boxes filled with old books. He glanced at the top volumes. *Demons of Ancient Mesopotamia* and *Witchcraft in Modern America.* Not exactly standard high-school research topics.

Feeling queasy, Dem pressed back as Willow, Xander, and Oz walked in and took chairs around the central table. Xander set down a cardboard tray full of doughnuts. Buffy shuffled out of the office and sat beside Willow, who had activated a computer. Mr. Giles followed to stand at the head of the table. Dem didn't know what was going on, but he suspected something foul. He was also positive he had uncovered the unknown quantity that bound Buffy and her friends together.

The librarian.

Buffy forced the haunting image of Angel's obliteration to the back of her mind. As always, she desperately wanted the prophetic dream vision to be wrong. They never were, although the events she saw and experienced subconsciously did not always mean what they seemed to on the surface. But they sometimes did. Her best and only hope of averting Angel's final annihilation was to pay attention to Giles. She had to know what she was facing in order to fight it.

"—The obsidian smoking mirror belonged to Tezcatlipoca, the Aztec god of death, darkness, destruction, and destiny." Giles sighed. "Since he was also a shapeshifter with a preference for the jaguar form, he may be responsible for recent events."

"Like using the park as a deli?" Xander asked.

Buffy almost smiled. Xander's sarcastic humor was a defense mechanism that usually took the edge off everyone's jitters. It wasn't quite working for her this morning. Maybe because she didn't know what was going down in demonville—yet.

"And the cemetery." Willow looked up from the monitor screen. "And the mini-mall on Baxter. Johnny Spardo works at the convenience store there and, uh—he saw the cat get one of his customers . . . in the parking lot."

"Fast food for the predatory," Oz quipped.

Willow's tongue anchored the corner of her mouth as she typed a command. "But—I can't find any police or news reports about the attacks."

"And still nothing on Mr. Coltrane?" Buffy glanced over her shoulder.

Willow shook her head.

"So what's Tezcat's agenda?" Xander reached for a jelly doughnut, saw Giles frown slightly, then picked up a glazed.

"According to Aztec myth," Giles explained, "he was one of four gods created by Ometechutli and his female aspect, Omecihuatl. When Ometechutli decided the world needed a brighter sun, he made Tezcatlipoca the *first* sun, which is symbolic of an *age* in Aztec terms. However, Tezcatlipoca utilized his favored jaguar form and devoured all the people. Consequently, the honor was passed on to Quetzalcoatl, the second sun."

Buffy flinched. Angel had vanished in a bright flash of light in her dream. Sunlight would fry him into cinders as surely as a stake through the heart would turn him to dust.

"Is that significant?" Oz asked.

"Symbolically, perhaps." Giles took a jelly doughnut from the tray, but he didn't eat it. He shook his doughnut hand for emphasis as he talked, causing powdered sugar to sift off onto the table. "Quetzalcoatl destroyed the world with hurricanes. Tlaloc and Chalchiuihtlicue were lesser gods appointed as the third and fourth suns. They wrought havoc with fire and flood. A human was chosen to be the fifth and current sun, which will most likely be destroyed by earthquakes—according to ancient prophecy."

Xander scowled. "Does anyone else feel just a little concerned because the Hellmouth is in southern California, land of shake, rattle, and roll?"

"I'm not at all sure earthquakes are the problem, Xander." Giles started to bite into his doughnut, then changed his mind and set it on a napkin.

"Then what is?" Buffy asked bluntly. "Not that I don't find the mythical history lesson entertaining, but—could we get to the point?"

"Uh, yes—of course. Sorry to run on." Giles looked at her quizzically, sensing that she was more upset than annoyed. "Quetzalcoatl was a benign deity opposed to human sacrifice. He was forced into exile by Tezcatlipoca, the god of all things dark and demonic, who used the power of the smoking mirror."

"What kind of power?" Willow asked tentatively. "I mean, it, uh—must be pretty potent to make another god run, right?"

Giles nodded. "Tezcatlipoca could read thoughts, and he used that power to his advantage. He could not only foresee the future in the mirror, he was able to manipulate individual fate as he chose. He used the mirror's power to tempt potential allies and destroy his enemies."

"So did he tempt or destroy Quetzalcoatl?" Oz asked.

"Both actually. Quetzalcoatl was tempted into"—an embarrassed flush crept up Giles's neck—"an incestuous indiscretion, and vanished at sea filled with remorse. The Aztecs thought Cortez was the returning Quetzalcoatl."

Buffy held up her hands. Giles had OD'd on research and was wandering too far afield again. "Okay. Loose jaguar. Could be this Tezcatlipoca guy. Missing Aztec artifact that might be a mirror. Could be this smoking mirror. Obviously related. How? Exactly."

"Theoretically—" Giles sat down. "The Aztec gods moved of their own volition and often injected themselves into ordinary objects to maintain surveillance over their subjects. It's possible Tezcatlipoca became trapped in his own mirror, which was stolen from the Aztec capital Tenochtitlan by the Spaniards and buried with them here."

"Trapped how?" Oz asked.

"Like most of the Aztec gods, his strength was constantly renewed through human sacrifices." Giles paused thoughtfully. "Perhaps warring with Cortez's forces reduced the number of rituals they were able to perform in his name, thus weakening and imprisoning him in the glass."

"But—" Willow's brow creased in a puzzled frown. "If he couldn't get out of the mirror five hundred years ago . . . well, how did he escape now? If the jaguar is in fact this, uh, Tezcatlipoca person, of course."

"I'm not entirely certain," Giles said, "but he may have had enough energy for a single emergence that he didn't want to waste. The lives of a few Spanish soldiers would not have sustained him long. However, what was an unpopulated wilderness then—"

"Is a thriving monster market now!" Xander sighed. "Sunnydale smorgasbord."

"Yes, well, that's one way to put it." Giles didn't

smile. "But I suspect the slaughter of Sunnydale's residents may not be the only problem Tezcatlipoca presents."

"Okay, I'll bite." Buffy sagged. "What else?"

"He may be planning to conquer the sun by some means other than earthquakes, which would result in unending darkness." Giles took off his glasses and rubbed his eyes.

"Now there's a thought to make a vampire's day." Leaning forward, Xander rested his arms on his knees.

"So much for my floundering college plans." Buffy slumped. "I won't have time for school if I'm killing vamps twenty-four hours a night."

"Uh-oh." Willow froze.

"Uh-oh?" Oz started.

"Uh—on the news this morning—" Willow seemed to shrivel in her chair. "There was a story about sunrise being ten minutes late. Almost ten minutes. More like nine minutes and forty-seven seconds. The announcer said a computer glitch had made a mistake in the calculations."

Oz pointed at the computer. "Can you look up what time the sun rose two days ago and yesterday? And today."

Nodding, Willow attacked the keyboard. "Tuesday . . . 6:39. Yesterday it came up at 6:37. Today—" She leaned toward the screen, then sat back slowly. "—6:45."

"Instead of 6:35," Oz said.

"Oh, boy." Buffy exhaled. "We're in trouble."

"Don't you people ever go home?" Cordelia breezed through the doors toward the table. She stopped beside Willow. "Did you get it?"

"Your pith helmet? Well I, uh, found an online store

than sells them, but I . . . couldn't order one." Willow shrugged.

"Why not?" Cordelia looked offended. "I *know* there's room on my card."

"But *I* didn't know the last four digits of your social security number," Willow explained. "And it's, you know—a security thing?"

"Oh, right. Let's do it now, then. There's still time—"

"We're a bit busy at the moment, Cordelia," Giles snapped impatiently, evidence that he was extremely concerned about the developing situation. "You'll have to wait."

"Fine! I'll wait." Irritated, Cordelia sank into an empty chair and folded her arms. "What's going on?"

"You mean before you wrecked our train of thought?" Xander glowered at her. "Let's see. Delayed sunrise, prelude to perpetual night."

"You're kidding." Cordelia shifted uneasily when no one answered. "Okay, you're not kidding."

"In my dream this morning Angel was killed by the sun. Incinerated. Vaporized. Whatever." Buffy studied the faces watching her, gauging their reactions. They all knew her dreams were based on events that had not yet happened, but would. Giles gazed back stonily, perhaps guarding against revealing his true feelings. He tolerated Angel, but would rather see Angelus eradicated. The others didn't appear to be particularly upset by the prospect of losing him either. The evil Angeles had hurt all of them in one way or another.

"You're certain it was the sun, Buffy?" Giles asked evenly.

"Pretty sure. I mean, there was a bright light and he just . . . disappeared."

Giles lowered his gaze to study the uneaten doughnut. "Was that the entire content of the dream?"

Buffy shook her head and gave them a quick rundown: temple, masks, scream, knife, roar, blood, Angel. "And then I woke up."

"I am *so* glad we're not psychically linked, Buffy." Cordelia grimaced.

"I know you probably don't want to hear this, Buffy, but aside from Angel's apparent demise, I find your dream somewhat encouraging." Giles did not look at her until he had finished speaking.

"Encouraging?" Xander looked at Oz askance. "Did you find any of those things even remotely encouraging?"

Oz shook his head. "Not really."

"Me neither." Willow pushed her hair behind her ear. "Except . . . as far as I know, there aren't any ruined stone temples near Sunnydale. That's good . . . I think."

"Yes, well—perhaps. Buffy's dream would also indicate that the sun *does* rise at a critical moment." Giles paused, detoured by a stray thought. "Although I rather think it would be obscured to prevent visible light from shining through, as opposed to being destroyed—"

"Giles—" Buffy pleaded.

"Hmmm? Oh, yes." Giles continued. "When Tezcatlipoca threatened the world with eternal night during the time of the Aztecs, Huitzilopochtli fought him back every morning so the sun could ascend. Unfortunately, Huitzilopochtli required multiple daily human sacrifices to accomplish the task."

"I think we need an alternative plan," Xander said.

"Yes, quite." Rising again, Giles resumed pacing. "And we must also confirm that the entity prowling Sunnydale is, indeed, Tezcatlipoca. Assuming that's the case, we'll need more information to devise a plan to defeat him—one that doesn't call for ritual mass murder."

"I second that motion." Oz raised his hand.

Giles nodded. "Buffy and I will go to the site after school using the field trip as a pretext. If my theory is correct, I suspect we'll find . . . evidence."

"Can you be more specific?" Buffy asked. "So I know what to look for?"

"I'd rather not."

Catching the slight jutting of Giles' chin, Buffy didn't press. When he stubbornly withheld information, he had good reasons. Besides, if she wasn't looking for something in particular, she'd be more alert and suspicious of everything, which made annoying sense. It reduced the chances that she'd miss a small but vital clue.

"Oz and I are free this afternoon," Xander said. "Four pairs of eyes are better than two."

"No, absolutely not." Giles instantly segued into stern authority mode. "Tezcatlipoca had great influence over young adults because of his power to manipulate destiny. He *lured* people to evil, and teenagers—even those with your unique experiences—would be much too susceptible to his temptations. For the time being, the site is off-limits to everyone but the Slayer."

"So the field trip is off?" Cordelia threw up her hands.

"I'm leaning toward canceling, yes," Giles said.

Willow brightened. "Oh—so then, maybe it was a good thing I couldn't order your pith helmet, Cordy."

Cordelia, however, wasn't quite ready to abandon the helmet quest. "Doesn't that online company have a return policy?"

* * *

Dem hugged the far corner of the cage, terrified that the librarian would discover him after the students left. Having eavesdropped on the whole unbelievable discussion, he was convinced that Giles was insane. Maybe he was one of those deluded millennium fanatics who thought the world was doomed. The librarian was certainly smart enough to know that the twenty-first century didn't actually start until 12:01 A.M. on January 1, 2001. For whatever reason, Buffy and her friends had bought into his psychotic fabrications about ancient gods and the imminent destruction of the sun, and were pathetically unaware that their mentor was using them for some undisclosed evil purpose.

And *he* was late for class.

Easing forward, Dem watched as Giles returned to his office. With his mouth covered in powdered doughnut sugar, the librarian didn't look like much of threat, but then, even diabolical villains with hidden agendas had to eat. It was definitely safer to assume the man wouldn't appreciate having his questionable ethics exposed by a nosey kid. With luck, he could get out of the library without being seen.

Clutching his books to his chest, Dem took a deep breath and dashed out of the cage. He was halfway to the door before Giles's voice turned his feet into cement.

"Did you need something?"

Swallowing the lump in his throat, Dem slowly turned around. "Uh—well, I, uh, didn't know you were here, but . . . well, here you are!"

So lame! He was no James Bond, but then the librarian wasn't a crack detective, either. Giles didn't seem to suspect that he had been there for a while. Which wasn't hard to believe, given the librarian's intolerant attitude toward interruption. He had only needed that one initial experience to get the message. Kids probably came into the library and left almost immediately all the time.

"Yes?" Giles cocked his head and squinted. "You're in the History Club, aren't you?"

"Uh—yes, sir." Dem nodded and smiled weakly. "I, uh, thought I'd, uh—read up on Cortez!"

"Commendable. Second case on the right." Giles waved toward the upper level of reference books, then frowned again. He started to say something, then hesitated as though he had decided against it. "Don't you have a first-period class?"

Saved!

"Oh, yeah! I, uh—didn't realize it was so late." Nodding inanely, Dem backed toward the doors. "I'll check out, uh, Cortez—later."

"Yes, well—as you wish." Shaking his head, Giles retreated back into his office.

Dem left assured that Giles thought he was just another clueless geek. Which was fine. He was still stinging with the embarrassment of being knocked unconscious during the jaguar encounter last night, and now he had a chance to make up for it. Buffy would have to respect him after he saved her from the mad librarian's scheme—whatever it was.

And he'd find that out soon enough.

When he followed her and Giles to the archaeological site that afternoon.

Chapter 8

"No! Wait, Hazel—" Joyce stood in the middle of chaos, a victim of her own ambition. A class-four tornado would have done less damage to the small chic art gallery than she had managed in the past twenty-four hours. Crated and uncrated paintings were stacked everywhere. Those they had taken down to make space for Juan Hernandez's canvases were destined for storage in the back room. A few of Juan's pieces had been hung or placed on easels, but the arrangement seemed haphazard, without focus. Not acceptable.

Hazel Atkins peered at her over the rim of a large framed painting of the magnificent Templo Mayor, the architectural center of Tenochtitlan before Cortez destroyed it in 1521. The vibrant colors and detail, executed in a primitive style, perfectly captured the glory of the Aztec Empire at its height, and Joyce wanted it to be the focal point of the exhibition. She just couldn't decide where to put it to produce the desired effect. She'd have to get her act together soon, since it was after three and the show opened at seven tomorrow!

Hazel rested the frame on the floor and rubbed her aching arm. A robust widow of sixty and Joyce's primary patron, she had graciously volunteered to help set up and co-host the weekend's event. At the moment, the wealthy, good-natured woman probably regretted her generous offer.

Juan, tall and darkly handsome with brooding Latin eyes, leaned on an unopened crate. A hammer dangled from his hand. Joyce had toyed with the idea of introducing him to Buffy. Aside from his "hot hunk" appeal, he had an artist's sensitivity and a fun sense of humor. However, after due thought and consideration, she had decided playing matchmaker was a bad idea. Her stubborn daughter would resist any maternal meddling in her romantic affairs, and Buffy's calling as the Slayer would not be advantageous for Juan's artistic career.

Right now, the young man looked worried and hesitant about offering an opinion regarding the display. Although his work was about to make its professional debut, Joyce was running the show.

"Okay—" Taking a deep breath, Joyce smiled to alleviate the tension. "I think we're going about this all wrong."

"I agree. Let's take a break." Making sure the temple painting was stabilized against the wall, Hazel headed for the coffee station they had set up outside Joyce's office door. The gallery was closed to the public until the reception the following evening.

Juan set the hammer down and joined them. "Is there any of that stooble cake left?"

"Strudel." Hazel beamed with pleasure. Childless, she had developed a motherly affection for the artist—

and he had become addicted to her homemade pastries. "There's plenty."

"Eat it all, Juan. My waistline won't stand a second helping." Joyce poured herself a cup of muddy, over-done coffee, then rolled her eyes in exasperation as the telephone rang. "Excuse me."

Juan pulled up a folding chair. His brown eyes twinkled as Hazel handed him a paper plate piled high with apple strudel. *"Gracias."*

"Hello?" Joyce perched on the edge of her desk, amused by Hazel's fussing and Juan's adoring acceptance of her attentions. "Buffy! Hi, honey. Sorry I had to leave before you got up this morning. We're absolutely swamped trying to get ready for tomorrow. Are you okay?"

"I'm fine. I just wanted to let you know I might be late for dinner. Giles and I are going out to the site after school. To, uh—make the arrangements for the field trip."

"The Spanish archaeological site near Coyote Rock, right?"

"That's the one." Buffy's lighthearted tone put Joyce at ease. It had been far too long since she had been involved in an activity that wasn't life threatening.

"I'll probably be late myself. We're a little behind schedule here, I'm afraid. Have fun." Joyce hung up with a wistful smile.

"I did not mean to overhear, but—" Juan shrugged sheepishly. "Did I understand correctly that there's a Spanish ruin near here?"

"Yes. An old campsite or something. It's a few miles outside town. They've uncovered the remains of some soldiers that date all the way back to Cortez. Or so I've heard."

"Cortez?" Juan set his plate aside. "Would it be inconvenient for me to take an hour or so tomorrow morning? I would like to visit this place. To do some sketches."

"No problem." Joyce glanced past him at the disarray on the gallery floor. "As long as we have this disaster under control. Do you have any ideas?"

"Actually, yes!" Rising, Juan strode into the center of the floor and took command. "We shall arrange everything in the manner of an Aztec city. Templo Mayor in the center surrounded by the other interior and exterior temple pieces, surrounded by the peasant scenes and so on and so forth. This works for you, no?"

"This works for me, yes!" Joyce slid off the desk, feeling re-energized. As the Slayer's mom and a Sunnydale resident in the know, she didn't have many days when all seemed right with the world. She wasn't going to waste a single precious moment of this one. "Let's get those other paintings into the storeroom first, though."

"I was going to suggest that." Grinning, Hazel gave Juan a thumbs-up.

"Juan, could you sketch a diagram of an Aztec city before you leave tonight?" Joyce's creative energies had also clicked into gear. "I'd like to have fliers available at the door to explain the display layout."

"*Muy bien!*" Juan nodded vigorously. "An excellent idea, *Señora!*"

The ruts in the dirt track leading to the archaeological site were deeper and more tire-threatening than the potholes around the Sunnydale docks. Buffy gripped the edges of her seat as Giles tried to steer his aging Citroën DS on a course that wouldn't rip out the undercarriage. Her teeth jarred in her jaw when he hit a particularly insidious depression. A clanking noise indicated that the grumbling old car was in dire danger of falling apart around them.

"Maybe we should walk the rest of the way, Giles. Get some exercise . . . a little fresh air. Prevent unnecessary dental bills."

"It's only another half mile or so." Giles hunched forward to peer through the windshield. He kept a white-knuckled grip on the steering wheel with his left hand, downshifted with his right, and winced as the car rumbled over a series of waffled ridges in the hard ground.

"Is this a macho thing? Man against the ruts?"

"No, not at all." Giles flicked her an annoyed glance. "Since we don't know what we might find, I thought it would be prudent to have the car parked as close as possible. In case it becomes necessary to leave in a hurry."

"Giles, if we have to make a fast getaway, we'd make better time on foot."

"Oh, yes, well—I suppose you may be right." He sighed. "So let's hope it doesn't become necessary."

"Right." Buffy nodded. "Heaven forbid we'd have to abandon this junkyard relic you insist on driving."

"It's a classic."

The discussion and the dirt track ended on a level area that had been assigned the dubious designation of parking lot. The actual dig area began another hundred yards up a meandering path. Several cars and pickup trucks were parked at random between scrub bushes and large rocks. Buffy noted that Mr. Coltrane's rusting red Colt clunker wasn't among them. As the Citroën's motor coughed off, she wondered if most history-oriented teachers preferred old wrecks.

"Don't slam the door," Giles cautioned as he slid out and pocketed the keys. He tossed his tie and suit jacket into the back seat and pulled on a cable-knit V-neck sweater.

"I wouldn't dare." Buffy winced as the door squeaked closed. Following Giles's example, she gave it a shove with her hip to secure it.

As they started up the trail, Giles looked back with a quizzical frown. "Dem Inglese—he was with you in the park last night?"

"He was jogging and stopped to make small talk while I was patrolling. Why?"

"He came into the library this morning." Shoving his hands in his pockets, Giles studied the ground as he walked. "I found that odd, since I don't believe I've ever seen him prior to the History Club meeting. How much of your encounter with the jaguar and Angel did he witness?"

"None. He hit his head on a tree and was unconscious the whole time."

"Curious—"

"Not really." Buffy shrugged. "I think he just has a crush—on me."

"Really?" Giles grinned. "Captivated by the Buffy charm, is he?"

"Not funny." Buffy didn't point out that humorous banter was a violation of the strict Watcher code of conduct—all work, no play. However, the uncharacteristic teasing was better than the awkward discomfort she felt whenever Angel was mentioned. "Dem's a nice guy, but I don't need any complications in my life right now."

"Probably wise."

Buffy used the ensuing silence to get a feel for the

site and the crew before their presence became known. Several middle-aged and elderly men and women were working in the deep wash that cut through another flat stretch of land at a slightly higher elevation. String marked off sections of the dig inside the gully and under a rock ledge at the base of a long, gradual slope. A water truck pulled away from the storage tank behind a large tent. Apparently unconcerned about getting stuck or mauling a few sapling trees, the driver steered a course around the dig site that would connect him with the dirt track below the parking area.

"Everything appears normal—for an excavation of this type." Giles gaze focused on Lucy Frank when she stepped out of the tent to hand a worker a clipboard.

"I'll have to take your word for that." Buffy gaze swept the whole area, then settled on the tall rock formation just below the crest of the hill. She had hiked up to Coyote Rock from a different direction a couple of times since moving to Sunnydale, and she hadn't given the unusual natural structure more than passing notice. Today it seemed ominous . . . a stone totem of something evil.

"Those rocks—" An involuntary shudder rippled across Buffy's shoulders. "I want a closer look."

"Giles!" Lucy Frank shouted and waved from the tent.

Returning the greeting with a casual nod, Giles sighed. "Perhaps I can keep Ms. Frank occupied so you can explore without undue interference."

"Lucy," Buffy prompted. "She wants you to call her Lucy."

"Yes—" Giles nervously adjusted his glasses. "I must remember that. Let's see what we can find out, shall we?"

Buffy hesitated as Giles moved ahead, startled by the realization that the young woman made him uneasy. Was this a good thing or a bad thing? Considering Lucy's warm smile as they approached, it was potentially a very interesting thing. Although she was wearing jeans, boots, a red-and-white checkered shirt, and a wide-brimmed straw hat, the archaeologist bore a striking resemblance to Jenny Calendar, which could work for or against her with the heartbroken librarian. On the other hand, Giles and Lucy shared a passionate interest in the past, which might offset the troublesome aspects of her appearance. Either way, the romantic twist created some comic relief to offset the darker elements of the developing Aztec situation.

"What a pleasant surprise!" Eyes sparkling, Lucy grasped Giles hand but didn't shake it. "What brings you out here today? A scouting expedition, I bet."

"More or less, yes." Giles gently pulled his hand free and folded his arms. "I, uh—thought it might be a good idea to check things out a bit before I descend on you with my student horde tomorrow."

"Well, your timing's perfect. I was ready to take a break, and I can't think of anything I'd like better than giving you the grand tour." Lucy glanced at Buffy. "And this is—"

"Buffy Summers," Giles said. "One of the History Club members."

"Nice to meet you—Buffy." Lucy's smile dimmed and the nuance in her tone made it perfectly clear that she thought Buffy was a ditz. That assumption was going to make Buffy's job a lot easier.

"Yeah. Like, same here." With an exaggerated sigh, Buffy looked away as though she could care less about Lucy or the site. On a table beside the tent, human bones and rusted pieces of metal armor had been arranged for classification and labeling. "Ohmigod! Are those skeletons? I mean, like for real? Ewww."

Giles looked at her as though he had just instantaneously transported into an alternate universe where she had never outgrown the totally awesome, ever so cool, cheerleading persona of her pre—Buffy The Vampire Slayer days. *Like, stake that, vamp boy!* The thought was amusing, but she didn't grin.

Lucy wasn't amused. "Those *skeletons* were once soldiers in Cortez's army—five hundred years ago."

"Well, *they* obviously had a bad day." Rolling her eyes, Buffy leveled Giles with an accusing glare. "So we're going to, like spend the *whole* weekend digging up old bones and stuff? I mean—seriously?"

"Seriously, Buffy." Giles coughed to keep from laughing. "Perhaps if you wander around a bit, you'll get a better idea of how—fascinating an excavation can be."

"I so doubt it." Looking bored, Buffy turned to leave.

"Don't touch anything!" Lucy snapped. "Please."

"Like I'd deliberately touch pieces of some old dead guy?" Shaking her head, Buffy stepped up to the table and made a show of looking grossed out.

A ringing cell phone drew Lucy back into the tent. "Come on in, Giles."

Giles silently applauded Buffy's performance, then stepped through the canvas door flap. Curious, Buffy moved to a plastic window near the back of the tent to eavesdrop on Lucy's side of the telephone conversation.

"No, Mrs. Baine. He left right after I got here this morning and I haven't heard from him since. I'm sure there's nothing to worry about. He's probably poking through the university archives or something. Yes, Mrs. Baine. If he contacts me, I'll let you know immediately. Good-bye."

"Is there a problem?" Giles asked.

"No. Professor Baine is always forgetting about the time when he's doing heavy research. You'd think after twenty-some years of being married his wife would remember that." Lucy laughed. "Are you married?"

Buffy clamped her hand over her mouth to muffle an exclamation of surprise. Apparently, Lucy had been more than a little captivated by the Giles charm, which defied definition by teen standards. Buffy resisted the temptation to peek through the plastic, but it wasn't hard to imagine Giles' dumbfounded expression.

"Uh, well—no. No, I'm not . . . married."

Tight, embarrassed smile, Buffy thought, *followed by a quick change of subject.*

"Is this the excavation catalog?"

Nervous tremor in the voice, probably pushing at his glasses.

"Yes, it is. Coffee?" Lucy asked.

Nonchalantly shifting position, gracious acceptance of the offer, then back to a safe topic. . . .

"Yes, if it's no trouble. Mind if I have a look? At the catalog."

Maybe she knew Giles too well, Buffy mused. This was exactly how he had responded to Jenny when they first met. Like a babbling idiot. But although the Giles and Lucy show was entertaining, she had a more important mission. At least he wouldn't have any trouble keeping the archaeologist busy. If she began wondering what had become of Buffy the bimbo, maybe he'd be forced to ask her out to dinner as a diversion. Nothing short of imminent disaster would give him the nerve.

Unless Lucy asked him first—which was exactly how Jenny broke the romantic barrier.

Easing back from the tent, Buffy ducked behind the large water tank. Since nothing on the actual excavation site had struck her or Giles as strange, there was no reason to waste time on a closer inspection. Her Slayer instincts had always served her well and they were pulling her toward Coyote Rock.

However, if she made a straight-line ascent, she would be in full view of the camp until she reached a collection of large boulders just below the tall formation. Although all the volunteer workers seemed engrossed in painstaking brushing and scraping at various locations, caution seemed advisable. They weren't sure what was going on, or whether anyone connected with the dig was involved.

Buffy headed for one of two portable latrines that had been set up a short distance beyond the water tank. From there, thick clusters of brush and stands of scrub trees would provide sufficient cover for the uphill trek. Much more efficient than moving through the more distant, surrounding woods.

Except for an elderly man in a baseball cap, no one gave her a glance as she paused outside the blue cubicle. Aware of his interest, she opened the door, then quickly closed it again as though she couldn't bring herself to enter the disgusting chamber. The old man looked away. Buffy quickly slipped around the unit, crouched and darted behind a dense tangle of brush and briar. As she started to move upward, a depression in the soft dirt caught her eye.

Paw prints. Large. Feline. Headed up the slope toward Coyote Rock.

She didn't question the mysterious "knowing" that

had drawn her toward the stone fortress, although the uncanny sixth Slayer sense that mysteriously tapped into some universal databank still amazed her at times.

Buffy looked for the old man and didn't see him. She had to assume he would begin to worry and start looking for her when she didn't emerge from the porta-potty after a few minutes. Pressed for time, she moved swiftly and silently, tracking the cat's weaving course through the undergrowth up the incline. As she climbed, a distinct feeling that she was being watched increased.

The middle-aged man and two younger people, a red-haired man and a dark-haired girl who were probably Professor Baine's students, were standing guard on the downhill side of the boulders, scanning all avenues of approach in a 270-degree arc. She couldn't tell if they were protecting another excavation site or something more sinister. Either way, they didn't want anyone getting close to Coyote Rock.

Buffy considered retracing her steps to come in from the far side of the slope. However, as she recalled from previous excursions, that ascent was steep and covered with loose shale that could break free and give away her position and intent. It seemed wiser to return to the camp unseen and without arousing unnecessary suspicion.

Keeping down, Buffy circled back so it would appear that she was returning from a stroll near the woods.

Dem almost had a heart attack when Buffy swung wide on her descent from the hill and came within twenty feet of his hiding place in the trees. He held his breath as she turned back toward the camp and released it slowly when he was sure she was out of earshot. He had ridden his mountain bike out from town and had arrived several minutes before Buffy and the librarian. From his position in the woods, he had witnessed almost everything that had transpired.

Nothing unusual—until Buffy had seen something on the ground that startled her. He had been on the verge of shadowing her surreptitious climb up the slope when she had suddenly decided to turn back.

Dem shrank back instinctively when the librarian and Lucy Frank emerged from the tent. Buffy had just cleared the blue latrine, and broke into a jog when Giles waved her to hurry. After a quick handshake with Lucy, Giles urged Buffy away in the opposite direction. The archaeologist returned to the tent when they were out of sight.

From Dem's perspective, their trip had been a waste of time. Nothing odd was happening that he could see. The old people working in the gully certainly didn't look like members of a dangerous cat cult. However, Lucy had been really glad to see Giles so it was possible they were partners. Maybe in a scheme with Mr. Coltrane! Teachers were underpaid—why wouldn't they risk stealing priceless antiques to sell on the black market? The missing history teacher was probably in L.A. setting up the deal. He had taken the Aztec mirror to back up his ability to deliver.

Dem's mind raced as all the pieces began to fall into place. Giles would need people he could trust to dig up, pack, and transport additional pieces, which is where Buffy and her friends came in and why the librarian didn't want the original members of the History Club included on the field trip. The escaped jaguar gave him an excuse to cancel and a premise for his fantastic story about a renegade Aztec god! Giles had successfully manipulated his young followers into cooperating without revealing what he was *really* up to!

Bolstered by the power of his own brilliant deductions, Dem decided to do a little investigating of his own. He wanted to know what Buffy had found.

Confident that he couldn't be seen, Dem darted from the trees and sprinted around bushes to the dense thicket behind the porta-potty. He stopped short of the spot where Buffy had been crouched and looked down.

A rush of cold fear sent him stumbling backward with a choked yelp. The imprint of the huge paw meant that the killer cat was nearby! Maybe that's why Buffy had turned back. Because she saw the cat.

Struggling to breathe, Dem looked up the slope. He didn't see a dark form skulking down the incline, but that didn't mean the jaguar had moved on. It might be sleeping in the sun—if his cry and thrashing around hadn't alerted it to the presence of fair game! His flight response engaged instantly, and Dem whirled to run toward the safety of the camp. Panicked, he cried aloud again when he just missed a collision with Lucy Frank.

"What do you think you're doing?" The young woman blocked the path, her hands on her hips and her dark eyes narrowed suspiciously.

"There's—a cat." Dem stammered between gasps. "It killed some people—last night. It's around here somewhere—"

Lucy didn't seem fazed by the information. "You look familiar. Have we met?"

Nodding, Dem glanced over his shoulder, then back into the woman's unnerving stare. "Dem Inglese. The, uh—History Club meeting. I was there—"

"The question is what are you doing here—*now?*"

"Uh—biking." He pointed toward the woods. "I left it over there and, uh—I thought I saw someone I knew. Buffy—"

"She just left."

Dem shrugged. "Doesn't matter. She doesn't like talking to me anyway."

"But you like her." Ignoring his befuddled reaction to the astute observation, Lucy looked toward the towering rock and motioned for him to follow. "Come on. Let's walk."

Dem hesitated.

"No cat," Lucy assured him. "Jaguars hunt at night."

"You know about it? There wasn't anything in the papers or on the radio—"

"I chased it off this morning." Lucy snapped impatiently, then turned to go back to the tent. "But if you don't want my help with Buffy this weekend, that's okay, too."

"No! I do—" Licking his dry lips, Dem started up the slope. He didn't know what Lucy had in mind, but she *was* a woman. It couldn't hurt to listen to her advice. His zero batting average with girls couldn't get any worse.

Lucy fell into step beside him and clamped a hand on his shoulder.

"There's just one problem about this weekend, though," Dem said.

"What's that?" Removing her hand, Lucy signaled a man near the rocks ahead. The man nodded, then vanished down the eastern slope with two other people.

"Uh—Giles didn't tell you?" Dem asked, surprised.

"Tell me what?"

"That he's thinking about canceling the field trip." Sensitive to subtle shifts in people's moods, an odd benefit of always being on the outside looking in, Dem faltered when Lucy tensed.

"Why?" Her voice seethed with controlled anger.

"Uh—because of the cat and—"

"That idiot!" Fuming, Lucy grabbed Dem's hand and quickened her pace. "Guess I'll have to pay Mr. Giles a visit and talk some sense into him."

Given the intensity of Lucy's reaction, Dem didn't go on to explain the librarian's bizarre theory about the Aztec jaguar myth. The only thing that mattered was that she obviously wasn't working with him. Buffy first. Then he'd worry about Giles's questionable motives and his own theories about Mr. Coltrane's disappearance. He stumbled over a tuft of grass and yanked Lucy to a halt so he could retrieve his fallen glasses. "Sorry."

She just shook her head and continued up the hill. When they reached a ring of large boulders in front of the stone tower, she pointed to a rocky ledge. "Sit down."

"Sure." Swallowing nervously, Dem sat and leaned forward as Lucy continued on around the boulders toward the distinctive rock formation. Although it was much taller and wider with unusual angles and ledges produced by millennia of erosion, the tapering, randomly sculpted monolith gave him the same eerie feeling he associated with Stonehenge. It seemed to radiate with an unnatural, mystical force. He dismissed the disquieting feeling as simply an overactive imagination stimulated by killer-cat attacks and weird talk of magical ancient legends.

When Lucy returned a moment later, she had something round and golden clutched to her chest. She stood before him, calm and silent, her brown eyes boring through the layers of emotional insulation to the core of his tormented soul.

Dem flinched when she took off his glasses.

"You're quite handsome, you know."

No, he didn't know. A surge of anxiety about her intentions sent an erotic shiver down his spine. He wouldn't mind being seduced by an older woman, but his complete lack of experience would surely turn his initiation into the worst humiliation of his bumbling life.

"Why don't you wear contacts?"

"Uh—" Dem lowered his gaze as she gently touched his cheek. "I have some, but—uh, I just never, you know, thought"—he was so flustered, he didn't realize she had stepped back—"they'd make much difference."

"You're wrong. Look."

Dem looked up at his own face reflected in a black glass swirling with wisps of smoke. Without his glasses the image should have looked fuzzy, but he was so shocked by the subtle difference in his appearance he didn't wonder why he saw sharp, focused detail. As he stared, his reflected image shifted again. The uncertainty evident in his soft, brown eyes became a hard glint of confidence. His tucked chin tilted upward, exuding daring rather than timidity, strength rather than weakness.

"This is how you really are, what you really look like. Strong, self-assured, commanding. This Dem can have anything he wants, *anyone* he wants."

Entranced by Lucy's hypnotic tone, Dem could not tear his gaze away when his image receded slightly. Blue-gray mist drifted over a carved stone background adorned with gold and silver. Buffy was kneeling at his feet, her head bowed in obeisance.

His perspective changed abruptly and he was looking through the reflected Dem's eyes. Far below Buffy a throng of people held their arms out to him in supplication. Their chanted words whispered through his consciousness.

"*. . . master of the depths, ruler of the dark, mercy to your humble servants. . . .*"

Above him, highlighted by the flames of a hundred torches, the jaguar roared. A heat flowed through Dem's veins, infusing him with a magnificent, eternal energy . . . the power of life and death.

"This Dem is a god! One with Tezcatlipoca, lord of the night and master of destiny! The honor is yours, Dem Inglese—if you pledge yourself to his service."

Dem's first impulse was to reject the temptation. As much as he longed to be the confident presence portrayed in the images, he feared the power behind the promise, sensed a threat to his identity.

The essence within the mirror sensed Dem's hesitation. Drawing on the boy's memories, Tezcatlipoca amplified the feelings of helpless inadequacy and isolation that tormented him, then contrasted those feelings with the overwhelming sense of absolute control and strength inherent in the proposed union.

Confronted with the distorted extremes—remaining a meek, ineffectual victim or becoming a powerful, commanding force—Dem's resistance dissolved. Unaware of the ancient god's insidious manipulations, he nodded. "Yes."

Chapter 9

The Bronze was busy, considering the early hour. Not jammed, but crowded enough so the white noise of conversation was audible over the alternative hit song booming from the speakers. Cue sticks cracked against pool balls. Pinball machines clanged and whistled, and laughter echoed off the cavernous brick walls. The sounds melded to create the opening strains of Sunnydale's symphony of the night, a raucous farewell to the sun as it dove for the western horizon.

Buffy paused inside the door and inhaled the conflicting aromas of fresh coffee and stale beer, popcorn and sour milk, mold, dust, and age. The fragrance was peculiar to the establishment, teasing and assaulting the senses, not quite repugnant, almost pleasant in its familiarity. Like the hangout itself. Classic and modern movie posters in various stages of decay were plastered here and there on the walls. Bumper stickers and graffiti adorned the large supporting pillars, the calling cards of patrons past and present. Bare overhead lights, stacks of empty beer kegs, mismatched stools, tables and chairs—all contributed to the comforting lack of thought and design. The appeal of the senseless décor wasn't difficult to understand. It reflected the confusion and chaos in the lives of the predominantly teenaged clientele.

With a couple hours of daylight still to go after Giles dropped her off, Buffy had called Willow and arranged to meet her. Some downtime to fall back and recharge seemed like a good idea, especially since the Slay-erettes would be spending the weekend shoveling dirt and quite possibly trying to avert another Hellmouth disaster. Although she didn't see Willow, Buffy headed for the hidden alcove table her friend favored whenever Dingoes Ate Your Baby was playing.

Bad Deal, a new band in town, was setting up on the raised stage. They had gotten a four-chord rating from Oz a few weeks ago. Not great, but could be worse. One of the perks of playing this low-paying dive was that the featured group didn't have to worry about packing the place. The Bronze had a monopoly on young-adult nightlife in Sunnydale.

The lead singer, a good-looking but arrogant hunk, winked at Buffy as she passed. She looked away and kept walking. She had changed into black pants and a belted black leather jacket over a lacy gold top with a daring V neckline, and was pleased with the attention even though she wasn't interested. Black was appropri-ate for her plans. Classy black with gold just made her feel better about everything. Besides, there was always a chance she'd run into Angel.

"Hey, Buffy!" Smiling brightly, Willow scooted over in the vintage, vinyl booth seat scavenged from a demolished diner. "You look dressed to kill! I mean . . . kill in a good way. Like with guys . . . but not literally!" Appalled, she sighed. "Maybe I should just carry a sock to stuff in my mouth."

"And deny us all the joy of Willow wisdom? Not." Grinning, Buffy sat down, leaned back, closed her eyes, and relaxed. "Perfect."

"Pretty close. It would be if Oz was here. Not that you're not great company, Buffy! You are—for a girl, I mean—do you know what I mean?"

Buffy nodded. "Yes. Is that scary?"

"Probably." Willow paused. "I got you a soda, but if you'd rather have something else—"

"No. Soda's great." Buffy sat forward and picked up the plastic cup Willow pushed in front of her. "So where is Oz?"

"He and Xander are changing the oil in the van. Tuning and gassing it up. Throwing out a month's worth of uneaten French fries and soda cans. And most important, cleaning the back seat where Devon, you know . . . got sick last week."

"I'd rather not know." Buffy had enough gross things disturbing her sleep without adding the Dingoes' lead singer's gastric distress to the cast.

"Oh, well—anyway, Oz wants to make sure the van doesn't die a long overdue-death *this* weekend. Just in case."

"Good idea. The trip may do in his shocks, though. Really rotten road. Giles's Citroën barely made it out alive this afternoon." Buffy frowned. "Oz isn't a closet history fanatic, is he?"

Willow shook her head. "Uh-uh, no. Why?"

"Never mind. Bad theory."

"Oh." Willow looked at her guardedly. "Anything else—interesting happen?"

"Happen? No. Interesting. Maybe." Buffy finished off her soda and sighed. "Dr. Baine seems to be missing now, and I found large cat prints near Coyote Rock."

"Not cool. So—will that affect the field trip? Is it still on?"

Buffy nodded. "For us—not for the History Club. Giles was adamant about canceling, even if we're just dealing with a man-eating animal, not the Aztec demon of darkness."

"Oh, good. Getting away for the weekend will take my mind off not hearing from M.I.T."

Buffy ignored the college comment. "Giles was going to call Oz when he got back to the library. Since the other club members aren't going, we'll need our own gear—"

"Who's not going where?" Cordelia appeared behind Willow, frowning. A casual, loose-fitting powder blue sweater and blue jeans accented rather than diminished her appropriately feminine curves. "And please don't tell me the trip to the excavation site is a no go."

Buffy looked Cordy in the eye and smiled. "The trip to the excavation site is a no go."

"No way!" Cordelia's dark eyes flashed, signifying much sound and fury and terrible consequences.

"Not entirely, though!" Willow jumped in. "We're going. Buffy and me—and Oz and Xander."

Pulling a chair from a nearby table without asking if anyone else was using it, Cordelia sat and folded her arms defiantly. "I just paid a hundred and fifty dollars for a pith helmet. That's a little much for a wall decoration, even for me. Besides, if I hang it in my dorm room at Stanford, I'll feel like a *complete* fake if I can't honestly say I wore it working on a real archaeological dig. I'm going."

"But—the cat thing is out there." Willow cast a helpless glance at Buffy and shrugged.

"I'm going. How horrible can a *cat* person be compared to most of the creeps the Hellmouth has spit out?" Considering the matter settled, Cordelia turned to Willow. "Speaking of pith helmets—did you get the shipping confirmation?"

"Not yet." Willow wrinkled her nose. "We can go check again now—if you want."

"I'll drive." Standing, Cordelia headed toward the door.

"Coming, Buffy?" Willow's eyes pleaded.

"Yeah, but just long enough to pick up the tranquilizer gun. There were too many people at the site to do any serious poking around today. Less chance of being seen after dark."

"And the gun is for—"

"Cat insurance. I found out the hard way that a stake against a hungry jaguar is about as effective as a toothpick against a brick wall."

"Always better to be prepared." Willow nodded toward Cordelia, who was glowering at them from the door. "We'd better go."

"Right." Buffy grabbed Willow's arm as she started to dash off. "There's just one other thing—"

"I'm *not* putting a 'nice' spell on Cordelia. Xander already asked and uh-uh. Not gonna happen 'cause I know I'd screw it up. And we'd probably *all* end up being too nice to kill vamps or something, and everyone in town would *die.* And I couldn't live with that on my conscience. No, thank you." Willow scowled to underline her determination.

"Not what I had in mind." Buffy urged Willow forward slowly. "If you see Angel tonight and he asks where I am? You don't know. I don't want him going any place where he could get caught out in the open at dawn. Got it?"

"Oh, yeah. Your dream. Angel crisp—" Willow winced, then made a zipping motion across her mouth. "Got it. Vacuum sealed. Not a word."

"Okay." Relieved, Buffy charged ahead, braced for a blast of Cordelia indignation.

Lucy was pleased with her choice, even though Dem was still disoriented. She studied him as he walked down the slope in front of her, noting the stumbling gait and nervous glances he cast back and his annoying habit of pushing up his glasses, which he had put back on after the connection with the mirror was broken. She smiled to reassure him, a temporary necessity to keep him focused. After his initiation as Tezcatlipoca's *ixiptla* at dawn tomorrow, the boy would essentially become the human embodiment of the deity, and all aspects of the shy, uncertain teenaged geek would be gone.

Lucy swayed slightly and paused, dizzy from exhaustion. She had been awake since long before dawn, and the events of the day had drained her. However, Baine was no longer a problem and all the workers had been wooed into blind obedience through the power of the mirror. This evening, many of their friends and relatives would be exposed to the mirror and added to the ranks. With Dem soon to be anointed as the *ixiptla,* all the preliminary preparations for Tezcatlipoca's reign of darkness were complete. Nevertheless, there was still much to be done and no time to rest. Drawing on an inner reserve of will, Lucy plunged down the hill to catch up.

Rolf intercepted them before they reached the water

tank. Freckles and a head of shocking red hair made him look younger than his twenty-one years. Belittled by Baine in class and on the site, he had gladly embraced the gruesome task of impaling the dead professor's head after she had subjected him to the mirror's spell that morning. "We've got a problem."

Lucy waited for an explanation.

Rolf looked at Dem suspiciously, then looked away when Dem held his gaze without wavering. "That detective is back. Asking questions about Professor Baine. He's waiting for you in the tent."

"I'll handle it. Come on, Dem."

Rolf bowed his head and stepped back to let them pass.

Leaving Dem outside, Lucy slipped through the canvas flap and found Dwayne Thomas thumbing through the site findings catalog. "You wanted to see me, Detective?"

"Yes." Thomas eyed her narrowly. "Professor Baine is missing. According to his wife, you were the last person to see him. When he left here this morning."

Lucy shook her head and sighed, feigning exasperation. "Did you check with the university? He told me he had some research to—"

"He never got to the campus. No one's seen him in the library or the archives or his office. He didn't show up at his afternoon class and his car's not parked in his assigned space. Or anywhere else on school grounds for that matter."

"That is odd." Frowning with worry, Lucy eased past the detective to the camp stove and set a kettle of water to boil. "Would you like some coffee? Or tea, perhaps?"

"No, thanks." Thomas took a deep breath. "I'd like

your permission to look around the area. I can get a warrant, but I'd rather save us both the time and trouble."

"Of course." Abandoning coffee as a means of detaining him, Lucy turned slowly and smiled. "It'll be dark before long. Would you like a lantern?"

"The sun won't set for another hour, and I've got a flashlight if I need it. Thanks." Thomas took a step toward the entrance.

Moving quickly and without hesitation, Lucy grabbed a large rock weighting a stack of papers on a tray table and struck the detective in the head. He staggered. She hit him again and calmly eased back as he crumpled to the ground.

Dem threw the flap back. "What happened?"

"We're having company for breakfast." Setting the rock aside, Lucy rolled the unconscious man over and removed his gun and a set of handcuffs. "Get Rolf."

Dem obeyed without question and returned in less than a minute with the red-haired college student. Following Lucy's instructions, they lifted the man's dead weight into a chair and watched silently as she cuffed his hands behind his back. She gave Rolf the 9mm weapon.

"If he gives you any trouble, make him inhale some of this." Lucy reached for a small bowl filled with *yauhtli* powder, an anaesthetizing hemp drug used by the ancient Aztecs to numb their sacrificial victims. "I might be gone awhile."

"No problem." Rolf sat on a chair facing Thomas with the gun firmly gripped in his hand.

Lucy searched the detective's pockets for his car keys, scribbled directions to a warehouse district in L.A. on a scrap of paper, then waved Dem to follow her. Having to deal with another police investigation right now was an inconvenient irritation, but one she had expected and planned for. She had just foolishly hoped it would take longer for Ruth Baine to realize her husband *had* vanished. She couldn't simply hide the detective's official unmarked car the way she had Dan's old Colt and Baine's Taurus sedan. Her solution, however, would keep the cops away from the site for at least another day. After that—nothing the police did would matter.

"Henry! Eleanor!" Lucy met the old man and the plump spinster as they climbed out of the gully.

"Got another car to ditch, eh?" Henry pushed back the brim of his Minnesota Twins baseball cap and grinned.

Eleanor nervously wiped her hands on her extra-large sweat pants. "Are you sure you want me, Lucy?"

"Yes." Lucy handed the directions to the old man. "I want you to follow Henry to L.A., Eleanor, so he has a ride back. Park the car someplace where it will be easily spotted, Henry, and don't forget to bring the keys back with you."

"Consider it done. Let's go, Ellie."

"But I'm a mess!" Flustered, Eleanor wrung her hands.

"Nobody's gonna see you but me, and I don't give a damn whatcha look like! Let's go."

Eleanor's resistance dissipated as Henry stomped away. She bustled after him.

Lucy turned to Dem, who had watched the whole exchange with aloof disdain. Although his transition wasn't complete, he had apparently absorbed some of Tezcatlipoca's arrogance during the connection with the mirror. "Come on, Dem. I'll give you a ride home."

"My bike—"

Lucy almost refused, then realized it would be easier if the boy could return on his own in the morning. "All right. Go get it. I'll wait."

As Dem strode away at a leisurely pace, Lucy sighed. She was glad she had picked up a few things from her apartment and checked into a Sunnydale motel last night. The demands on a high priestess were time-consuming and trying. If Tezcatlipoca's chosen representative didn't take too much of his own sweet time retrieving the bike, she might have time for a bath in her room before she dropped in on Giles. Instinctively, she knew that subterfuge or force wouldn't work with the librarian, who was more complex and confident than his mild-mannered exterior would suggest. An attractive, charming woman, on the other hand, would be able to manipulate him quite effectively.

Some cats like to play with their prey before the kill.

Looking out on the world from the empty, infinite limbo within the mirror, Tezcatlipoca marked the seconds and mourned the years as the enemy sun dipped lower in the sky.

Four hundred and seventy-nine lost years.

Drained of his strength during Cortez's conquest of the Aztecs, he had fled into the mirror to wait until fate delivered him into the realm of another nation eager to serve his will and whim. As it was before, it would be now. A few would be rewarded and enriched. Most would give up their lives to feed his power. That was the way of a god, a truth long understood by mortal men.

But the waiting had been long and he was not a patient entity. Trapped in the glass, he had gained energizing life force when Diego de Garcia had died holding the vessel that contained him, but there had been no avenue of escape while buried under tons of earth and rock. Although he had the power to infect the human mind with visions of real and potential futures, he could not create such entertaining diversions for himself. Time spent abandoned and adrift, an incorporeal being awash in nothingness, had created a ravenous hunger for blood and vengeance.

Blood to restore his strength.

Vengeance for the lost centuries.

This he remembered as the last rays of light faded from the glass.

Gathering the wisps of his consciousness, Tezcatlipoca coalesced into smoke and rose into the night. Transforming into the jaguar was easier this time, his power enhanced by the heart of the human sacrificed in his name that dawn. He stretched, relishing the feel of sinewy muscle and the stench of decomposing flesh nearby. The cat was swift, strong, and savage, the most favored of his forms—except the human . . . but assuming a man's shape required more than the hunted prey that sustained the beast. Regaining his human aspect would demand many ritual sacrifices in the tradition of the ancients.

And the time was near . . . but until then, the cat had its own needs.

Tezcatlipoca raised his nose to the wind, testing scent. The musk of those humans working in the camp wafted on the evening breeze, tempting his predatory nature. The god rejected the urge. The High Priestess had enslaved them for other purposes, and replacing them would only delay his complete emergence.

Leaping from the rocks, Tezcatlipoca bounded down the hill and through the nearby forest, eager to hunt. The world had changed since the days of Montezuma. The people had multiplied and created wonders far beyond anything the Aztecs had imagined. But they were still human—susceptible to suggestion, intrigued by magic, intimidated by power, and helpless against the brutal might of the jaguar.

Except for the girl and her fanged warrior, a man who had lived and died—and yet had neither remained dead nor returned to life.

Tezcatlipoca had sensed many of these bewildering creatures on his forays through the human town. They were like him in many ways, fast and strong demons of death that stalked the dark. He did not fear them. And since their dead flesh and bloodless veins were of no use to him, and as they kept a respectful distance, he let them be.

Except for the one with the girl.

That one he would destroy for daring to defy his right to kill—after the girl's heart was paid in tribute.

He slowed his pace when he reached a concentration of dwellings on the outer edge of the town. Unlike the peasants he had known, these humans did not awaken and sleep on the sun's schedule. Light that was not fire shone from their windows. He paused to watch, fascinated by the strange activities that occupied the people of this new world. Young women spoke into machines that carried messages to distant ears. Children watched boxes that displayed moving pictures. Mothers cooked without flame and drew water from metal tubes. Men tinkered with the metal wagons they rode at great speeds everywhere they went. No one wandered the dark beyond locked windows and doors. He moved on.

Padding silently over hard streets, Tezcatlipoca skirted the place where a crowd of younger people had gathered. Following the jaguar's instincts, he looked for prey that had been separated from the herd. Drawn by a salty tang that reminded him of Lake Texcoco, he prowled a waterfront, keeping to the shadows cast by massive ships that moved without oar and sail. Human sounds mingled with strange music spilled into the quiet when a door on a corner building opened. Two men wearing funny yellow hats that looked like upside-down bowls emerged.

Tezcatlipoca crouched, saliva dripping from his fangs in anticipation of fresh game.

The men staggered down the walkway and paused, swaying erratically as they glanced up and down the street.

"Where'd ya put it, Max?"

"Put what, Steve?"

"The car, you lunkhead!"

"Don' 'member." Max laughed. "Guess we gotta walk."

Steve shook his head. "Uh-uh. I heard there's a killer cat loose in town."

"Killer cat, huh? I ain't ascared of no cat." Max stumbled into the street, ignoring Steve's warnings to return. "Here, kitty, kitty—"

Hidden in shadow, Tezcatlipoca eased forward.

Throwing up his hands, Steve stepped into the street to retrieve his companion.

The jaguar sprang. The man fell under his weight with a terrified cry that turned into a choked gurgle as fanged jaws crushed his exposed throat. Empowered by the first taste of blood, Tezcatlipoca tore flesh from bone and cartilage and looked up. Recovering from his initial shock, Steve started to back away.

He didn't get far.

One of the not-living creatures leaped from a darkened doorway and grabbed the man from behind. A dark human face grinned at Tezcatlipoca, then shifted suddenly. A bony ridge appeared between eyes that glowed with a demonic green and golden light. Roaring, the creature sank its fangs into Steve's neck and held on until the body collapsed in a lifeless heap at its feet.

Poised over his own kill, Tezcatlipoca watched as the creature's face shifted back into a human mask, then snarled as it boldly ambled toward him. The creature held up its hands in a placating gesture, but kept coming. A metal ring hung from a pierced ear and it wore the matching jacket and trouser costume preferred by modern males. When it stopped, it tugged on the wide gold cloth knotted around its neck, then shoved its hands into forest-green pockets.

"Tezcatlipoca, I presume. I'm Mr. Trick."

The jaguar crouched, wary and wondering how the strange demon knew his name. No one who hadn't been touched by the mirror should know of his return, and no one in his service would dare tell. This Mr. Trick was unlike any demon he had encountered before, however, and it aroused his curiosity.

"Now that we've had our hors d'oeuvres, I'd like to discuss a matter of mutual cooperation and benefit."

Tezcatlipoca dragged his kill deeper into the shadows and ate while he listened.

Chapter 10

"This is far enough, Oz." Buffy pushed a dangling plastic skeleton aside and lifted her Slayer bag off the floor behind Oz's seat. The turnoff to Coyote Rock was just ahead. She appreciated the ride out from town, but driving any closer would alert the people in the archaeological camp.

"You sure you want to get out here?" Oz steered the van onto the shoulder of the paved back road and peered through the windshield. Visibility was almost zero, in darkness lit by a mere sliver of moon. "It's a mile hike up to the site."

"Take my word for it. That wannabe road is the automotive equivalent of the elephant's graveyard. If we searched, we'd find the rusting innards of all the old clunkers that came here to die."

"I have to drive it tomorrow." Oz's bushy eyebrows twitched with concern.

Buffy smiled sympathetically. The van was more than just cool transportation for Oz. It was a diary written in boy toys, a rolling museum of accumulated stuff that told his life story. The only things he cared about more were those that lived and breathed—and maybe his guitar.

"True, but there's no sense running the gauntlet more than once if you don't have to." Opening the door, Buffy slid out and grabbed the tranquilizer gun stashed behind the passenger seat. "Are you going back to the library?"

"Not right away. Xander's on the phone trying to beg and borrow the camping gear on Giles's list. We'll stop by after we've collected everything." Oz leaned across the seat as Buffy started to push the door closed. "What about you? How are you going to get back?"

"It's only a few miles going cross-country. I'll be fine." Waving, Buffy shouldered her arsenal and darted into the brush.

Sitting at the computer behind the book counter, Willow logged back into the safari-gear site for the umpteenth time since she and Cordelia had returned to the library. The company's computer system was still down. "Sorry, Cordy."

"I'm not leaving here until I *know* my order was shipped." Disgusted, Cordelia stormed back to the table to finish her trig homework. She shot an angry glance back at Willow. "Online shopping will *never* replace the mall."

"I never have *time* to go to the mall." A frown hovering between thoughtful and petulant creased Willow's brow. "Okay, so . . . I never hung out at the mall much *before* Buffy came to Sunnydale, but—I've only been back a couple times since we blew up the Judge and, you know, turned him into a zillion little pieces. Which was a really good thing 'cause no one can ever put him back together again, but—"

"I remember the Humpty-Dumpty rocket routine, but the Judge is like permanently off the Slayer hit list." Cordelia paused, confused. "So what's your point?"

"Nothing. It's just that . . . I can't go into the mall now without wondering . . . if we found *all* the pieces." Willow shuddered. "Like I expect to find a sliver of him in my strawberry milkshake or something."

"Oh, there's a flavor of the week. Demon Dunk." Annoyed, Cordelia folded her arms. "Thanks, Willow. Now I'll never be able to drink another milkshake at the mall."

"Sorry." Withering slightly, Willow welcomed the interruption when Giles came out of his office. She liked the sweater look. The touch of casual softened the British sternness permanently etched on his face.

Giles handed her a scrawled note. "Would you type this up and print it, please? I'll need four or five copies to post around the school."

"Sure." Willow scanned the field trip cancellation announcement. "Won't the other kids in the History Club be upset? I mean, when they find out we're still going and they're not?"

"That wasn't a point of consideration." Giles leaned against the counter and rubbed his weary eyes. "Since my Tezcatlipoca theory hasn't been proven, I may be overreacting. However, with two people missing and a killer jaguar using Sunnydale as its primary hunting ground—" He straightened up suddenly when the library door opened.

"Am I interrupting?" Lucy Frank stepped inside.

Willow couldn't decide which of the two adults was more enchanting. Giles because he was gawking like a speechless schoolboy—or Lucy, who had traded in jeans and boots for a clinging blue knit dress. The jaguar wasn't the only one prowling Sunnydale, but at least Lucy's intentions weren't deadly.

"Are you busy?" Lucy looked directly at Giles.

"Uh, no. No, we're not. Please come in."

"Thanks." Acknowledging Willow and Cordelia's curious stares with a nod, Lucy paused by the librarian and hit him with a verbal two-by-four. "Are you free for dinner?"

"Dinner?" Giles stammered the word, as though the concept of going out to eat was as alien to him as e-mail.

Cordelia rolled her eyes. "He's free."

"Yep." Willow nodded and didn't back down when Giles admonished her with a scowl. "You know what they say, Giles. You are what you eat. And, well— you've been living on jelly doughnuts lately."

"I adore jelly doughnuts." Lucy grinned. "But tonight I have a craving for Italian."

"Italian works," Cordelia said. "The pesto pasta at Mario's got five stars in last Sunday's restaurant-review column."

"Yes, well, I'm sure the cuisine at Mario's is excellent, but—" Giles hesitated, which Lucy read as an imminent refusal.

"Actually, I do have an ulterior motive."

"You do?" Willow reacted spontaneously, then winced.

Lucy laughed and cocked her head coyly. "Yes, but my price for telling is some charming company over a real meal. Camp food and takeout gets monotonous after awhile."

"Which is why I was going to suggest the Naples Terrace," Giles said.

"All right." Lucy smiled, pleased. "I'm ready whenever you are."

"Just give me a moment to, uh—get something from my office." Giles glanced at Willow as he turned. "Come along, Willow. I have those—reference notes. For your assignment?"

Willow was about to ask what assignment, then realized he didn't want Lucy to hear whatever he wanted to tell her. Maybe he was going to yell at her for interfering in his social life! She jiggled nervously as he pulled his wallet and keys from his suit coat pocket, then relaxed when he gave her another paper.

"A computer search of those words might turn up some additional information on our Aztec friend," Giles explained. "I won't be gone too long, and you know where to reach me if something happens."

Willow exhaled, unaware that she had been holding her breath. "Right. I'm, uh, sorry if I—you know, said something out there I shouldn't have."

"Yes, well—that's another discussion." Giles paused at the door and lowered his voice. "I only accepted because Ms. Frank might be able to shed more light on the disappearances of Mr. Coltrane and Professor Baine."

"Right." Willow didn't believe that was his only reason. "Fishing expedition. Got it."

"Good. I'll be back in an hour or so."

Willow waited until the couple left before leaving the office. Cordelia looked up as she walked by. "I'll keep trying and let you know."

Easing back onto the stool, Willow checked to make sure Cordelia's attention was on math, then signed back onto the web. Before she tackled a new information search with Giles's keywords, she tried the police files to see if a missing-person report had been filed for Dr. Baine. None had . . . but a Detective Dwayne Thomas had been sent to the site that afternoon for undisclosed reasons. Maybe to investigate the professor's disappearance even though it wasn't "official." In any event, the Department hadn't heard from him since he left three hours ago.

Maybe Detective Thomas hadn't found anything suspicious and had just stopped to eat on his way back to the station.

And maybe he was vanishing guy number three!

Two in one day? Definitely not good.

Even though Buffy could take care of herself, she was a long way away without any backup. Except the tranquilizer gun. What if it jammed? Could happen. If Angel hadn't been in the park last night, she could have ended up as Slayer cat kibble. Angel wouldn't think to look for her at Coyote Rock, and she had promised Buffy not to tell him. Bad move. But *somebody* had to let Buffy know that someone else was missing from the site . . . maybe. It just wasn't wise to take any chances.

Willow picked up the phone and dialed. Oz had called from Xander's house forty-five minutes ago, after he got back from dropping Buffy off. No answer. She tried Oz's number. No answer there either. They were probably driving around getting all the gear Xander had scrounged for the weekend.

"Cordelia. We have a problem . . . maybe, kind of." Willow had a really bad feeling she couldn't ignore. It was an acquired Hellmouth thing.

"They didn't send it, did they?" Furious, Cordelia threw down her pencil.

"No! I mean, I don't know—about your helmet. It's Buffy."

"What about her?"

Willow really didn't want to ask Cordelia for a favor,

but there wasn't anyone else. She explained in a rush. "Somebody's got to go tell her about the missing detective."

"Why?"

"Well—" Another possibility hit Willow. The Slayer wasn't exactly on good terms with the local authorities. "What if he's not really missing? What if the police are in on it? Whatever it is . . . that's going on."

"We don't *know* that anything's going on," Cordelia reminded her coldly. "Nothing weird anyway. Except for a big cat using the streets as a grocery store."

"Yeah! Exactly, and—I don't know when Xander and Oz will get here, and Giles just left and I can't reach him. Besides, I don't want to spoil his first dinner date in ages. You've got a car."

"I've also got homework," Cordelia countered stubbornly.

"But—Buffy can't just pound a cop!" Willow pressed, trusting her instincts. "I mean, if they decide to haul her off to jail for, uh—trespassing or carrying a concealed stake or—she's got a gun! No permit!"

"All right! Going is better than sitting here and being babbled to distraction." Rising, Cordelia grabbed her purse off the table.

"Great, but, uh—don't park too close to the camp."

"I know I'm going to regret this." Sighing, Cordelia rummaged in her bag for her keys. "So while I'm gone, the least *you* can do is check my calculations and make sure I got the right answers."

Willow nodded. "I can do that."

There was blood in the air. Human blood. The scent drifted on a whisper of wind, taunting the hunger Angel refused to satisfy. The jaguar was not fasting. He sensed the beast even from a distance, knowing it was not a beast of noble, jungle breeding, but a thing born of evil. The cat was stalking Sunnydale, unchallenged by vampire or Slayer. And Buffy was nowhere to be found.

Frustrated, Angel sprinted through the cemetery gates and ran for the library. Giles would know where Buffy was and what she was doing, and he would want his help. When the Slayer's life was at risk, the librarian had no compunction about setting aside his simmering hatred for Jenny's murderer. Intellectually, he knew Angel was not responsible for the atrocities Angeles had committed, and all too often his vampire strength and speed had been the Slayer's survival edge. Giles was no fool.

But *he* was.

He could not purge Buffy from his heart, and his love threatened both of them. For the better part of two hundred and fifty years, he had carved a path of blood, terror, and pain across the world as the reviled and feared Angeles. A gypsy curse had smothered the demon and condemned him to an existence of self-loathing that had reduced him to a street bum feeding on rats and skulking through alleys—until a wisp of a girl had stolen his silent heart.

Buffy was his salvation and his doom.

Protecting her gave him purpose.

Passion would destroy him.

He burst through the doors of the school library like the black avenging angel he had become. His long, black duster settled around him as his dark gaze took in every detail of the room. Giles wasn't there, but Willow jumped off her stool with a startled yelp.

"Angel!" Willow's small, white hand fluttered to her chest. "Uh—hi!"

"Where is everyone?"

"Out. Uh—" She darted around the counter and hesitated, looking frantic. An idea seemed to strike her suddenly, lighting up her pixie face as brightly as the candle-lit windows of old Dublin on All Hallows Eve. "Want some tea? Oh—no, of course you don't." She laughed nervously. "I forgot. Vampires don't drink tea . . . or anything else except blood . . . not that you do! No." She paused. "Do you?"

If not for his worry, Angel would have smiled. Willow's genuine innocence was refreshing in a jaded, cynical world. "Do you know where Buffy is?"

"Uh—Buffy?" She hesitated again, then nodded. "It's just that, well—she made me cross-my-heart-and-hope-to-die promise not to tell you, but—"

Angel's countenance darkened with alarm. "Why?"

"It's not bad!" Willow shook her head vigorously. "I mean, not bad in the sense that she, uh—doesn't want to see you or anything. Just bad like—in this nightmare—she had and—"

"Buffy dreamt about me?"

Willow nodded.

"It's all right, Willow," Angel said gently. "You can tell me."

"Uh, well—" Fighting inner turmoil, the girl started to pace. He didn't interrupt her rambling monologue, knowing she would get to the point eventually. "That's good because Buffy's out there by herself. Almost. I mean, Cordelia went to warn her, but we don't know what's happening and it might be too much for them to handle alone. And maybe there's nothing to worry about . . . but we don't know, you know?"

"Out where?"

"Coyote Rock. Wait!" Willow called him back

as he turned. "Buffy didn't tell you because she dreamed . . . she dreamed you died. Or whatever it's called when a vampire, you know—gets turned into burnt toast by the sun. If anything happens to you, Angel, she'll never forgive me for telling."

"She dreamed that?" The Slayer's dreams were prophetic, but he'd rather be annihilated than abandon Buffy if she needed him.

Willow sighed, nodding slowly.

"I promise I'll be careful. Cross my heart and—whatever." With a curt nod, Angel left.

Following the path cut by the water truck, Buffy had skirted the parking area and main camp without being detected. Halfway up the slope, she looked down to check on the guards. Blazing camp lights illuminated the gully and tent area. Most of the workers had gone home. The red-haired man and the younger woman she had seen that afternoon had just finished a patrol and sat at the tent table drinking coffee. With luck, no one had been assigned to guard Coyote Rock.

Buffy studied the ground as she moved forward, avoiding noisy dry brush and loose rocks that would alert the sentries to the presence of an intruder. Moving quietly over wilderness terrain, the darkness lit only by a slim crescent moon, was a true field test of her Slayer abilities. So far, she was passing, and as near as she could tell she was alone on the hill. No nocturnal animals scampered through the undergrowth foraging for food, and she felt no twinges warning of more sinister company. Although the jaguar could be lying in wait, she did not sense it, and assumed that it had returned to the heavily populated streets of Sunnydale to hunt. Which was odd, when she thought about it, since two perfectly good human entrees were lounging less than a quarter-mile away. She filed that observation for later consideration, as she reached the line of boulders just below the stone tower.

Slipping sideways through a break between two massive stones, Buffy paused on the far side to take a flashlight from her pack. With the tall rocks behind her to block the glow, she aimed at the ground, flipped the light on, and crept forward with the tranquilizer gun tucked under her other arm. The light helped, but it still took a few minutes to pick her way through the dark, natural stone labyrinth. Low tangled branches clawed at her coat and legs, and she paused when a piece of loose shale shifted under her heel with a crunching sound that seemed louder than it was in the eerie quiet. Taking the cautionary hint, she angled the flashlight beam ahead of her to check the footing and froze when the circular light captured a man's boot.

Since becoming the Slayer, she had seen far too many bodies that had been punctured, mutilated, withered, and otherwise violated in ways too numerous and obscene to remember. Nevertheless, she had not been prepared to find the remains of two headless bodies tossed in a pile like so much garbage. The cat had obviously gorged itself on one of them. The other man had had his heart cut out. The heads were grotesquely displayed on eight-foot pikes at the base of Coyote Rock several feet further on.

Dan Coltrane and Dr. Baine.

She took no comfort in knowing that the history teacher wasn't a thief. The left side of his face had been torn away by jaguar fang and claw. The professor was a stranger reputed to be an arrogant, self-indulgent tyrant, but he hadn't deserved to be brutally slaughtered and defiled with a knife. To have their severed heads mounted like big-game trophies was a final humiliation, which flaunted the killer's complete lack of respect for their stolen lives. Only the need to keep her investigative intrusion a secret prevented her from pulling the heads down.

A glint from a narrow cut in the tower caught her eye, but as Buffy took a step toward it a cold shudder rippled across her shoulders and the fine hairs on the back of her neck sizzled with alarm.

Vamps.

There were several . . . and although they were still some distance away, they were closing in on her position from all sides.

Setting the gun on a large, flat stone, Buffy turned off the flashlight and unshouldered her bag. She stuck two stakes in her back pockets and gripped another. A twig snapped to her left, on the western side of the hill she had just climbed. Poised on the balls of her feet and trusting her senses, she waited. A stone rolled down the incline. When a dark figure jumped down from a tall rock to her left, she whirled with the stake drawn back to strike. She stayed her hand a mere inch from a fuzzy, blue sweater.

"Duh, Buffy! It's me!" Cordelia hissed indignantly. "The last time I looked, 'Stake Me, I'm Undead' was *not* tattooed on my forehead."

"Cordelia! What are you doing here?"

"I'm asking myself the same question. I was elected by a committee of one to come warn you that—" Cordelia's eyes widened and she uttered a weak cry as Buffy drew the stake back again and suddenly shoved her aside.

The vampire sneaking up behind the girl looked as

surprised as Cordelia when Buffy drove the stake into its heart. She could almost hear the mental "oops" that impaled its thoughts a split second before it vanished in an explosion of dust.

"It never ends with you, does it?"

"Nope." Buffy tossed Cordelia the stake and pulled another from her pocket as two more vamps charged from the boulders. A quick kick to the stomach knocked the female off her feet.

Cordelia jumped on top of the downed demon and drove the stake into her chest without stopping to think. She grimaced as the vampire disintegrated underneath her, then gasped again when she stood up and saw the pikes. "Ohmigod! Is that Mr. Coltrane's head?"

Buffy didn't have time to confirm the obvious. Spinning, she landed a solid foot on the male vampire's chin, then lunged toward him as he staggered backward. He ducked to the side, whirled, and roared as he grabbed her from behind. Buffy whacked him in the head with the stake, surprising him into loosening his hold. Slipping easily out of his grasp, she pivoted and landed another kick that sent him reeling backward.

Cordelia used the two-handed, lip-biting, eyes-almost-but-not-quite-closed technique to stake him in the back. Then, squaring her shoulders defiantly as he flashed out of existence, as she shook dusty vampire residue off her weapon she muttered, "I'd rather be doing my math."

Sensing another vamp behind her, Buffy rammed her stake backward. The demon vanished in a cloud of dust before it touched her.

"I thought you guys were on vacation!" Cordelia fumed, her gaze fastened on the ring of boulders behind Buffy.

Buffy turned slowly to see another ten to twelve vampires approaching from behind and on top of the tall boulders. They looked hungry after their long, unexplained week of abstinence.

"Isn't this a little much for the two of us?" Cordelia asked.

"Yep." Buffy opened her stance, daring the undead hoard to attack.

"I was afraid you were going to say that." Adopting a position that made her look like a skinny sumo wrestler, Cordelia gritted her teeth and gripped her stake. "This is not what I came out here for."

"What did you come out here for?" Buffy didn't take her eyes off the surrounding vamps.

"I'm too petrified to remember," Cordelia snapped.

"Just stay behind me."

"Right. Like that's supposed to make me feel better?" Cordelia's sarcasm was laced with a tremor of fright. "Eleven against two? The odds are not in our favor."

Buffy had to agree. She wasn't feeling too great herself, even though the vamps seemed hesitant. Like they were afraid . . . of what? Certainly not one Slayer and an admissions candidate for Stanford. Coyote Rock? Or the jaguar that probably wasn't a jaguar? Last night, Angel had said that the vamps in the park had not interfered with the cat's hunt. Maybe there was some kind of taboo associated with his lair, too. Still, if the vamps' hunger won out over the intangible chains of fear, there was no way she could take all of them on her own, even with Cordelia's help.

Two males and a female sprang toward her.

Then again, she wouldn't know until she tried.

Buffy stood her ground until the last second, then

sprang to the side staking the outside male. The other male skidded and turned to face the Slayer, snorting particles of his doomed companion out of his flaring nostrils. He was built like an NFL linebacker, and his demonic facial distortions did not obscure the ugliness he had borne in life. Bulbous nose, squinty eyes, no chin, and flabby cheeks. Buffy suspected he hadn't left his hostile emotional baggage behind during his transition into the ranks of the undead.

The female barreled toward Cordelia.

"I don't think so." Stuffing her stake in her waistband, Cordelia scrambled up the staggered rock shelves at the base of the stone tower.

Buffy's hand flexed on her stake as the huge male lunged toward her, then nimbly jumped back. Apparently, he *had* played football. In her peripheral vision, she saw Cordelia brace herself against the tower wall, grab a large rock and drop it. The primitive bomb missed the climbing vamp, but the surprise made the demon lose her balance and fall. Unfazed, the vamp stumbled to her feet and started up again.

And Bubba launched his incredible bulk toward Buffy.

She kicked, but the blow was a major miscalculation. The giant vamp grabbed her foot and pulled. Buffy fell on her back with a thud. Dazed, but still clinging to her stake, she shook her head and realized that her opponent hadn't been born with an abundance of brains, either. His massive hand was clamped around her ankle, but he looked perplexed, like he couldn't figure out what had happened to her bitable neck.

Unfortunately, the rest of the horde wasn't as mentally challenged. With one potential snack cornered on the rock and the other downed, whatever unknown imperative had been holding them back lost the battle of control. The eight remaining vampires threw themselves into the fray for the kill.

"Hey! Bubba! Is this what you're looking for?" Buffy tilted her head to expose her neck and wasn't at all surprised when the hulking vampire dropped her foot. She was on her feet and burying the stake on his broad chest before he realized his mistake. "Touchdown."

The odds, however, were still dangerously stacked against them. The female vamp was within a foot of reaching Cordelia, who couldn't climb higher on the sheer face of the stone tower. Two other vamps were scaling the ledges at the base, and Cordy had run out of loose rocks.

Buffy ducked and rolled past the vampire on her left, spun and threw another off-balance with a fist to the chin. A third grabbed her hair and yanked her backward. His free arm closed around her upper arms and chest as he pulled her head to the side. Ears ringing with the ferocity of his roar, she bent forward to flip him over her head and winced as he ripped several strands of her hair from her scalp. Two more vampires flanked her as the startled vamp on the ground staggered to his feet.

Cordelia's frantic scream cut off abruptly.

Buffy's heart lurched. Cordy was a major thorn in the brambles of her mixed-up life, but she couldn't imagine losing her. Enraged, she swung her stake to the left. Another vamp gone. The crazed creature on her right tackled her around the legs and threw her to the ground.

"Finally! Here!"

The unexpected sound of Cordelia's peeved voice

seeped into Buffy's consciousness as she rolled over to repel the vampire falling toward her with fangs bared. It impaled itself on her raised stake and disappeared. Through the dissipating specks of its final moment, she saw Angel catch the stake Cordelia threw down to him. He stabbed the persistent female, then quickly dispatched the two he had pulled off the tower.

The surviving four fled for safety in the woods.

Buffy took Angel's extended hand and got to her feet, her thoughts clearing in the backwash of subsiding adrenaline. "You have to get back to Sunnydale, Angel. Now."

"The sun won't be up for hours, yet, Buffy."

"Willow told you about my dream, didn't she?" Buffy's temper flared. "She promised she wouldn't tell you anything."

"Pardon me for mentioning this, but if Willow had kept that promise, we'd be rising from our graves tomorrow night on the wrong side of this war." Shaking her head, Cordelia glanced down the hill. "I hear voices."

"The camp guards." Buffy grabbed the tranquilizer gun and her pack off the flat rock. "Let's get out of here."

Taking the lead, Buffy headed back down the dark western side of the slope. She wouldn't relax until Angel was safely back in town, with access to plenty of dark daytime retreats. And, considering the gruesome evidence of foul play the site workers had been guarding at Coyote Rock, she was certain Lucy Frank and maybe even all the volunteers as well were up to their unbitten necks in murder and mayhem. Maybe it was because they had formed a cult devoted to Tezcatlipoca and his savage demands, perhaps at the direction of the ancient god himself. Either way, as long as the camp people thought their activities were still a secret, Giles's options for dealing with the problem remained open and flexible.

"Where'd you park, Cordelia?" Buffy had taken a course that steered well clear of the water tank, then turned east to parallel the camp.

"Just off the dirt road not far from the highway." Cordelia cursed as she tore her sweater free of a branch. "I sure hope Giles is enjoying his dinner date. He owes me one."

"Giles has a date?" Angel asked, surprised.

Buffy turned to face Cordelia. "With whom?"

"Lucy Frank. Don't ask me why, but she really seems to like him."

"Let's just hope dinner doesn't translate as fresh heart of Giles on the menu." Buffy broke into a run and angled back toward the truck trail.

Chapter 11

Giles studied Lucy Frank over the rim of his coffee cup. Vivacious, outspoken, knowledgeable, warm, and witty, she had kept him jumping through mental and emotional hoops all through dinner. They'd discussed everything from Charles Dickens to the gladiatorial aspects of American football and European soccer to the global impact of recently extinct insect species in the Amazon. Intelligent and ambitious, she aspired to scientific greatness, yet had a realistic perspective on the difficulties of making a mark in a highly competitive field with diminishing opportunities. The Coyote Rock archaeological find had given her an unexpected edge. . . . Under different circumstances, he would have enjoyed her company, but even aside from the realization that he wasn't ready to fill the empty space Jenny had left in his life, he had the feeling Lucy was hiding something. Cleverly, to be sure—but there were subtle clues embedded in her body language and responses that were impossible to hide.

"You don't seem worried." Giles sipped his steaming almond coffee, noting the slight hesitation as Lucy sliced her cheesecake with the side of her fork.

"I'm not really." Lucy rested the fork on the small plate and smiled as she looked up. "Garret Baine *is* an absent-minded professor with a one-track mind. When he's focused on a particular problem, nothing diverts him from solving it."

"Even so—" Giles set his cup down. He needed answers, but not at the risk of appearing suspicious. Lucy, however, was anxious to put his concerns for student safety to rest, and saved him the trouble of pressing.

"I'd be willing to bet Dr. Baine's in L.A. right now, hoping to catch Dan Coltrane trying to sell that artifact."

"Los Angeles is a rather large territory for one man to cover alone."

"Yes, it is." Lucy leaned forward slightly, as though intensity would add merit to her theory. "But there are only a dozen art and antiquity dealers there that would risk fencing a rare museum piece that's easily traced."

"A dozen, you say?" Giles feigned a surprised reaction. "I had no idea there was that much demand for the priceless and stolen. Perhaps I've been immersed in education at the high school level too long."

"That would keep you out of touch with the academic mainstream, wouldn't it?" While Lucy paused to take another bite of cheesecake, Giles signaled the waiter for the check. "Anyway, there's a huge black market, and Dr. Baine knows who those dealers are. I gave Detective Thomas several names and addresses to check out. He'll find Baine. Dan, too, probably."

"Detective Thomas?" This time Giles's surprise was not fabricated.

Lucy nodded. "He came out to ask me a few questions after Mrs. Baine called the police in a panic over her delinquent husband. She couldn't file an official missing-person report because he hasn't been gone long enough, and Thomas probably wouldn't have bothered looking into it except for Dan taking off the way he did. The rat."

"Yes, I found Dan's actions rather disturbing myself." That much was honest, Giles mused. However, although Lucy's theory about the absent men made sense, it seemed too pat and convenient.

"I still can't believe it." Sighing, Lucy pushed the rest of her dessert aside. "But the point I'm trying to make is that there's no reason your history students have to pass up a wonderful educational opportunity this weekend. I'm actually quite a good archaeologist. In fact, they'll probably learn more with *me* in charge of the dig—" She faltered, then qualified the remark. "—In the event Dr. Baine doesn't return tomorrow. I don't know if you're aware of this or not, Giles, but the professor wasn't happy about having a bunch of teenagers underfoot all weekend."

"Really? No, I wasn't aware of that." Giles took the check when the waiter returned and pretended to read it while he considered her extreme interest in the school field trip. There was, of course, a remote chance she viewed the student expedition as an opportunity to get to know him better. Odd as that was to contemplate, the possibility wasn't without validity, given her bold and flirtatious attitude since they had first met. Still, modesty and caution would not allow him to accept that as the explanation. For one thing, there was the matter of the guards that Buffy had seen stationed near the rock formation that afternoon.

"How many kids are there?" Lucy asked. "I thought I counted ten."

It was a logical question, even though the History Club was taking care of its own supplies and gear. Yet it triggered a chilling flash of concern that overshadowed the otherwise enjoyable evening.

"Actually, only five will be able to make it."

"Five?" The timbre of Lucy's voice sharpened.

If Giles had had any doubt about her ulterior motive, it was dispelled in that moment of unguarded anger and distress. The dinner invitation had been issued with one and only one objective in mind: to make sure he didn't cancel the overnight camping trip, a possibility he had not mentioned to her that afternoon if memory served.

"Yes, uh—are you finished?" Giles asked casually, and placed two twenty-dollar bills on the table with the check. Lucy recovered her congenial demeanor so quickly he couldn't tell if he had betrayed his own anxiety. "I don't want to rush you, but I do have a bit of work to catch up on at the library before school convenes in the morning."

"Yes, of course." Lucy placed her napkin on the table. "Thank you so much for joining me, Giles. It was lovely."

"My pleasure." Walking behind her toward the exit, Giles felt a curious disappointment. Whatever nasty business was being orchestrated at Coyote Rock, everything suggested that Lucy Frank was a primary player in the enemy camp.

Willow blinked to clear her blurry vision. She had been staring at the monitor so long the words had started running together and made absolutely no sense. Suddenly she spotted the missing detective's name in the police files, which jolted her from the stupor created by a prolonged and fruitless search. Then the shuffle of feet outside the library door kicked her into wide-awake gear.

"Giles? Buffy?" She slipped off the stool when nobody answered, suddenly wary. "Oz?"

Still no answer.

All the good people just barged in. They didn't lurk.

"Okay—first rule. Don't panic." Willow's anxious gaze flicked around the familiar surroundings which had become a haven of reason in the midst of weird and troubled times. Although, they'd been attacked by all kinds of demons in this room too, in spite of their best precautions. The library wasn't monster-proof and she was alone. "This could be a problem. Like talking to myself, only worse."

Something jostled the door.

Willow fumbled under the counter for a stake among the various weapons Giles kept stashed for emergencies. She added a small bottle of holy water and a cross for good measure and clutched the vampire repellents to her chest as she scooted from behind the counter. She hesitated, not quite sure what to do next. She'd feel pretty silly if Xander and Oz walked in and found her standing there armed and desperate, especially since the weapons all worked against vampires and they hadn't seen one in a week. What if the skulking intruder wasn't a vamp? What if it was the jaguar? Or what if it was a lot of vamps? They had to start feeding again sooner or later, didn't they? She hadn't exactly perfected her staking technique, and Buffy always prepped the undead guys with a pre-oblivion battering first.

"When in doubt—hide. Excellent idea."

As Willow turned toward the book cage, the doors

smashed open. Three male vampires stood in the doorway, glaring at her with creepy green eyes and sneering to show off their fangs. She was suitably impressed.

"Don't come any closer. I'm, uh—armed!" Holding out the cross, Willow defiantly raised her chin and stepped backward toward the cage on trembling legs. Three against one. Not fair and not a chance. She looked past them down the long corridor. Empty. Nobody was rushing to her rescue. So—bluff! She waved the bottle of holy water and stake gripped in her other hand. "And, uh—I know how to use these, too. So just—watch it!"

The tall vamp in the center laughed. "I'm so scared."

"Well—you should be." Nodding, Willow backed up another step. Why hadn't they attacked? This was a good sign—wasn't it? "I'm a witch!"

"And I'm bored." The spokesman for the deadly trio leaped toward her, covering the intervening space in three strides.

Clicking into fight-or-die mode, Willow scalded his gaunt cheek with the cross. Shrieking in pain, he hit her arm and the cross went flying into the cage. She grabbed the stake and ducked under his arm, head-butting one of the other vamps in the stomach. His fist closed on her hair.

The tall vamp clamped onto her shoulder and yanked her around to face him. The blackened cross mark on his face smoked. Scared and angry, Willow jabbed at him with the stake and missed. The third vamp pulled the stake out of her grasp.

"Gotcha." The tall one standing in front of her grinned.

Not funny, Willow thought, frantic as the second vamp tightened his hold on her hair and pulled her head back. This was exactly the moment when someone should race in to save her. No one did. She popped the top on the bottle of holy water.

The tall vamp jumped back.

Holding the bottle tightly, Willow jerked her hand backward, sending a stream of holy water over her shoulder to splash the vamp with the painful grip on her hair. He screamed and let go and began to claw at his scorched face. Even as she turned to run, she realized there was no escape from the stronger, faster demons. She kicked to no avail when two arms closed around her chest and gritted her teeth when the tall vamp whispered in her ear.

"Game's over."

"It doesn't hurt to be ready for anything." Xander cast a satisfied glance at the camping equipment and supplies jammed into the back of Oz's van. If they needed it this weekend, they'd have it. If they didn't need it, so what?

"There's prepared and there's excessive. This is excessive." Oz locked the doors and headed across the school parking lot.

Xander had been a soldier once. Okay, so it had only been for a few hours one Halloween, but the tactics and strategies of successful military maneuvers had stuck. He was right. Oz was wrong. "It's not like we're dealing with your basic camping scenario here, Oz. We've got vampires, an Aztec jaguar god with a taste for people, and who knows what other demonic boy scouts, as well as the black widow spiders, poisonous snakes, and scorpions one can expect to find at a slumber party in the southern California wilderness."

"Uh-huh. Mosquito netting won't stop any of those

things, but the machetes might prove useful—if we have to hack our way through a jungle."

"That could happen. This is the Hellmouth, remember?"

"I keep trying to forget." Oz hesitated and sniffed.

Xander frowned, his anxiety about sharing a sleeping bag with mate-murdering lady spiders and not-so-particular snakes forgotten. Oz's sense of smell was extremely acute, a side effect of the latent werewolf within. When Oz's nose twitched, he usually smelled trouble.

"Willow—" Oz bolted.

The jaguar? Xander dashed after him and stumbled to a halt when Oz paused at the corner of the building. The front doors opened and three vampires dragged a struggling Willow down the steps.

"Look who's back in business."

"Yeah, but she hasn't been bitten, yet," Oz whispered. "Why not?"

"Maybe they forgot the salt." Xander joked, but a mixture of relief and trepidation flooded him. Willow wasn't a lost soul, but considering that the local vampire population hadn't had a square meal in over a week, the vamps' failure to feed was unnerving. Apparently, they had other plans.

"You didn't happen to bring a stake or two with you tonight, did you?" Oz asked.

"I'm not in the habit of packing." Xander licked his lips as the kidnappers hauled their reluctant hostage down the front walk. "Okay. Here's the plan. We rush them. They let Willow go, and then we all make tracks for the library and the vampire busting supplies."

"You're kidding, right?"

"No, but I'm open to a better idea."

Oz sighed. "Don't have one."

"On three?"

"Screw that." Shrieking like a banshee in pain, Oz burst out of hiding and raced toward the vamp holding Willow.

"Ramming speed." Xander barreled toward the two vamps bringing up the rear and plowed into them, which resulted in no damage whatsoever to the vampires. He, however, suddenly found himself in a brutal headlock. He was no Jesse Ventura, even though they both had a knack for snappy patter. The vamp intent on crushing his windpipe was built like a rock, and he was too busy trying to breathe to talk.

Oz bounced off the tall guy and danced out of reach when the vamp grabbed for him without loosening his grip on Willow. Feisty little witch that she was, Willow kicked her captor in the shin, which also had no discernible effect. The vamp pinned her arms and muzzled her with his hand.

And the entire tableau froze.

"Okay. Here's the deal—" Oz's gaze darted to Willow, to Xander, then settled on the tall vamp with the cross mark emblazoned on his face. "You let them go. I'll let you go."

"That sounds like a plan I can live with." Xander rasped, then coughed when Gibraltar boy tightened his hold. "You're a vampire, not a python."

"Better plan." The tall vamp motioned to his unoccupied partner, then growled at Oz. "You die. We eat."

"Care to reconsider that option?"

Buffy? Xander gagged as the thug with the vice-grip twisted to look behind him. Buffy, Angel, and Cordelia walked out of the shadows, all of them armed and disheveled with dirt and assorted bits of wilderness debris clinging to their clothes and tangled hair. The Hellmouth had pulled out all the stops tonight.

"I'd reconsider, if I were you," Cordelia said.

"Good advice." Buffy nodded. "We haven't filled today's vamp-kill quota, yet."

"But we're working on it." Cordelia smiled.

Angel didn't talk. He sprang toward the vamp who wasn't holding someone hostage and staked him. Another undead became really dead in a *whoosh* of dust.

Snarling, the tall vamp held Willow's white neck at fang-point. Oz responded to the threat by the only means available. He charged and sank his teeth into bloodless vamp thigh. The thought made Xander's stomach churn. Only the iron arm still clamped around his throat kept the bile down and saved him from additional humiliation. On the plus side, Oz's bite-me tactic worked. Yowling, the outraged vamp released Willow to pull Oz off his leg.

Oz latched onto Willow's hand and pulled her clear as the injured vamp hobbled toward the street. Angel's thrown stake zinged passed the huddling couple and buried itself in the fleeing vamp, obliterating it with an anticlimactic *poof.*

Which, Xander realized, left him the only one in imminent danger of dying in the next few seconds. No one else seemed to be particularly worried about that possibility. Then again, if someone moved against Gibraltar boy, the vamp could snap his neck in that split second before he vaporized.

"Are you all right?" Willow anxiously touched Oz's face.

"I'm fine. What about you?"

"I'm fine." Willow nodded and recoiled when Oz leaned in to kiss her. "Uh . . . maybe you should . . . brush your teeth first?"

"Speaking of teeth—" Xander glanced at Buffy.

"Oh, right." Buffy hefted her stake and scowled at the vamp. "I am the Slayer. Guess I should slay. Unless, of course, *you* want to make a deal."

The vamp shifted uncertainly. His arm flexed.

Black dots swam in Xander's field of vision.

"Not sure?" Buffy sighed. "You have three choices. Stake, stake, or let Xander go and maybe I'll miss."

The vamp dropped Xander and ran.

Xander sank to the ground with all the grace of a rag doll. As he passed out, he wondered if he would sustain permanent brain damage from oxygen deprivation.

Buffy picked another piece of twig out of her hair and glanced across the table at Cordelia. Cordy had gone to the rest room to repair her damage, and looked amazingly fresh and unflustered as she corrected her math homework. At the far end, Oz and Willow were engaged in relieved clinging accented by poignant eye contact. Xander's lips were moving in a silent litany of calculations and facts to determine if his mental and memory faculties were intact. Angel had gone home to appease her anxieties about his welfare.

"Good, you're all here." Giles strode into the library and toward the table with a pensive frown. His preoccupation with whatever was on his mind was so intense a long moment passed before he realized that the assembly was unusually quiet and subdued. "Did I miss something?"

"The vamps are back in town and ready to party." Xander rubbed his chaffed throat.

"Who was attacked?" Everyone raised a hand.

"Where?" In the absence of a free chair, Giles sat on the edge of the table.

"Right here," Willow said softly. "Three of them. I thought I was done for, but—they didn't even try to . . . you know, bite. I'm glad, but—it was a little weird."

"Kidnapping seemed to be the order of the day." Oz gripped Willow's hand.

"Kidnapping? Are you certain that was their intention?" When Oz nodded, Giles stood up and ran his fingers through his hair. "That's rather difficult to believe, after their extended period of inactivity."

"For what it's worth," Xander said, "they were perfectly willing to put the bite on Oz and me—until Oz got in the first nip."

"I wouldn't recommend it, except as a last resort." Oz grimaced. "Vamps are vile."

"The horde that hit Cordelia and me at Coyote Rock were *definitely* intent on feeding," Buffy said, "but they acted like they weren't sure if they should. It's hard to describe."

"They were hesitant?" Crossing his arms, Giles focused on Buffy.

"Only until hunger overruled whatever was holding them back. Couldn't have been the jaguar. He wasn't there."

"The jaguar was back in town as well, I'm afraid. I drove by one of his kill sites on my way here from the restaurant." Giles studied the floor, then looked up suddenly. "Why were you at Coyote Rock, Cordelia?"

"Huh?" Cordelia's expression blanked.

"I asked her to go." Willow shifted uneasily, as though she was guilty of something horrendous and was confessing. "At the time, it, well—it seemed like a good idea to let Buffy know that someone else had . . . disappeared."

Cordelia slapped her forehead. "That was it! The missing cop!"

"Cop?" Giles leaned across the table to peer at Willow. "This missing officer wouldn't be Detective Thomas, would it?"

"Yeah, but—" Willow slid down in her chair. "—He's not missing. His car was found in L.A."

"You mean I almost got killed and totally trashed a cashmere sweater for *nothing?*" Bristling, Cordelia bent her arm to show the loops of pulled blue threads on her sleeve.

Buffy refrained from pointing out that without Cordelia's help, she would have been hopelessly outnumbered.

"L.A." Giles ignored Cordy's misguided outrage, too. "That would corroborate Lucy Frank's account concerning the detective, although I'm not completely convinced she told me all she knows about Mr. Coltrane and Dr. Baine."

"She didn't." Buffy exhaled slowly. "They're dead. I found the bodies near the rock tower. The cat got Mr. Coltrane. Dr. Baine's heart was—missing."

Xander eyed her narrowly. "Define 'missing?' "

Buffy clarified. "Cut out with a knife and nowhere to be found."

"Totally gross, but not as gross as using their skewered heads as garden ornaments." Cordelia shuddered.

Willow groaned. "I won't sleep at all tonight—not with visions of disembodied hearts and, uh, headless corpses dancing in my head."

Giles straightened slowly, his face ashen. "Actually, all this makes disturbing sense given my hypothesis regarding Tezcatlipoca. The professor's heart was undoubtedly removed and fed to the jaguar before it stopped beating."

"Is that an educated guess, Giles?" Xander asked.

"Yes, based on the historical record about Aztec culture." Giles disappeared into his office and returned with a chair. "The Aztecs were quite barbarous. Their practice of ritual sacrifice took different forms, depending on the deity. Victims to the god of fire, Huchueteotl, were bound and hurled into a fire. Those dedicated to the rain god were drowned. The bodies were then thrown from the top of the temple and decapitated. The, uh . . . heads were displayed on pikes at the base of the pyramid."

"I may not sleep tonight either." Xander shook his head in a futile attempt to dislodge the uncomfortable images.

"Yes, well—the ritual used to empower the gods of day and night is significantly more savage. I believe we discussed the fact that Huitzilopochtli, the sun god, required multiple daily sacrifices in order to fight off Tezcatlipoca's night. The victims' beating hearts were wrenched from their bodies with a stone knife."

Buffy started. "Dr. Baine was killed as a ritual sacrifice to the *sun* god?"

"No. The method of religious murder for Huitzilopochtli and Tezcatlipoca was identical. Day and night remained equally powerful. Unfortunately, Huitzilopochtli has *not* returned to maintain that balance." Giles leaned back. "Did you find the mirror, Buffy?"

"Negative. I thought I saw something glinting in the rocks, but then the vamps attacked and I got kind of busy."

Giles nodded. "So we can't be certain Tezcatlipoca has returned, either."

"Maybe he hasn't." Buffeted by incredulous looks, Buffy defended her supposition. "What if the people at the site have just gotten carried away with the whole Aztec thing?"

"A cult? That is a possibility." Giles considered it. "Someone could have turned a killer jaguar loose to lend credence to the prophecy."

"I read something about a prophecy," Willow said. "On the net, but . . . I didn't think it applied."

"What prophecy?" Oz asked.

"That the Aztec Empire would rise again on August 13, 1999—478 years after the fall of Tenochtitlan, the Aztec capital Cortez destroyed."

"They missed the deadline," Xander said.

"Maybe their calculations were off," Oz suggested.

"Perhaps, but the actual date is irrelevant to present circumstances." Giles looked at Buffy. "And—I have good reason to believe that we're dealing with Tezcatlipoca himself, aside from the site's proximity to the Hellmouth and the other supporting evidence."

Buffy wasn't close to being convinced. "And that reason is—"

"Lucy Frank was subtly but unmistakably upset when I told her there would only be *five* students on the field trip."

"I'm not getting the importance of that?" Xander frowned, puzzled.

"The size of our group would only be vital if the cult is based on the god's *actual* return," Giles said.

"I don't want to know." Cordelia wrapped her arms around herself. "Why?"

Giles didn't pull his punch. "Tezcatlipoca needs multiple ritual sacrifices to completely restore himself."

"He's doing a pretty good job of stuffing himself on Sunnydale residents," Oz said.

"Yes, but that only sustains the physical *jaguar* incarnation." Giles pushed at his glasses. "His power is derived from the ritual. The greater the number of sacrifices, the greater his strength."

"Which," Xander said dryly, "begs the question—will *five* beating hearts meet his minimum daily requirement?"

Funny, Buffy thought, but she didn't laugh.

Furious, Mr. Trick glowered at the five miserable creatures cowering before him. He checked an urge to shove them all into the flames blazing in the fireplace at their backs. "You *dare* to call yourself vampires?"

All eyes stared at the floor.

"You're stronger and faster than any living human—with the exception of the Slayer—"

The Rock nodded and shuffled his foot. He was a dunce, but smart enough to keep his mouth shut, Trick noted.

"—And yet, *fourteen* of you couldn't kill her and her insufferable friend?" Trick stepped up to an average-looking male, an accountant before his demise as he recalled, and demanded an explanation. "Well?"

The pitiful excuse for a demon stammered, "The outsider came."

"Really?" Trick smiled. "How many of you were still *present* when he arrived?"

The accountant shrugged. "Seven. Maybe eight."

"That is pathetic." Sighing, Trick turned away. It was highly inconvenient that the Slayer had found the evidence of Tezcatlipoca's return at the site. Secrecy would have made the final phase of the operation so much easier. Nothing, however, could prevent the inevitable from happening—unless the jaguar was deprived of the hearts he required to maintain his strength during the interim. Trick whirled on the Rock.

"I promised Tezcatlipoca a special treat for his predawn feast tomorrow!" Trick's face morphed as he unleashed his vampire rage. "One of the Slayer's own to seal the bargain! How could one small teenaged girl escape from a big lug like you?"

"Well, the Slayer came." Rock sighed. "And this guy bit Edward—"

"Bit him?"

"In the leg. Right here." Rock poked his thigh. "And he let her go."

"Out! All of you. Now!" Seething, Trick pointed to the door, then marched out of the room. He had to contact Lucy Frank while there was still time to make up for the deficit in the morning's head count.

Chapter 12

Lucy poured a cup of coffee and set the kettle back on the camp stove with a weary sigh. Rising at three-thirty in the morning on less than four hours sleep yet again was putting a severe strain on her endurance. Somehow, she would muster the energy to get through one more grueling day. The ultimate rewards were more than worth the effort. Slipping on a sweater, she left the tent with cup in hand to check the daily offerings.

Rolf had been forced to keep the detective drugged and gagged. Considering Mr. Trick's midnight call, those precautions had saved them a lot of unnecessary trouble. The suave vampire had ID'd that clever little Buffy as the Slayer, a notorious troublemaker who had been snooping around Coyote Rock. It was unfortunate she had escaped to report her findings about their recent activities to Rupert Giles, but the situation would have become infinitely more complicated if the girl had discovered that Detective Dwayne Thomas was a captive and not in Los Angeles looking for Dr. Baine.

Pausing at the edge of the illuminated gully, Lucy glanced up the dark slope and shivered. It was not a physical response to the invigorating chill in the predawn air, but a stirring of passion unlike anything she had ever felt before.

Tezcatlipoca.

She alone had seen his face—the glorious countenance of an all-powerful entity, whose human form had left her breathless. The desire he had evoked transcended the mundane scientific aspirations and daily concerns that had driven her life. She had never had a relationship that had survived more than a few weeks, had never met anyone who truly appreciated her intelligence and ambition, had never expected to find anyone who could tap the reservoir of passion buried so deep for so long.

Until she had looked into the smoking mirror and seen the dark and brooding Aztec god.

She had pledged herself without hesitation, and had no qualms about the decision. She was the instrument by which Tezcatlipoca would regain his power and reenter the world as a man after centuries of confinement. In return for her loyal devotion, she would reign over the darkness beside him, his only consort.

Lucy laughed softly as she continued toward the rock ledge at the base of the hill, amused by the irony. Before Tezcatlipoca, she would have been genuinely attracted to Rupert Giles. Beneath the shy and awkward surface of the academic she sensed a smoldering, uncommon strength. However, since Giles was only bringing half his students that afternoon, his heart would also contribute to Tezcatlipoca's emergence. Intelligent and strong, the librarian was more than worthy of the honor. The same could not be said for the men she had conscripted last night.

Seeing her approach, Rolf stood up and stretched. Carrie was curled into a ball on the ground, sound asleep by a small campfire. Lucy made a mental note. Subjects from the camp's ranks would have to replace the missing field-trip students. She would make the final selection tomorrow.

"Is there more coffee?" Rolf asked.

"Yes, plenty. Go on." Lucy nodded toward the tent. "Just don't be too long. The preparations for this morning's ceremony will take some time."

Nodding, Rolf handed her the detective's gun and jogged away.

Lucy sat on a squat rock and stared at her three drugged captives: the detective, a homeless drunk, and a middle-aged hitchhiker. She had been asleep in her motel room when the strange man who called himself Mr. Trick had shown up at her door. Certain that a dusting of the *yauhtli* powder in her fist could instantly subdue any man, she had invited him in. She hadn't believed his story about an alliance with Tezcatlipoca until he had shown her his grotesquely ridged vampire face. Curiously, she had not been alarmed, and Tezcatlipoca's partnership with the undead had been a logical move that had already proven useful. If Mr. Trick's minions hadn't been maintaining surreptitious surveillance over Coyote Rock, she wouldn't have known that Giles was aware of altered circumstances at the dig. Now she would be prepared to deal with whatever problems arose because of it.

The loss of the girl was another matter. Trick had failed to deliver as promised, forcing her to find substitutes in the middle of the night. They were inadequate, and she risked bringing Tezcatlipoca's wrath upon herself if her revised plan did not appease him. She was certain it would.

This dawn his *ixiptla* would be initiated. Tomorrow the god, in conjunction with his human surrogate, would know the young Willow intimately—before the jaguar devoured her heart.

Full of energy and anxious anticipation, Dem left his bike in the crowded parking area and jogged up the trail to the site. He hadn't slept much. All he had been able to think about was the power he would have as Tezcatlipoca's representative—and Buffy. After today, she would be his . . . willing or not.

Dem paused at the top of the path. A hundred lanterns blazed, illuminating the entire dig. Fifty or sixty men and women were gathered along the rock shelf on the far side of the deep wash. All of them wore white bathrobes or knotted bed sheets. Some had feathers or beaded jewelry woven into their hair. When they saw him, they lowered their eyes in deference to his elevated position. A surge of elation washed over him as Rolf walked toward him with his head bowed. He wouldn't have any problem getting used to this. No problem at all.

"The High Priestess requests your presence at the tent." Rolf spoke softly, without looking at him.

Dem didn't bother to answer. As Tezcatlipoca's chosen, he didn't have to. Rolf followed a discreet ten paces behind as he walked sedately toward the woman, taking in every detail of her strange costume. The feathered headdress and the provocative white garment that hung loosely from her left shoulder looked familiar. This *felt* right. He did not lower his gaze or speak when he stopped before her.

"This way, please." Lucy did not raise her eyes until her back was turned. Holding a primitive torch that smoked and sizzled, she walked slowly toward the hill.

Tense with excitement, Dem fell into step behind her. As they began the ascent, he sensed that the rest of the assembly was following. He did not look back. Somehow a display of curiosity seemed inappropriate given his new status, but that did not negate the unanswered questions ricocheting through his mind. He had no idea what to expect.

The pungent aroma of damp grass and earth wafted through the cool air, calming him. He had never spent much time in the wilds and yet, the sounds and scents emanating from the dark terrain were known to him, as was a profound dread of the sun. His element was the night.

The jaguar's roar reverberated off silent stone sentinels as Lucy guided the procession through the maze below Coyote Rock. In the flickering light of her torch Dem could just make out the black silhouette of the jaguar on a ledge halfway up the stone tower. A mere two nights ago, the animal had almost killed him. Now they shared a symbiotic joining. With each step, the empathic link to the cat intensified. He was aware of two entwined, yet separate streams of power. One was the physical strength inherent in primal muscle and bone. The other was generated from the cosmos itself, an immense energy that flowed through all time and all things and could be molded and directed at Tezcatlipoca's will.

Dem followed as Lucy climbed the natural steps on the lower portion of the rock formation, his heart quickening in his chest when they reached the ledge just below the jaguar's perch. He did not follow Lucy's lead and bow, but met the jaguar's golden stare. The cat's only acknowledgment was a slight flick of his tail.

Lucy wedged the end of her torch in a crevice, then picked up the gold-framed black mirror that had been leaning against the stone wall. With her back still to him, she gripped the glass in two hands and raised it over her bowed head. Shifting patterns of golden light shimmered across sleek black hide as the cat began to dissolve. Solid flesh transformed into a haze of gray smoke, then coalesced into a snaking plume. Dem caught the scent of burning wood and molten metal as the smoky stream streaked into the glass. When Lucy turned and lowered the mirror to Dem's eye level, he set his jaw to curb any outward signs of fear and surrendered to Tezcatlipoca's will.

The gray plume drifted around the outer edge of the black surface, moving faster and faster as it spiraled into a whirlpool at the center. The vortex pulled at Dem's mind, drawing his consciousness into an arena of fire that raged within the obsidian depths. Indistinct dark shapes writhed in and around the flames, howling and screeching as their ghostly extremities clawed at his terror. Blazing rocks exploded, showering him with a brimstone hail. Tongues of liquid lightning broke through the surrounding ebony, daring him to flinch. Dem's disembodied spirit responded as though he was still physical in nature, and he fought the overwhelming urge to cower from the horrors that tormented him.

When he was suddenly cast adrift in an eternal dark, he rejected the helpless panic that threatened to consume him and focused on a solitary point of light. The light expanded, taking form as it enlarged. He saw himself dressed in a more intricate version of Lucy's costume. The white fabric split to expose his chest and a gaping wound. Raw flesh opened and closed over an empty cavity beneath his ribs.

He had no heart.

Still Dem did not flinch.

The repulsive image faded and another figure appeared in his place.

Tezcatlipoca, with large black eyes as bottomless as his dark domain. Shining black hair, adorned with multicolored feathers and beaded gold, fell in ebony cascades down his back. No blemish marred the smooth bronze skin. A golden jewel hung around his neck. His arms boasted many golden bracelets. Bells on golden chains circled his ankles. He carried a blue, yellow, and green feathered fan in his left hand and four arrows in his right. Full lips parted in a smile revealing even white teeth, which slowly elongated into the jaguar's fangs. Except for the fangs and the glowing eyes, the beast was invisible against the black background . . . until it sprang.

Instantly transported back to Coyote Rock, Dem took a faltering step backward. He barely saved himself from falling off the ledge as spears of blue-gray smoke erupted from the black mirror and pierced his body. The power of Tezcatlipoca flowed through his veins, filled his senses, and seeped into every cell as they fused. The bond was sealed and unbroken when the smoke escaped through his eyes and nose and the jaguar reformed on the ledge above.

Larger than his stature now, Dem glared at Lucy as she lowered the mirror. She trembled under his scrutiny and fell to her knees at his feet. Dem looked down, his glance falling past her to the people on their knees at the base of the tower. None of them met his gaze, which was as it should be. Flaming torches branded the scene into his memory. When Lucy began to intone an incantation in the language of the ancient Aztec, he raised his eyes to the dark sky. He did not look at her as she removed his shirt and jeans or twitch when she knotted a white cloak heavy with gold and rare gems over his left shoulder. When she held up an ornate feather headdress, he inclined his head to receive it but did not meet her eyes. When the natural rock formation began to shift, changing form as past and present intersected and ordinary reality was infused with magic, he did not move.

He was still Dem Inglese—and more. Infinitely more.

He turned and followed the jaguar up a long flight of stone steps that rose over the terrain suspended in midair. On a landing near the top, the jaguar moved to the left of a large, rounded stone. Dem recognized the *techcatl* and walked around the altar to the right to join the jaguar behind it. Lucy stopped beside the sacrificial stone and picked up a knife with a gleaming, obsidian blade and a jeweled gold hilt. The people stood, released from their humble groveling for the ceremonial culmination of Dem's initiation and Tezcatlipoca's ritual feeding.

On the ground, Rolf and Carrie dragged three bound men through the throng of Tezcatlipoca's followers. The people chanted, softly at first, then louder as the frenzy for blood mounted. Dem saw the shadowy wisps of old Aztec souls flitting through ghostly temples and courtyards superimposed over the maze of boulders as Rolf and Carrie forced the gagged detective to mount the steps. The man's eyes widened with fright, and he struggled to pull free of the younger red-haired man's grip. The arrogance Dwayne Thomas had flaunted yesterday was not in evidence today. On the ground, one of the other two men tried to run and was quickly subdued. The older one wept.

A gray sheen maimed the dark in the east, harbinger of the enemy dawn.

Dem watched with cold detachment as Rolf and Carrie heaved the kicking detective over the rounded stone on his back and pinioned his arms. The jaguar beside him tensed as Lucy held her hand palm up under the man's nose and blew a dusting of *yauhtli* powder in his face. His struggles ceased as the anaesthetizing drug took effect and he offered little resistance as Rolf ripped open his dirt streaked shirt. Lucy raised the knife.

Aware that his own as well as Tezcatlipoca's power flowed from sacrificial blood, Dem ignored the sour taste in his mouth when the High Priestess plunged the blade between the man's ribs.

Juan Hernandez cringed behind a large rock halfway up the slope, his pad and pencils scattered and forgotten on the ground, his thoughts on horrified hold. He mentally rewound, looking for solid footing to escape the hallucinogenic shock of the sacrificial slaughter he had just seen. Anxious about his opening that night, he had risen early to sketch at the archaeological site to calm his nerves. He had left a message on the gallery answering machine, assuring Joyce that he'd be in before noon to help with the final preparations for the show. He had not expected to blunder into a reenactment of Aztec ritual murder that was so startling that his creative mind was imagining ancient architecture and surreal beings that weren't really there.

Another scream rose above the rhythmic chanting that pounded in Juan's ears. He clamped his hands to his head to blot out the sound, yearning for dawn and the sanctuary of light. He had timed his arrival to coincide with the rising of the sun at 6:32. The illuminated readout on his watch read 6:43. The stubborn darkness pulsed with the steady cadence of the chant, refusing to relinquish the world to light.

A third scream shattered the trance.

Unable to accept the unthinkable, Juan risked taking another look over the top of the boulder and immediately regretted the impulse. The executioner tossed the beating heart she had just harvested. The jaguar caught it, ate it, then roared. The ferocious sound echoed off the rocks and stone stairway as the cat changed into smoke and disappeared into a flat object the High Priestess was holding aloft.

Juan ran his hands over the rough ground, searching for his dropped pencils, pad, and flashlight. He had to get out of there before the insane horde realized he was an eyewitness to the atrocities they had committed in the name of an ancient Aztec god. Dawn had been delayed, and his mind reeled with the implications as he crept backward down the slope, staying low to the ground.

The ceremony was not simply an acting-out of misguided devotion to an old religion. The dark lord Tezcatlipoca, master of death and destiny, was back—and fighting his perpetual war against light. Only this time it looked like Tezcatlipoca might win.

"Good morning." The male voice leaped out of the darkness, braking Juan's desperate flight. "Although morning is a little late today, isn't it?"

Speechless with fright, Juan stared into the perverted face of a dark vampire whose villainous visage was incongruous with its tailored suit and flashy tie. Several others of its evil ilk surrounded him, their distorted features flickering in the erratic light of torches carried by the procession descending the hill.

"What? Cat got your tongue?" The creature grinned. "No, not today. Tomorrow."

Juan dropped his sketching supplies as powerful hands grabbed him from behind.

* * *

Buffy sat up with a cry, shaken awake by the dream. There was no question of the portent in the rerun. Angel had been destroyed in a burst of sunlight.

"Buffy?" Her mother glanced in the door and flicked the light switch on. "You okay?"

"Yeah." Buffy squinted and shielded her eyes from the glare. "Bad dream."

Frantic and slightly harried, Joyce knotted her bathrobe belt. "Don't dawdle. We overslept."

"But it's still—" Buffy glanced at her clock radio and shut up. She did not want to needlessly worry her mother. "I'll hurry."

"You're on your own for breakfast," Joyce said apologetically. "I've got twenty hours of work left to do before the opening tonight and less than twelve hours to get it done in."

"I'll manage." Slipping out of bed, Buffy went to the window. Six-fifty and still pitch dark outside. She wondered who had died to stop the sun from rising on time today.

And who would die tomorrow if Giles didn't figure out how to declaw Tezcatlipoca.

In the dream, Angel was killed by the sun, which probably indicated that they would defeat the god of darkness.

But what if Angel went to ground for the duration? Would that alter the outcome? What price would they pay for making *sure* Angel wasn't a victim of their victory? A win for Tezcatlipoca and a world condemned to perpetual darkness?

The sun had just cleared the horizon when Lucy dropped Dem off in front of the school. The campus was buzzing with speculation about the discrepancy between predicted sunrise and the actual event. Emotions ranged from indifference to fear. Although he was anything but indifferent, Dem pretended not to care as he strode up the walk, scanning for the original members of the History Club. None of them were in sight and he moved quickly through the groups scattered around the lawn toward the school. He was not surprised by the flurry of interest his passing evoked from several classmates. The connection with Tezcatlipoca had broken into his own suppressed potential, amplifying his confidence and shoring up his bearing. He ignored the whispers and curious glances until Cordelia Chase stepped in front of him. He tried to move around her, but Cordelia was persistent and impossible to ignore.

"Excuse me, but—do I know you?"

Dem gave in and paused. A brief exchange would ultimately prove more efficient than coping with the tempestuous aftershocks of a confrontation. "Dem Inglese. History Club."

"No, couldn't be." Cordelia shook her head, then peered at him intently. "Did you get taller or something? Change your hair? You look—different."

"Contacts." Dem revealed nothing of the intense pleasure he derived from her attentive admiration, a feeling that was not steeped in any desire to call her friend or win her approval. She was a self-centered snob, and he had not forgotten how she had callously cut him down at the History Club meeting. He would have his revenge tomorrow when she was cut up by Lucy's knife.

"Oh, you ditched the glasses." Cordelia nodded. "You should have done that a long time ago. Better late than never, I guess."

"I am late. Excuse me." Dem brushed past her. He

did not look back, but he could imagine Cordelia's outraged indignation at the abrupt dismissal.

Dem found Chance, Sienna, Kilya, and Bart in the student lounge. He sat down without waiting to be invited.

"Read that!" Furious, Kilya shoved a paper into his hand, then jumped up, crossed her arms, and stalked back and forth in between the two couches. "It was posted on the bulletin board this morning."

"Would you, like, *believe* they cancelled the field trip?" Sienna rolled her eyes and sat back, disgusted. "I mean, Chance and I had *plans*, you know?"

"Don't remind me." Devastated by the lost opportunity to spend two relatively unsupervised nights with Sienna, Chance put his arm around her shoulders and sighed.

Bart stared out the window, keeping his own silent counsel.

"Sienna and I already did the shopping! With our own money! Is the school going to pay us back or what? I mean, it takes us hours and then they *cancel?*" Kilya snatched the paper from Dem's grasp and slapped it with the back of her hand. "Can they do that? No notice, no nothing?"

"Actually," Dem said calmly, "Mr. Giles is responsible for the cancellation, but—"

"Ohmigod! Dem!" Sienna gawked open-mouthed, then gushed. "Whoa! What miracle makeover machine did you pop out of?"

Kilya started and cocked her head, as though seeing him for the first time. "From geek to hunk for nineteen ninety-five? It was worth it."

"You were saying something about the field trip," Bart reminded him.

"Yes." Dem smiled. "I happen to be friends with the person in charge of the dig."

"So?" Chance asked warily.

"So there's nothing stopping us from going on our own, if you're up for it." As Dem expected, the prey couldn't resist the bait.

"I didn't bust my butt grocery shopping to sit home all weekend," Kilya said.

"And we've got the gear." Chance extended his hand to shake Dem's. "We're in."

Buffy stared at Xander's tapping fingers until she couldn't stand the nervous beat another second. Her hand shot out and over his, quieting the drumming and bringing Xander to full alert.

"Thank you." Giles didn't look up from the pad on the table before him.

"Sorry." Xander tucked his hands under his armpits. "Guess it's time to call the regularly scheduled emergency meeting of the Slayerettes to order, huh?"

"Charter members only." Using the energy of thought, Willow moved a stack of books in a triangular pattern across the table. Buffy suspected the telekinetic exercise wasn't doing much to distract her. In the middle of the night, Willow had come to the disquieting realization that she had narrowly escaped becoming jaguar granola this morning. It was the only thing that explained the vamps' restraint last night.

"Yeah, it's been a long time since it's just been the four of us," Xander said. "I could care less why Cordelia hasn't graced us with her esteemed presence, but what's Oz doing?"

"Reloading the camping gear in the van so some of

s will fit." Zipping the books to an abrupt halt in front f her nose, Willow sat up as Giles finished his calculaions.

"Thirty-three minutes and fourteen seconds." Giles ossed his pencil on the pad and rubbed his eyes. He ad been up most of the night working on the Tezatlipoca puzzle.

Willow stared at her clasped hands. "Does that mean hat, uh, somebody else . . . died?"

Buffy recognized the signs of survivor guilt in Wilow's numb expression, shortness of breath, and fretful iddling. She felt the same way every time she wasn't round to save someone. She also knew there was nothng she could say to make the despondent girl feel better.

"Uh, yes, Willow. Probably more than one, since unrise was delayed for better than a half hour." Giles uickly pressed on so Willow wouldn't feel obliged to omment. "We must assume Tezcatlipoca is gaining trength at an exponential rate."

"Exponential. I know that word." Xander looked at Buffy. "What does it mean in English?"

"Cat-guy's power infusions could be doubling or etter with each successive sacrifice," Buffy said. "In a utshell."

"More or less." Giles cocked an approving eyebrow, hen reverted back to his more familiar the-end-of-theworld-is-near face. "We have to act quickly—but we do have time to act."

"Confidence. I like that." Xander nodded, then eyed Giles pointedly. "Why are you so sure we have time?"

Giles picked up his pencil and turned it end over end as he explained. "For one thing, I believe the mirror is in the vicinity of the dig. The jaguar has not been sighted during daylight, which suggests that Tezcatlipoca must remain within the glass during those hours. At least until he reaches his full strength."

"In which case there won't be any daylight," Xander said.

"Yeah." Willow propped her chin on her hand and sighed despondently. "And we'll all develop a vitamin D deficiency because . . . well, because ultraviolet light from the sun makes our bodies make vitamin D . . . from egg yokes and stuff. So our teeth will fall out—if we're not, you know . . . sacrificed first."

"Without the sun we may all be too depressed to care." Xander sighed.

Buffy focused on Giles. "So we have to do whatever we're going to do before sundown."

"Yes." Giles circled one of his calculations with the pencil. "After sunrise tomorrow, it may be too late."

"And we have to do what?" Buffy tensed.

"Find the mirror and break it before Tezcatlipoca emerges from the glass tonight."

Buffy had been prepared for the usual complex and dangerous rigmarole that seemed to be the universally accepted means of undoing a demon. She was convinced that something somewhere put a lot of time and effort into making things as difficult as possible for the good guys.

Just find and break the mirror?

There had to be a catch.

Chapter 13

Juan Hernandez was missing. Buffy fumbled with the phone in Giles's office, and recovered before Joyce had paused to take a breath. She had called the gallery to wish her mother luck with Juan's debut and to appease her concerns about the jaguar with a midnight craving for people munchies. As it turned out, her mom had been so busy getting ready for the opening she hadn't kept up with the local news and wasn't worried.

"You know how artists are, Buffy. They get so engrossed in their work they forget about the time. If it wasn't for Hazel's strudel, I'd have to remind him to eat." Joyce sighed tolerantly. "So when you see him, please remind him that the reception starts at seven."

"Sure. If I see him." Buffy hung up slowly with a sick feeling in the pit of her stomach. Juan had left a message on the gallery answering machine before dawn. Chances were better than even that he hadn't lived to see the sun rise.

"Problem?" Giles dropped his duffel bag in the doorway and glanced at his watch. He looked almost cool in jeans, a plaid flannel shirt unbuttoned over a gray T, and scuffed boots that were either survivors of his college years or thrift-store refugees.

"Not unless Juan Hernandez lost his head this morning. My mom's new artistic discovery," Buffy clarified in response to Giles's bewildered expression. "He went out to Coyote Rock to sketch. Hasn't been heard from since."

"Does your mother, uh—"

"Know that he may be one of Tezcatlipoca's heart donors?" Buffy shook her head. "And please don't tell her." Until she confirmed whether Juan was a corpse, a captive, or just lost in his work, she didn't want to ruin her mom's day. Bad news would still be bad news later.

"There wouldn't be much point, I suppose. Are you ready? I told Oz we'd meet him in the parking lot at a quarter to."

"Let's boogie." With a camping pack in one hand and her Slayer bag in the other, Buffy breezed past him out the door.

Giles followed, muttering about the proliferation of incomprehensible American teen slang.

Oz's reorganization had failed to yield additional passenger space, and Willow was sandwiched between him and Xander in the front seat of the van. Oz's hair color of the day was a neon, probably-glows-in-the-dark red that clashed with Willow's burnished auburn. Cordelia pulled in five minutes later with her new pith helmet perched at a jaunty angle on her head.

"Sorry I'm late but I had to wait for UPS."

"Yes, well—" Giles tossed his duffel and Buffy's camp pack into the trunk of Cordelia's car, then slid in the front seat as Buffy climbed into the back. "We're late. Ms. Frank expected us an hour ago."

"*Lucy,* Giles." Buffy looked at him askance. The librarian's assignment was to keep the archaeologist distracted while everyone else searched for the mirror. "A romantic diversion is going to totally bomb if you keep calling her Ms. Frank."

"I don't recall saying anything about a *romantic* diversion," Giles said, annoyed. "I was thinking more along the lines of appealing to her need for scientific recognition and respect."

"Actually, scientific probably has a better chance of working." Cordelia threw the gearshift into reverse. "No offense, Giles, but you're not exactly toting a full load of sex appeal."

"That's oddly comforting coming from you, Cordelia." Giles lurched in the seat as the car sped backward and stopped suddenly.

In the rearview mirror, Buffy saw Cordelia frown, not quite sure whether she had just been insulted or not. Now seemed like a good time to mention a minor modification in the game plan. "I have to stop by Angel's place on the way out of town, Cordy."

"Angel's?" Giles snapped his head around. "Why?"

Buffy pulled a folded paper from her Slayer bag. "To leave him a note. Informing him that he's grounded for the next twenty-four hours. Slayer's orders."

"I see. If he stays in, he cannot possibly be incinerated at sunrise."

Buffy nodded, noting the anxiety twitch at the corner of Giles's mouth as he averted his gaze. He understood her reasoning, but thought that any effort to change the outcome foretold in her dream was futile. Still, he didn't object.

Ten minutes later, the note had been taped to Angel's door where he couldn't miss it, and they were headed toward the site with Oz's van following hard on Cordy's rear bumper. No one said much until Cordelia stopped by the turnoff into the site and Giles issued his last-minute instructions.

"Smash the glass immediately if you find the mirror before sundown, Buffy."

"And after sundown?"

"Once the sun sets Tezcatlipoca won't be in the mirror, and we'll be faced with one of two possibilities." The worry lining Giles's brow negated his even tone. "He'll have to retreat if he's not at full strength by dawn. If the mirror is broken, he'll simply choose another receptacle—and we won't be able to find him."

"And the second?" Buffy asked.

"If tomorrow's ritual sacrifices succeed in restoring him, he won't need to hide."

Because it will be dark forever.

Nodding, Buffy got out. As Cordelia and Oz drove on up the dirt track, she slipped the Slayer bag over her shoulder and headed cross-country toward the eastern woods. It was a longer route over rougher terrain, but there was less chance the dig guards would see her if she accessed Coyote Rock from the steep southern side of the hill. As she darted into the cover of the trees, she still couldn't dispel the uneasy feeling that had nagged her all day. By keeping Angel out of the equation she might be giving the advantage and the win to Tezcatlipoca. As much as she loved Angel, she wouldn't be able to reconcile saving him if thousands of others had to pay with their lives.

The bad feeling was pervasive, underscored by the caustic banter between Xander and Cordelia and acknowledged by Oz and Willow's grim silence. Everything "felt" wrong. As he led the way up the path to the dig, Giles's neck and forearms prickled as if the air were charged with a physical and ubiquitous malevolence. Consequently he was only mildly surprised to see Dem Inglese and the other History Club students sitting at the table by the tent.

"What are they doing here?" Cordelia grabbed Xander's shirttail and dabbed away the perspiration beaded on her forehead.

"They're not using other people's clothes as sweat towels." Xander yanked his shirt free.

"A miscalculation on my part, I'm afraid." Giles dropped his duffel and pretended to rummage through it while he analyzed the unexpected complication.

"Did you forget to post the notices?" Willow asked.

"No. I put them at key points throughout the building. They must not have seen them." Giles rose as Lucy climbed out of the gully.

"Their S.A. isn't up to army standards for sure. Situational awareness," Xander explained in response to the blank looks. "It's a military thing."

"A little soldier exposure goes a long way, doesn't it?" Oz quipped.

Xander shrugged. "Right now, I'd settle for knowing what cereal Dem, the used-to-be-a-geek guy, had for breakfast this morning."

Perplexed by the comment, Giles glanced at the group by the tent. Bart chewed on a pen with a book open in front of him. Probably doing his homework. Nothing unusual there. However, while Chance refilled a water glass from a pitcher at the far end of the table, Sienna sidled closer to Dem and kissed him on the cheek. Kilya was vigorously massaging Dem's shoulders. Highly unusual. The shy boy seemed totally at ease with the attention, and if Chance was concerned about sharing his girlfriend's affections, he didn't show it, as he gave the water glass to Dem. Intriguing and disturbing.

Xander looked at Dem, then at Willow. "You, uh—didn't do any—"

"No way! No more messing around with love spells and potions and, uh, mushy stuff for this witch. Except for Oz." Willow started. "But I, uh, don't mean messing around in a magic way. I mean—no, that's not what I mean. I mean, we don't mess around . . . at all. Right, Oz?"

"Right," Oz agreed blandly.

Cordelia cut the awkward moment with a knife aimed at Xander. "Some people don't *need* magic to be irresistible."

"Oh, right, Cordelia." Xander scoffed. "And who kept dragging whom into the school janitor's closet for the sole purpose of necking? Before *and* after Willow's spell turned me into a woman magnet?"

"Hey, Giles! Get a move on!" Lucy shouted, then laughed. "You're late."

"Well—" Giles picked up his bag. "As they say in the theater, it's showtime."

"I just hope we're still around for the curtain call," Willow said. "I've kind of gotten used to having my head attached to my shoulders."

"Me, too." Oz grinned. "I'd hate to break up the set."

Lucy didn't wait for them to catch up, but jogged ahead and disappeared into the tent. Moving at a slower pace, Giles paid strict attention to the surroundings. For the most part, nothing seemed much different today than it had yesterday—except that there were three times as many dig volunteers who weren't digging. They were watching the new arrivals with more than passing interest. The guards on the hill were standing on boulders in full view instead of keeping a low profile. As they approached the table the disquiet he felt segued into alarm when the other members of the History Club glared with undisguised animosity.

"Hey! How's it going?" Xander raised his hand in a gesture that almost qualified as a wave. His greeting was met with cold stares.

Dismissing Xander with an annoyed glance, Dem impatiently waved Kilya away and frowned as he looked toward the parking area.

"Chilly out here, isn't it?" Xander faked a shiver.

"Frigid," Oz said.

Giles glanced at the camping gear strewn in front of two smaller tents newly erected at the base of the hill. Sienna and Kilya had abandoned bangles and leather for jeans and casual tops more appropriate for a working weekend in the great outdoors. They had come prepared to stay, and if his sprouting suspicions were correct, nothing he could say would convince them to leave. "I see you're all settled in."

"No thanks to you, Mr. Giles," Kilya growled.

Dem's angry glance aborted further comment, subduing the outspoken girl with an authority that reinforced Giles's assumption. The dramatic change in the boy's attitude and appearance was easily explained if he was Tezcatlipoca's *ixiptla,* a meld that transferred an essence of the demon psyche into the human host. Seduced into service by the mirror, the others would treat the *ixiptla* with the same fear and deference as they would the demon. The evidence supported the theory, and Giles's bad feeling burrowed in for the night.

"We're *so* glad to see you, too." Cordelia bristled.

"That hat is like totally dork, Cordelia." Sienna rolled her eyes.

"No, it's not." Willow rushed to defend the pith helmet she had worked so hard to get. "Everybody's wearing them in, uh—Africa."

Lucy's timely intrusion prevented an escalation of the verbal war. "I'm glad you finally made it, Giles."

"Yes, sorry we're late. A slight delay getting our supplies together." Giles tensed as Lucy took an uncomfortably obvious head count. He was one head short of his promised five. "Buffy couldn't make it."

"What?" Dem exploded to his feet, outraged. "Why not? Go get her!"

"Apparently the new look didn't include an attitude wrench, huh, Dem?" Xander rocked back on his heels as Chance took a threatening step toward him. Bart stood up, fists clenched.

"I want Buffy here, and I want her here *now.*" Dem glowered at Giles, expecting immediate and unquestioning compliance with his demand.

Lucy flinched. Giles didn't. "I'm afraid that's not possible—"

"You dare defy me?" Dem's question was not issued as an empty threat. Reacting to his loud burst of temper, the dig workers dropped their tools and quickly closed in to surround them.

Giles realized, a bit late he conceded wryly, that he had greatly underestimated how far the situation at the site had progressed. Lucy Frank and Tezcatlipoca's other converts were no longer concerned with caution or secrecy. "Perhaps we'd better leave."

"No," Lucy said evenly. "You really must stay."

"No, I think we should go. I'm definitely feeling a drop in the, uh, warm fuzzies count." Smiling tightly,

Willow turned. A large, grim-looking man moved in front of her and folded his arms.

"Guess it's too late to circle the wagons." Xander glanced over his shoulder. "Yep. Way too late."

Oz dropped his backpack. "Okay, but I'm not staying without a fight."

"I don't recommend that," Lucy said evenly. "You can't win and we wouldn't want to insult Tezcatlipoca by offering him bruised goods tomorrow morning, now would we?" She blew a dusting of fine powder into Oz's face.

Oz coughed and shook his head. Giles grabbed his arm when he swayed, but he couldn't stop the boy from sinking to the ground in a drugged daze.

"Oz!" Willow gasped and knelt before him. "What was that?"

"*Yauhtli* powder, I suspect," Giles said. "It's a derivative of hemp and quite effective as a pain-killing, anti-stress agent. The Aztecs were only one of many pre-Columbian cultures that used it."

"Let's talk, Giles." Lucy nodded toward the tent. "Privately."

Outnumbered four-to-one by mesmerized fanatics, Giles nodded his assent. Lucy wouldn't hesitate to use the drug, and unclouded reason was his only edge besides Buffy. From the top of the hill, the Slayer would see what had happened and realize she had to locate the mirror on her own. He could only hope she remembered their discussion about Aztec ritual and didn't forsake the search to attempt rescue. No serious harm would come to anyone until just before dawn.

"And we're expected to do what?" Cordelia warily eyed the students and surrounding workers. "I don't do short sweet trips to lala-land."

Rising, Dem moved to confront her with astonishing speed and grace. He spoke with the mocking arrogance of an unrivalled, superior being. "Sit down and be quiet, Cordelia, and you can contemplate your very short and not so sweet future with a clear head."

"I've got news for you, Dem. There's a lot more to being cool than contacts. You are still a loser." Stubbornly defiant, Cordelia pulled a chair out from the table.

"On the ground!" Dem clamped onto Cordelia's wrist and pointed toward a shelf of overhanging rock opposite the deep wash. "Over there. All of you. Leave your stuff here."

Giles saw another man lying on the ground by the ledge. He wondered if the prisoner was Joyce's missing artist. "Do as he says, Xander—" He looked at Lucy. "For now."

Nodding, Xander helped Willow pull Oz to his feet and caught him under the arms when he sagged on jelly legs. Cordelia took a haughty lead as Chance, Bart, and several volunteers herded the captives toward the gully with shoves, sticks, and insults. Stumbling between Xander and Willow, Oz looked much like a wilted carrot, his shocking red-haired head lolling listlessly to the side.

"What about Buffy?" Again, Dem's question was not a question, but a demand delivered with blatant menace.

Lucy spoke softly, eyes downcast. "She will come. You told me yourself that she feels responsible for the safety of her friends. She will not abandon them."

"That's not a given, Ms. Frank."

"Isn't it? This way, Giles." Lucy smiled, bowed to excuse herself from Dem's presence, and turned away.

Loath to give the impression that he was at all cowed by her or Tezcatlipoca and his self-indulgent human puppet, Giles hesitated. Something sharp jabbed him in the ribs. Incensed, as much by his own failure to anticipate the possibility of a trap as he was by the Aztec god's deluded slaves, he yanked a trowel away from a surprised old man and threw it into the brush. He followed Lucy without a word or glance at Dem.

Furious, Dem strode toward the ledge to vent his rage on the captives. Sienna and Kilya scurried after him.

"Dem doesn't know, does he?" Inside the tent Giles sat in the folding chair he had occupied the day before.

"Know what?" Lucy sat opposite him, confident and at ease.

"That as Tezcatlipoca's *ixiptla* he'll be the culminating sacrifice tomorrow." By stating what he assumed to be fact, Giles baited Lucy into confirming the cult's intent.

"Of course not. None of them do."

Giles had suspected as much and didn't react.

"And they won't believe you if you tell them."

Giles shrugged, although he was inclined to agree with her assessment. Being endowed with immense power derived from magical sources was the ultimate teenaged fantasy. They would deny and reject anything that suggested Lucy's promise of fulfillment was a sham.

Lucy leaned forward and put her hand on his knee. "But your destiny does not have to be with a knife, Giles. I can substitute someone else. Carrie, perhaps."

"Yes?" Giles curiosity was genuine, although not because he was interested in whatever Lucy had to offer.

"Even an Aztec Empire rooted in darkness requires civil discipline. I'll need a Great Speaker to govern in the name of Tezcatlipoca."

"I thought the Great Speaker was a disciple of Huitzilopochtli, the sun—"

Lucy slapped him, hard across the mouth. "Never

utter that blasphemous name again. In my presence or anywhere."

Giles touched the cut on his lip with his tongue. "As you wish."

Lucy leaned back and reached behind her, catching Giles off guard as she whipped the obsidian mirror in front of his face.

As the dark glass captured his eye, Giles's first thought was to grab the artifact and smash it. But he couldn't move. He was drawn against his will through a smoky mist into the dark embrace of eternity.

Considering their size, the pebbles made way too much noise when they bounced and rolled down the side of a cliff. Buffy flattened herself against the rock face as much as her bulky Slayer bag would allow. From the woods, she had counted three guards standing on boulders below the rock formation. Trapped halfway up the sheer dropoff, she expected three heads to peer over the rim above. If she climbed up, they'd push her off. If she climbed down, they'd just shoot her.

Five minutes passed and no one appeared. She waited five more, then resumed the ascent.

The sun was plummeting toward the treetops as Buffy quietly picked her way to the top of the long ridge. With only an hour of good light left to find the mirror, time was putting on the pressure. Even so, she paused before moving down the steep northern incline to the large stones strewn haphazardly behind Coyote Rock. Three guards—the dark-haired girl, the red-haired man, and the middle-aged man she had seen yesterday—were standing on large boulders below the tower. From her significantly higher point of view she could see all the way down into most of the camp.

And she didn't like what she saw.

Dem Inglese and the other four kids from the History Club were standing outside Lucy's tent. There had obviously been a major screwup in the field-trip cancellation department. When Giles emerged from the tent a moment later, she didn't realize that anything was dreadfully wrong until two workers rushed forward and grabbed him by the arms. Giles didn't resist, and he didn't look at Dem when the boy stepped in front of him and poked him repeatedly in the chest. She couldn't tell if Giles was dazed or being stubborn, but Dem, infuriated by the librarian's audacious disregard, began shouting with a rage that scattered the other kids. Dem joined them by the table as the workers hauled Giles to an area at the base of the hill, which was blocked from view by scrub trees and the short dropoff to the rock ledge. Almost immediately, Xander walked into view, followed by an old man in a baseball cap. The old guy jabbed him in the back with a short tool of some kind to hurry him along. Lucy came out of the tent and escorted Xander inside.

Buffy ducked back behind the ridge to think things through. The plan had obviously fallen apart in a hurry—with a few unexpected twists to keep things interesting. Dem the doormat had suddenly turned into Dem the tyrant, and her suspicions about the whole dig crew being drafted into the cult had been confirmed. The dig crew had also tripled in size. Giles and her friends were prisoners and apparently being interrogated one by one. They were probably on the roster to be sacrificed at dawn.

Which was good, because she couldn't race to the rescue just yet.

She had less than an hour to locate and break the

mirror before the jaguar escaped the glass at sundown.

The introspective silence was beginning to unnerve Xander almost as much as his very weird and extremely upsetting encounter with the smoking mirror. A man Giles thought was Juan Hernandez, the artist Joyce Summers' gallery was featuring this weekend, was passed out on the ground several feet away. Giles, Cordelia, and Oz hadn't said more than a few words since they had returned from the tent. He inched closer to Giles along the rock ledge, his movement unnoticed. The guards were focused on the crimson western sky—probably because they didn't expect to see a sunset again. But not for the same reasons *he* didn't expect to see one again. Starting tomorrow, the guards would be living in a world of constant night. He'd be headless, heartless, and dead.

"Listen, Giles," Xander said softly. "I know you don't want to talk about it, but—I have to talk about it."

"Count me out." Cordelia scooted in the opposite direction.

"Still mad 'cause Kilya took your pith helmet?" Xander smiled.

"I *don't* want to talk about it!" Fuming, Cordelia folded her arms and turned her back to them. "Life was so much easier when I only cared about me!"

Interesting. Xander filed the comment. He'd ponder the significance later, when he wasn't facing imminent death by primitive heart extraction.

"Actually, talk would be good," Oz said. "I can't stop thinking about Willow."

"Yeah." Xander glanced toward the tent where Willow was currently being subjected to the disturbing effects of the black mirror. She had the most defined sense of right and wrong of anyone he had ever met. She couldn't sleep if her library books were overdue. A stolen kiss was the biggest sin she had ever committed, and she was still doing private penance. Nothing he could think of could tempt her to evil. Then again, he wasn't a demon with a passkey to her innermost desires and a knack for manufacturing futures made to order.

Not quite fully recovered from the effects of the Aztec knockout powder, Oz dropped his throbbing head in his hands. "I can't believe people *deliberately* use this stuff."

Xander shrugged. "I don't know about now, but five hundred years ago Aztec users didn't live long enough to have a *ya-hoo-tie* hangover. Which brings us back to the mirror. Giles?"

Giles sighed. "You want to know what I saw."

"For starters. I came much too close to giving in. I mean, I had almost forgotten how it felt to be a predator." Xander took a deep breath. In deference to his sensibilities and guilt, no one ever—make that rarely—mentioned the brief time he had been possessed by the spirit of a hyena. Only fate and good timing had prevented him from sinking his teeth into Principal Flutie, who had survived to give the rest of the pack detention for dining on raw pig, a.k.a. the school mascot. He still couldn't smell bacon without choking up about poor Herbert.

"You relived the experience through the mirror," Giles said.

Xander nodded. "In sense-around, stereo, and living color."

The distant woods burned in the glow of a dying day. Giles stared at the fiery panorama, removed and adrift in his own haunted memory. "You felt the enormous freedom of being driven by primal instinct unfettered by guilt, of having power over life and death. And you realized you could have it all back again, permanently, if you committed yourself to Tezcatlipoca."

"That about covers it, but heart surgery with a one-hundred-percent fatality rate just didn't strike me as a viable career move. I passed."

"As did I." Shaking off his tormented reverie, Giles rubbed his temples.

"Let me guess." Xander squinted thoughtfully. "College days. Living on the wild side of life, dabbling in the black arts, summoning demons—Eyghon in particular."

"Partly, but that wasn't how Tezcatlipoca chose to tempt me. He's much more insidious." Giles didn't wince as he fell back against the rock, bumping his head. "He offered to erase Jenny from my memory. No memory, no guilt, no pain. . . ."

"But if you forgot her, how much you loved her—" Oz raised his head slowly. "It would be like she never lived."

"Yes." The intensity of the Watcher's despair caught in his throat and glazed his eyes. "Exactly."

"So—Oz." Xander slapped his knees. "Your turn."

"Not much to tell. The werewolf me I never remember? I remembered. Didn't like it."

"Guess we're all too good—for our own good." Xander's mood darkened as the sun's orb slipped below the horizon. "Maybe today is the day evil finally wins."

"No." Giles straightened, composed and resolved. "Good will always triumph over evil when good is willing to sacrifice everything to prevail."

"It's the 'everything' part I'm having trouble with," Xander said.

"Speaking of good . . ." Cordelia pointed toward the tent. "There's Willow."

Oz started to jump up. Xander pulled him down as one of the guards glanced back. They'd lose a critical advantage if they were bound and gagged.

Willow trudged ahead of Henry, the old man wielding the trowel. She looked devastated, worse than if she had just failed calculus, which was not even remotely possible. When they cleared the end of the deep wash, Henry shooed her toward the ledge, then headed back to the tent with his trusty little shovel resting on his bony shoulder.

Xander moved over another inch to make room between himself and Oz. Since Willow had been returned, he assumed she had opted out of Tezcatlipoca's inner circle, too. "Welcome to the Victims of the Smoking Mirror Support Group."

"Was it terrible?" Oz asked gently.

"Well—sort of, but not really. I mean, if I never master advanced witchcraft, it's okay. Isn't it?" Willow didn't give anyone a chance to offer an opinion. "Of course it is. And—I'll survive if I'm not accepted at M.I.T., right?"

"Isn't the pertinent question whether you'll survive tomorrow morning?" Blunt, Xander realized, but relevant.

"Well, actually—no." Willow winced. "The really pertinent question is . . . will I survive *until* tomorrow morning."

"What do you mean?" Giles asked sharply.

"Yeah?" Cordelia snapped to attention. "Is this a group worry or a Willow-specific problem?"

"Uh, well . . . since I escaped last night?" Willow withered in the shadow of Oz's concern. "I, uh—I'm the, uh—"

"Just spit it out, Willow," Xander pleaded.

Willow shut her eyes and blurted in a rush. "I have to spend the night with Dem."

"Gross!" Cordelia shuddered. "Although he's not that bad-looking since he lost the glasses."

"Wait a minute." Oz controlled his panic with remarkable calm. "Spend the night like in . . . spend the *night?*"

"Yeah." Willow's head bobbed in the affirmative. "Like that."

"Whatever happened to the good old-fashioned tradition of sacrificing virgins?" Xander joked, a buffer against the thought of Dem Inglese or anyone forcibly violating Willow. He loved her—as a friend and in ways he would never again acknowledge—except in all-too-frequent traumatic moments of weakness, like this. If necessary, he'd suffer all the horrors of hell until the end of time to preserve Willow's dignity.

"That was my next question," Oz mumbled.

"I'm afraid this, uh, development fits the Aztec tradition." Giles shifted uneasily as all eyes turned. "Dem has been chosen as Tezcatlipoca's *ixiptla,* the highest honor the Aztec culture could bestow on a young man. For all practical purposes, an *ixiptla* is the embodiment of the god with all the god's rights and privileges."

"Lucky Dem," Xander muttered.

"Hardly," Giles said. "Centuries ago Tezcatlipoca's chosen representative enjoyed his elevated position for a year before being sacrificed. Dem only has until tomorrow."

"So do we, but we don't get any of Dem's cool perks!" Xander held up his hands. "Sorry."

"Yes, well . . ." Giles touched Willow's arm. "Dem doesn't know he's going to be killed, Willow. If you can convince him, the shock might break the hold Tezcatlipoca has over him. Then, perhaps, there won't be—a problem."

"I'll try, but—I'd rather die than, you know . . . and besides—" Willow smiled bravely. "Buffy's still out there. So—it's not over yet."

Xander turned to scan the slope behind him. The towering stone of Coyote Rock blackened as twilight faded into night. Buffy was probably lying low, waiting for the cover of darkness before making a move. Three lanterns flashed on, marking the positions of the guards. Not a problem. They wouldn't be able to stop the Slayer.

Buffy eased out of a large crack in the tower, as shadow and stone blended into seamless black. Muscles and joints complained after twenty-plus minutes of being sandwiched between slabs of rock, but she couldn't afford the luxury of a decent stretch to work out the kinks. The guards, whom she had gotten to know while eavesdropping from her hiding place, had become more alert with the setting sun. Eager even, she realized, as Carrie lit a lantern and moved to confer with Rolf. Doug, a middle-aged dentist with a healthy paunch, stood by his camp light, rifle at the ready in the crook of his arm.

Trying not to make any noise, Buffy carefully pulled her bag out of the crevice. Although the fearless trio hadn't heard the mini–rock slide, they had almost discovered her when she had literally stumbled over the latest additions to Tezcatlipoca's body dump. Only the newbie lookouts' slow response time had allowed her to slip unseen into the rocks, where she had spent the time *not* looking for the mirror and staring into the lifeless eyes of Mr. Coltrane, Dr. Baine, and three strangers. She assumed one of them was the missing detective, Dwayne Thomas. None were young enough to be Juan Hernandez.

Now, with the coming of darkness, Carrie, Rolf, and Doug had more to worry about than random hikers and a nosey Slayer finding the remnants of their barbaric religious rituals. If she had interpreted their idle comments correctly, Tezcatlipoca had forged an alliance with Mr. Trick. Before too long, the local vampires would be leaving their daylight havens and heading out of town by car and on foot to the site. She had maybe ten minutes before the area was overrun with famished, fanged guys. Long enough to get down the hill, but too late to prevent Tezcatlipoca from leaving the mirror. With luck, she wouldn't be too late to free Giles and the troops before Lucy Frank's undead reinforcements arrived.

Hugging the tower wall, Buffy moved toward the western slope, which afforded the most cover and an easier route down than she had taken to get up. A precious five minutes passed before she was slipping with Slayer stealth and speed through clumps of brush and piles of rock. She was thirty yards from the porta-potty when her senses sounded the alarm.

A stake was in her hand and her bag on the ground seconds before the first vampire barreled out of the darkness. She jumped to the side, twisted and kicked, simultaneously sending him sprawling and turning another into dust motes with a deft thrust of her stake. Two more jumped her before she took another breath. A knee to the groin discouraged one. The other clamped cold hands on her upper arms. She bent forward, flipping the heavy-set female onto her back. The stake drove into the body with a satisfying *thwap*. Dust to dust.

"Time!" A deep voice called.

On her feet with stake in hand, Buffy stayed her attack as two dozen vampires of assorted genders, ages, and sizes stopped closing the circle they had formed around her. Mr. Trick stepped forward.

"You're vastly outnumbered, wouldn't you agree, Slayer?"

"Not really. I like a challenge."

Mr. Trick sighed. "There's more where these came from, but I'm prepared to be reasonable if you are."

Buffy had no choice but to listen. She was good, but not good enough to take on this many vampires alone. "What's the deal?"

"Simple. You surrender without a fight, and I guarantee that you'll live through the night. Most of the night anyway."

"And your word is supposed to mean something?" Buffy had never met an honorable vampire, except Angel, who had a soul and wasn't there. That was the only fortuitous aspect of her present circumstances.

"Yes. Believe me, after all the dead hearts you've disintegrated with that lethal toothpick—" He glanced at the stake. "I'll take enormous pleasure in watching *yours* cut out at dawn."

Several of the surrounding vampires snarled through bared fangs.

Buffy dropped her toothpick.

"Grounded?" Angel skimmed Buffy's handwritten note again, then crumpled the paper. He dropped it in the gutter as he sped into the night toward Coyote Rock.

Chapter 14

As she walked into the enemy camp behind Mr. Trick, Buffy questioned the wisdom of surrendering peacefully—for all of five seconds. She had taken the only viable option, buying time and a chance to stop Tezcatlipoca subsequently, and maybe even survive. Granted, with the surrounding terrain infested with vampires and a mob of misguided pagans in control, it wasn't much of a chance, but fighting against impossible odds was included in the Slayer job description.

Battery-powered lanterns and torches burned a hole in the dark around the dig, and the air was thick with anticipation. Everyone had exchanged their regular clothes for knotted white bedsheets accessorized with feathers, gold jewelry, and other miscellaneous trinkets. The old man refused to relinquish his Twins baseball cap and trowel to a plump woman, who stomped off in a fit of pique. Any illusion of comedy ended there. Faces and eyes betrayed an evil malice, as the isolated groups coalesced into a single gathering, with a sole purpose. The chill of murderous intent entwined with the crisp bite in the night air, as the crowd parted to let Lucy pass. Her slim body was draped in a flowing white garment with an embroidered border, which billowed slightly as she walked. She wore a feathered headdress adorned with gold and precious stones and carried a gold-framed black object that had to be Tezcatlipoca's obsidian mirror.

Buffy considered and rejected a bold and suicidal impulse to grab the artifact. The risk would be for nothing if the jaguar had already left the glass. Instead, she glanced toward the hill as Giles and her friends were herded together at the edge of the deep gully. Xander propped up an unsteady young man with dark hair. She assumed he was the missing Juan Hernandez. She caught Giles's eye and returned an imperceptible nod, hoping he had a plan B. Because she was at a loss.

Mr. Trick dropped the Slayer bag on the table, then stepped up to Lucy with a slight inclination of his head. "High Priestess. I've brought a gift, a symbol of my esteem for the dark lord, Tezcatlipoca. I'm certain she will more than make up for the unfortunate incident last night."

Buffy shivered in the cold generated by Lucy's subtle smile as the vampire stepped aside.

"The *ixiptla* will be most pleased, Mr. Trick. Most pleased." The woman nodded with a quick glance toward the tent and immediately lowered her gaze, as did everyone else in the cult.

Buffy and the captive sacrifice pool stared directly at Dem as he swept onto center stage with Sienna, Chance, Bart, and Kilya at his heels. They were all dressed in makeshift variations of the traditional Aztec clothing, with the exception of Cordelia's pith helmet, which crowned Kilya's head. Dem, whose elaborate garb appeared authentic, gripped a feathered fan in one hand and four arrows in the other. No trace of the tongue-tied, awkward boy Buffy had first met was evident as he paused to survey the throng. He looked neither pleased nor impressed with their adulation as he turned to speak to Lucy. The new and not necessarily improved Dem was apparently limited to two moods: indifferent and angry.

Buffy stiffened when he whirled suddenly to face her. His stare bore into her with an almost painful intensity, a probing violation of her self and soul. She did not look away, but felt an immense relief when he broke the connection. Her better judgment kept a caustic insult at bay.

A restless urgency moved through the crowd like a stadium wave when Lucy raised the mirror over her head and turned and walked sedately toward the hill. Dem moved into position a few steps behind her with the fan and arrows crossed over his chest. The others pulled torches out of the ground and followed en masse, their solemn faces aglow with excitement. Mr. Trick faded into the night as two men with crude spears yanked Buffy out of the procession's path. Giles and company brought up the rear under the watchful eyes of several guards. When they came abreast of her, she was rudely shoved into the group.

"Buffy!" Willow looked at her with wide, desperate eyes. "You got—caught."

"Sorry. Too many vamps to solo and live." Buffy shrugged.

"Bummer." Oz squeezed Willow's hand.

"Maybe you haven't noticed, Buffy," Xander said,

"but present circumstances are not exactly conducive to longevity."

"Yeah, but we've got a few hours before the main event." Buffy eased back beside Giles. "What's the new plan?"

Giles raised an eyebrow. "I was hoping you had one."

"We're gonna die," Cordelia moaned. "Why do I let you people talk me into these things?"

"Because you're weak-minded and easily persuaded?" Buffy stumbled when a guard prodded her with the shaft of his spear.

"Be quiet!" The guard poked her again.

Sighing, Buffy concentrated on not tripping over rocks and roots as the torchlit parade moved up the slope. Escape was not out of the question. It wouldn't be too hard to overpower the three men behind them and run, and they'd be difficult if not impossible to find in the dark wilderness area. Except for the fact that there was a vampire lurking behind every bush. And then there was the mirror, which was still intact. Win or lose, they had no choice but to go with the program and hope fate gave them a break.

Joyce's worried frown changed back into a welcoming smile as Richard Wilkens entered the gallery. She didn't care much for the slick politician, but his presence at Juan's opening would benefit the artist and the affair. Guests who were likely to buy would be impressed, and the local newspaper always reported his public activities on the front page. "Good evening, Mayor Wilkens. So good of you to come."

"My pleasure, Ms. Summers. I happen to have an interest in Aztec culture, and I can't wait to meet your young Mr. Hernandez and see his work."

Joyce nodded and kept smiling even though the mayor's ingratiating seventy-five-watt grin gave her the creeps.

"Is he here?" Wilkens glanced around the crowded room.

"Actually, no." Joyce shrugged apologetically. "But I'm sure he will be shortly. Why don't you have some refreshments and, uh—mingle with your wealthier constituents until he arrives?"

"Excellent idea." Wilkens' smile brightened to one hundred watts when he spotted Lorne Michaels, owner of Sunnydale's largest real-estate agency, who was talking with the president of the First Street Bank and his wife. "If you'll excuse me. . . ."

"Of course." Joyce sagged as the mayor walked away and waved to Hazel, who immediately bustled over. "Did he call?"

"No." Hazel's eyes betrayed her deep concern. "You don't think anything happened to him, do you?"

"No, I'm sure he just lost track of the time." Actually, Joyce wasn't sure, but she didn't want her co-hostess moping about the reception while she was gone. "Can you handle things here while I go find out what's keeping him?"

"Yes, of course." The older woman smiled uncertainly. "Everything's under control."

Ten minutes of polite small talk later, Joyce finally reached her office. Grabbing her bag and jacket, she ducked out the back door. Coyote Rock was only a fifteen-minute drive, but it would be a long fifteen minutes. Too much time had passed since Buffy had left for the site with orders to remind Juan about the reception. Either one or both of them was in trouble.

* * *

While Lucy, Dem, and their cult entourage moved on toward Coyote Rock, Buffy and friends were detained when they exited the maze of boulders. Two men and a woman stayed behind with Carrie, Rolf, and Doug to make sure they stayed put. Juan was still groggy after multiple doses of *yauhtli* and collapsed on the ground. Oz sat beside Willow on a low, flat stone and put his arm around her.

Xander rubbed the back of his head, then folded his arms. "You know, Cordy . . . they say that adversity brings people closer together."

"They're wrong." Cordelia stormed over to the nearest guard. "Can I bribe you into putting me in solitary confinement?"

As Lucy and Dem began to climb the tall rock formation, illuminated now by the frantic light of torches set into cracks and crags, Buffy leaned into Giles and whispered. "There's no chance they're going to push the schedule ahead, is there?"

"No. The sacrifices must be made just before sunrise to be effective."

"Then what's going on? Why bring everyone up here now?" The temperature was dropping rapidly and Buffy rubbed her arms, wishing she had remembered to bring a jacket.

"Well, I'm not quite sure, but there is another slight problem"—Giles hesitated, which was always a bad sign in her experience—"concerning Willow." The butt of a rifle whipped out of the dark and rammed into his back. He fell forward, taking Buffy down with him.

"Shut up," Doug snapped in a low husky voice. "The ceremony's about to start."

Buffy eased out from under Giles and kept quiet until Doug was back on top of his boulder. The heavy silence that had settled over the crowd radiated outward to muffle the terrain and everything that crept, crawled, or slithered over it. She dared to whisper, "Are you all right?"

"Yes, I think so." Wincing, Giles let Buffy help him to his feet. "Let's, uh, shut up for now, shall we?"

"Good idea."

The night was crackling with expectation when Dem and Lucy reached a ledge halfway up the tower and turned to face the mob of anxious converts. As Lucy raised the mirror, a wisp of blue-gray smoke drifted out from the dark glass and elongated into a huge plume that rose to hover over the stone column.

Realizing Tezcatlipoca was only now leaving the mirror, Buffy suppressed a pang of regret as the plume spiraled around the natural monolith, wrapping the stone in a smoky blue-gray helix. The silence deepened, muting even the whisper of her breathing. She couldn't blame herself for not acting on insufficient information earlier, and yet, as the snaking plume pulsed and constricted, she wished she had taken the chance.

Maybe her only chance.

Buffy instinctively moved closer to Giles when the ground began to shake and a pattern of fine cracks split the surface of the stone tower. Oz and Willow stood up and backed toward them. Xander pulled Juan to his feet and grabbed Cordelia's arm to haul her into the dubious safety of the group.

"It's the earthquake, isn't it?" Willow clung to Oz.

"The one that's supposed to destroy the fifth sun?" Xander asked.

Buffy glanced up at Doug. He was too terrified or enthralled by the spectacle to care about a disrespectful dialogue among the prisoners.

Juan blinked, shaken from his daze. *"Que Dios nos ayude a todos!"*

Giles shook his head. "This isn't an earthquake."

Xander flailed his arms to keep his balance when a tremor shot under his feet. "Could have fooled me."

A rumbling crescendo broke the eerie silence as the smoky plume unwound from the tower and whipped around the stones at the base. Lucy and Dem remained calm and still on their precarious ledge, unfazed by the prospect of being buried under tons of crumbling rock. The crowd huddled together in small groups below, but they stood fast when the air undulated and suddenly increased in density. Buffy struggled to breathe under the suffocating pressure, and gasped when the weight lifted in a burst of deafening thunder. The temperature rose twenty degrees as the dark shimmered and stone turned to clay under an invisible sculptor's hand.

The boulders around the prisoners expanded and changed shape, turning into a wall of rough adobe behind them, then into four walls enclosing them. Buffy rushed to a window opening as straw thatch appeared overhead, blotting out the stars.

"Can we assume there's a logical explanation for this?" Xander jumped clear as a torch burst into flame on the interior wall.

Giles moved to the doorway. "I believe we're witnessing a recreation of the Templo Mayor complex, the center of the old Aztec capital at Tenochtitlan."

"That's logical." Xander shrugged. "Considering that an Aztec god is the interior decorator."

Cordelia scanned their crude prison with distaste. "His taste leaves a lot to be desired."

Juan stepped up to another narrow window slit and inhaled sharply. "Incredible."

Outside, Coyote Rock was absorbed into a huge, flattened pyramid with a base the size of a football field. Dem and Lucy were untouched when the ledge they stood on rose upward and stretched into a broad platform with a bench-shaped throne on the right and a large, slightly rounded stone on the left. Two trapezoidal structures supported by thick, low stone columns formed behind them. Two long flights of stone steps separated by a stone median and inlaid with mosaics formed below Lucy and Dem's position. Two wide landings with shorter flights of steps appeared at the base. Large stone carvings of snakes and frogs painted orange and green flanked the steps on each tier. A rack boasting the five skewered heads stood off to the side. Torches lit the entire temple and surrounding area.

The rumbling roar died away as the transformation solidified, and a cheer rose up from the throng gathered in the wide plaza in front of the finished temple. The bedsheets were gone, replaced with authentic Aztec capes, tunics, loose homespun trousers and sandals. Oddly, Kilya still wore Cordelia's pith helmet, a trophy that had survived the transition along with the heads. Long wooden tables laden with bowls of fruit, corn bread and roasted meats lined the eastern side of the courtyard.

"We're all still wearing jeans." Willow frowned. "How come our clothes didn't change?"

"*Never* question good fortune, Willow." Cordelia grimaced. "If I'm going to die, I'd just as soon go out in style."

"That's more accurate than you realize, Cordelia," Giles said. "Since we did not commit ourselves to Tezcatlipoca's service, we're not worthy of Aztec recognition. Not to mention that we're not expected to live to usher in his new age of darkness."

"Something else is happening," Juan said.

Buffy was only vaguely aware of Xander pressing next to her to look out. She was focused entirely on the temple, as the plume of smoke settled on the topmost structure to the left and condensed into the sleek, muscular form of the black jaguar. It was not Tezcatlipoca's immense power that struck terror in her heart, however. She stared at Dem as he took his honored place on the low stone and mosaic throne below the jaguar's perch, then shifted her gaze as Lucy began to descend the steps.

. . . The stone steps where Angel had stood before he vanished, in her dream.

Angel darted from the forest, ignoring the spectacular appearance of an Aztec temple on the distant hill. The woods and terrain around the archaeological site were crawling with vamps, all of them unaware that he moved among them, most of them distracted by the latest Hellmouth extravaganza. He counted six or seven in his immediate vicinity. Only one was between him and Coyote Rock—or what had been Coyote Rock until a few minutes ago.

Angel moved quickly and silently, a sharp, broken tree branch clutched in his hand. The male vampire in his path had no warning. Angel grabbed his shoulder, yanked him around, and drove the deadly wood into his chest. He moved on before the dust settled, intent on nothing but finding Buffy.

"What?" Buffy's mouth fell open. "That—that arrogant, no-good Aztec lowlife picked Willow to be his—his—"

"Lady of the evening?" Willow shrugged and

clasped her hands. "Or whatever . . . but I'm not gonna, you know . . . *do* anything. Because, well, because . . . I just can't. I'll—I'll throw myself off the top of the temple first."

Oz started to protest.

"You won't get the chance." Lucy interrupted from the doorway.

Willow whirled, mortified as Lucy pointed.

"That one."

Willow thought the shock might stop her heart right then and there, saving her from a last-resort plunge and a messy, though dignified, end. However, since things hadn't reached the last-resort stage yet, she shrank back as six husky guards barged in. "Wait. I'm not ready. Okay, so I'll never be ready. But—" She smiled weakly at the man who grabbed her arm. "Can't we, uh, talk about this?"

"I'm done talking." Oz pulled a torch off the wall and lunged to burn the guard holding Willow. He was pushed back at spear point and disarmed. Three other guards forced Xander, Giles, and Juan against the walls.

"And that one," Lucy said.

Cordelia gasped, then sighed with relief when Lucy's moving finger targeted Buffy. Willow's hopes rose when she saw *that* smile. The one Buffy got whenever she was *really* mad. The pseudo Aztec warrior had no idea that Buffy wasn't just some insipid teenaged girl who would squeal and give up without a fight. Willow winced in anticipation as he reached to take the Slayer's arm.

"I'm not ready, either." Buffy slammed the burly man into the wall with a right hook to the chin. The stunned guard staggered and slid to the floor.

"Idiot." Lucy stepped toward Buffy.

Willow saw the mound of *yauhtli* powder in the woman's open palm and realized Buffy was focused on the guard, just waiting to flatten him again if he dared get up. He didn't look like he was going to risk it, but Lucy wasn't at all intimidated.

Willow yelled, "Buffy! Behind you!"

Buffy spun to kick a split second before Willow realized her mistake.

"No! I mean—don't look!"

Reacting instantly, Buffy ducked under the high concentration of powder Lucy threw in her face, but she didn't escape the cloud entirely. She staggered as she inhaled the potent drug. Lucy grabbed her by the hair and yanked her out the door.

Willow thought about putting up a fight as the guard hauled her across the room but vetoed the idea. An elbow to the ribs or a swift kick in the shin wouldn't accomplish anything except make the guy mad. Besides, Buffy was zoned out on *yauhtli* powder now and as helpless as she was—temporarily.

Willow's mind reeled as she considered her limited options. Even though she couldn't preserve their honor with her fists, she was still thinking clearly. Maybe she could stall for time. Not a great plan, but better than no plan. As the guard shoved her outside, Willow looked back and shook her head to stop Oz from doing something stupid. Like volunteering to test the puncture power of a spear.

"Hey, Willow." Buffy swayed, then waved a limp hand as she vacantly looked around. "When did they redo the mall?"

"Buffy, listen." Willow hissed softly. They were halfway across the courtyard with Lucy leading the way and three armed men behind. Although the lighted plaza was crowded with cult members, dark flitting shadows that weren't connected to anyone's feet, and a few transparent people, they were all partying. If she and Buffy made a break for it, they could get lost in the crowd—maybe. Once they started up the steps, their current almost nil chance of escape would drop to absolute zero. "We're not at the mall. We're—"

"Hungry." Sniffing, Buffy executed an abrupt quarter turn toward the aroma of roast beast rising from the primitive buffet. A guard pulled her back into line.

Okay, Willow thought frantically. Their chance of escape was already zero. And the more she thought about it, the less confidant she was that Dem Inglese, ex-nerd and social outcast who'd probably never had a date, was going to pass on—you know. Blast! She couldn't even *think* the S-word! And when it got right down to it, she really didn't want to jump off a pyramid. So since desperate circumstances called for desperate measures, and she was pretty desperate—

"Buffy?" When Buffy turned, Willow slapped her. Buffy's eyes flashed—with surprise or anger? The Slayer didn't swing, but a hand closed around Willow's wrist and twisted her arm behind her back. "Buffy, I'm sorry, but—"

The guard tightened his grip, pinching her skin, then released her to mount the first, short tier of steps. She stole a glance at Buffy as they crossed a wide landing and ascended the second tier. Buffy rubbed the reddening spot on her cheek and looked the other way.

Numb, Willow counted the steps on the long stairway to keep from losing it in the face of overwhelmingly rotten circumstances. Buffy was spaced for who knew how long. The armed guards were dutifully watchful behind them. Lucy was caught in the throes of pagan fervor, and Dem was high on delusions of grandeur and the impending satisfaction of his adolescent sexual fantasies. Reason didn't work on irrational people driven by fanaticism and hormones.

Fifty. Give or take a step.

Willow inhaled a whiff of scented smoke from a small brazier at the head of the steps and sneezed as Lucy knelt before Dem. A guard prodded her in the small of the back.

"Kneel!" The threat of reprisal underscored the harshly whispered order. Lucy's eyes narrowed with warning as she rose and backed off to stand at Dem's left.

On the verge of hyperventilating, Willow took a deep breath and knelt. Before she bowed her head to prevent guard-induced whiplash, she noticed that Dem's gaze hadn't wavered from Buffy.

Responding to the pressure of a guard's hand on her shoulder, Buffy sank to her knees with an inane smile and stared at a flickering torch. When the black jaguar on the roof above them growled, she looked up. "Oh! Look at the big kitty!"

Dem smiled.

Willow wilted.

Chapter 15

Angel hung back in the shadows, beyond the glow of the camp lights that were spaced around the dig. He had detoured from a direct course up the hill when he saw a familiar car pull into the parking area, but he had not arrived in time to warn Buffy's mother away. She was in shock, in part from seeing a full-sized Aztec temple dominating the California landscape, but mostly from being hauled before Mr. Trick by a snarling, female vampire.

"Well, if it isn't the Slayer's mom." Mr. Trick grinned with satisfaction. "My new associate will be delighted."

Furious, Joyce tried to yank free of the female vamp's iron grip, a futile effort until Mr. Trick nodded his consent. She smoothed the skirt of a sleek, black dress and lifted her chin defiantly. "Where's my daughter?"

"Why don't I just take you to her. This way." Trick motioned for Joyce to move ahead of him.

Angel followed at a discreet distance. Joyce stumbled in her high heels, but was not a candidate for a quick feed, and the sleazy Mr. Trick was saving him the time and trouble of locating Buffy on his own. He didn't have difficulty keeping them in sight until they reached the outskirts of the Aztec complex. Unlike the temple and central plazas, the buildings on the perimeter had only been partially restored, creating a confusing jumble of incomplete walls, roofs, and narrow streets. The ghosts of Aztec warriors and peasants cavorted among the ruins, celebrating a conquered past soon to be avenged. They were harmless, but other more malevolent essences impeded his progress through the labyrinth.

Repulsed by Angel's salvaged spirit, shadow demons shrieked in his face and clawed at his long duster, a nuisance without teeth that cost him precious seconds. He lost sight of Joyce and Trick when they turned a corner. A bevy of shadowy wisps flew in his face, blinding him.

Disoriented still after batting the creatures away, Angel quickened his pace. He didn't sense the other vampire until it tackled him from a doorway and threw him to the ground. Pinned under the larger demon's weight, he fumbled for the pointed branch in his pocket. Fangs raked his cheek and a claw hooked his ear. Enraged by the pain and delay, he pushed the vamp to the side, drew the stake and struck. It disintegrated just as it was about to rip off his ear.

Spotting Buffy's mother and Mr. Trick moving between two rows of free-standing columns near the distant temple, Angel quickly closed the gap. He tracked them to a heavily guarded adobe building with a peaked thatched roof, and waited under a floating stone portal until Mr. Trick came back into view. Smiling, Trick sauntered across the plaza toward the western slope—alone.

The back wall of the building was solid except for a vertical slit in the center that was too narrow for an adult to squeeze through. Two guards stood at the front corners of the crude hut. Two others paced back and forth on either side. None of them checked the escape-proof back wall.

Silent as the ghosts hovering around him, Angel crept to the window. Giles was comforting Joyce just inside the front entrance. Cordelia dozed in a corner next to a young man he didn't recognize. Oz was pacing the length of the torchlit room and hitting the wall with his fist, before turning and retracing his steps. Xander stood at a front window, peering out. Buffy and Willow weren't there.

"Giles!" Angel called softly.

"Angel?" Releasing Joyce, Giles sprang to the window. He kept his voice low. "What are you doing here? I'm actually quite glad to see you, but—didn't you get Buffy's note?"

"What note?" Joyce frowned. "And where is Buffy?"

"Quietly, Joyce. Please." Giles pointed to indicate that the guards might hear.

"I got the message." Angel didn't waste time explaining why he had chosen to ignore it. "Where is she?"

"They, uh—took Buffy and Willow to the temple a few minutes—"

Angel turned to leave. The urgency in Giles's voice drew him back.

"No, wait! They won't be losing their hearts or their heads tonight, and there's—"

"Then why were they taken to the temple?" Angel asked.

"Let's just say that Dem won't be losing *his* soul because of it." Xander's answer was oblique in deference to Buffy's mother, but the meaning was crystal-clear to Angel.

"What does that mean?" Joyce looked from Xander to Angel to Giles, then back at Angel. "You lost your soul when you and Buffy—" Her hand flew to her mouth.

Angel diverted his attention to Giles before millennia of evolved maternal wrath erupted in Joyce and crashed down on him. "No one can force Buffy to do anything she doesn't want to."

"Ordinarily, that's very true." Giles nodded, then stared at the floor. "Except right now she's a bit"—he looked up nervously—"drugged."

"What?" Joyce's temper flared, but she aimed it directly at Giles. "Isn't courting mortal danger seven days a week enough? Now it's sex and drugs, too?"

"Joyce, believe me, I—I—" Giles fumbled for words that weren't there.

"I'll certainly never give her permission to go on a school field trip again!" Joyce's seething gaze dared the stricken librarian to point out that the comment was completely lame and immaterial.

"Could we discuss this later, Joyce?" Giles asked gently. "I really must speak to Angel before he dashes off to rescue Buffy and Willow."

Oz slammed his fist into the wall full force.

"Do you mind? Since nobody's doing anything to get us out of here, I'd like to get some sleep." Cordelia snuggled back into the hollow of Juan's shoulder.

"Of course," Xander said. "Beauty rest is so important the night before you have your heart cut out."

Out of patience, Angel melted back into the shadows.

Giles's frantic call did not lure him back this time. Whatever the Watcher had to say could wait until after Buffy and Willow were safe.

Angel smelled the jaguar before he saw the dark cat pad into the twisted walkways of its malformed domain. Cursing, he froze. The massive predator was stronger now, and he couldn't risk an injury. Apparently unable to distinguish his scent from that of the other undead nearby, the cat kept moving, intent on another hunting spree through the unprotected streets of Sunnydale.

The beast within Angel stirred as he cleared the corner of the prison hut and looked toward the temple. Two guards, one tall and lean, the other shorter and heavy-set, were escorting Buffy and Willow into a square chamber at the top of the pyramid. As three men with spears rushed him, rage set the vampire free, and he sent them sprawling across flat stones with the snap of a hand.

Whether by chance or agreement, the plaza area was free of vampires. Humans and ghosts scattered as Angel charged across the courtyard. Attracted to his rage, hell's nebulous denizens swarmed around him as he took the first tier of steps in one stride. He paused for a split second to disperse the annoying demon beasties with a fanged snarl, then cleared the landing and second flight of steps before another second passed.

The woman at the top called for additional forces from the ranks below, then realized they could not possibly muster and arrive in time. She ordered the solitary man on the landing to repel the demonic tempest racing up the steps. The man took one look, dropped his spear and cowered on the farthest edge of the precipice. The woman fled into the structure where Buffy and Willow had gone.

Angel fought the vampire's terrible hunger as he ran across the platform. The woman hiding within the walls would be easy prey—for someone else. He came to a startled halt when she unexpectedly leaped between two round columns supporting the wide doorway into the squat building.

"Be gone, rogue!" Her eyes were alight with a zealous confidence and conviction.

"Not without Buffy and Willow."

"They belong to the dark now."

"I don't have time for this." Angel darted to the right.

The woman matched his maneuver, moving behind the column. Her face contorted with wrath as she held up a black glass framed in gold. "No one betrays Tezcatlipoca!"

Angel recognized the artifact from Buffy's description—the smoking mirror she'd been looking for when the vampires had attacked her and Cordelia on the hill last night, the source of the power that threatened her now.

Maddened, Angel raised his fist to smash it, then staggered as a stream of cold concentrated smoke whipped past him and into the inky surface.

"See your doom, vampire." The woman hissed and thrust the mirror in his face.

Angel saw nothing but a swirl of smoke on black. He had no reflection, and he was losing control. Fangs bared, he drew back his arm, fist clenched.

Buffy leaned against the stone wall, content to let Willow jabber at Dem as he inspected the chambers.

"All of this—what's going on? It isn't what you think it is, Dem." Willow glanced over her shoulder at the guards flanking the door. "I mean—you may think you've got it made and that you're gonna rule the world when this is all over, but—"

"I do have it made." Dem glanced at a large, thick pallet covered with robes and fur pelts that lay on the floor of a smaller, inner chamber, then removed his feathered headdress and dropped it on a table stocked with fruit and sweetbreads. "I'm Tezcatlipoca's *ixiptla*. I can do anything I want. *Have* anything I want."

"For tonight—maybe, but tomorrow—"

"Tomorrow you die." Dem picked up an apple and leered at Buffy.

"Yeah? Well—it's your funeral, too!" Willow huffed when Dem laughed. "I'm not kidding. There's no such thing as a free lunch or a—a free orgy, either . . . which we're not going to have. An orgy, I mean—"

"Shut up, Willow." Dem threw the apple at her.

Willow ducked and the fruit smacked against the wall. "I will, but—it won't change anything. They're going to kill you, too, because—because that's what an *ixiptla* does. Get sacrificed—like everyone else . . . only they treat you better first and—and your body gets carried off the pyramid instead of thrown off. But you'll still be a head on a stick when it's all over—" Willow stopped talking and backed away as Dem took a threatening step toward her.

"Keep quiet!" Dem glared at her for a long moment.

Willow glanced at the guards, swallowed, and nodded.

Satisfied, Dem slowly walked over to Buffy. She smiled absently as he stroked her hair and reached for her hand. "Come on, Buffy."

"Sorry, Dem." Buffy's smile vanished. "I've got other plans." She clamped onto his arm, pivoted, and flipped him onto his back, knocking the wind out of him.

"Buffy! You're back!"

"Never left." Buffy whirled to take on the guards while Dem struggled to fill his empty lungs with air. The tall one charged. She ripped the spear from his grasp and kicked, sending him flying into the stone table so hard the fruit bowl rocked. The second, shorter man was more cautious, and circled the dim-witted girl who had suddenly turned into a focused, armed, and dangerous foe.

"You mean you were just pretending?" Willow asked. "To be totally out of it?"

"Pretty much." Buffy dodged as the guard jabbed with his spear. She spun and whacked him in the back with the blunt end of her spear, throwing him off balance. "I was groggy at first, but that—" The guard tried to duplicate her move and she whacked him again. He stumbled backward. "—Passed."

Willow shook her head and exhaled shortly. "I should have known. I mean, what's a little whoopee powder to the Slayer."

"A major headache." Wincing, Buffy opened her stance as the angry, second guard prepared to rush her again.

Gasping for air, Dem rolled onto his side. Willow picked up the apple from the floor and loomed over him. "Don't try anything, Dem, or I'll—I'll stuff this down your throat!"

The tall man near the table dragged himself onto all fours, then lunged forward. He grasped Willow around the ankle and pulled her feet out from under her. The apple sailed out of her hand as she fell with a loud grunt.

With Willow down, Buffy got serious. She snap-kicked the short guard in the stomach, then delivered a fist to the chin that put him on his knees. She hung onto the spear and jumped over Dem to stomp the first guard's wrist with her boot heel. He yelped and let go of Willow's ankle.

"Let's get out of here." Buffy hauled Willow upright and turned to flee. The sight of Lucy standing inside the door made her hesitate.

"What happened to your face?" Willow blurted.

A large, purple bruise darkened the young woman's cheek and her eyes gleamed with angry contempt, but she didn't answer. Her fist flexed on the folds of her gown, which she clutched tightly at her waist.

"Out of my way, Lucy." Buffy approached cautiously, in case more men waited in the foyer. No guards rushed in, but she was ambushed by surprise when Lucy pulled the obsidian mirror from under her gown and held it up. A glance and the glass owned her.

An unseen, virulent force stripped away the layers of emotional veneer that protected her deepest secrets and fears, exposing her to the violent horror of her nature and the vengeful fury of her enemies. Buffy ceased to exist outside an eternal night infested with screaming demons and vampires. Fangs and talons gouged and shredded her flesh, pecked at her bones and devoured her soul. Blood flowed freely from the wounds, pooled at her feet, and swelled into a thick red sea that dragged her down and down and down. . . .

Angel paused in the narrow stone corridor and closed his eyes against the irritating flicker of torchlight. Rage against the High Priestess had sent him blindly charging into the temple after she had taken a fist in the face to save the mirror. Furious over his failure to smash the offending glass and desperate to find Buffy, he had quickly become lost in a convoluted system of corridors and chambers. Now, anger and frustration made it harder to cage the beast, but determined calm prevailed with the fluid change of his facial features. He waited, listened, then moved upward toward the only sounds that whispered through the stone passageways.

He found Buffy in a large chamber near the top of the pyramid. She stood paralyzed, her eyes glazed, staring into the mirror the High Priestess held before her. Willow was there, too, unharmed but cornered by two guards. A boy wearing the finery of the Aztec aristocracy sat on a table, eating an apple and hungrily watching Buffy.

The woman yelped as Angel grabbed the back of her gown and tossed her aside. She rolled into a protective ball around the mirror as she hit the floor. Buffy stared straight ahead, lost in her own mind, a captive of Tezcatlipoca's manipulations.

"Angel!" Willow's face brightened with hope.

Her perky voice was drowned out by the sound of booted feet pounding stone as more guards mounted the temple steps.

A wisp of smoke drifted through the folds of the High Priestess's gown.

Another minute and he would be trapped between a horde of would-be Aztec warriors and the jaguar.

Angel latched onto Buffy and bolted back into the interior of the massive pyramid, ignoring Willow's plaintive cry.

* * *

Willow stared at the empty doorway. Angel had appeared and disappeared so fast, she wouldn't have been sure he had been there at all except that Buffy was gone, too. And she wasn't. She jumped as Dem leaped off the table and sacrificed another apple to his rage.

The half-eaten fruit splattered against stone as the *ixiptla* turned on the stunned guards. "Why are you just standing there? Go after them!"

The men hurried to do his bidding, but hesitated as smoke coalesced into an angry jaguar outside the chamber. The rustling, stomping sounds of other guards entering the foyer stopped suddenly. Even Dem exercised a measure of prudence and ceased his ravings when Tezcatlipoca roared, incensed at the theft of his prize.

Mentally stuffing a sock in her mouth, Willow watched silently as Lucy huddled on the stone floor before the agitated cat. It swiped at the woman's face with unsheathed claws. Two bleeding slashes opened on her cheek. No one moved, while the jaguar paced a restless circle testing the warm air for the escapees' scent. When the animal finally bounded into the night, scattering men with a frustrated, feline scream, Lucy got up slowly. She was still holding the unbroken mirror.

Dem resumed his tantrum. "I want Buffy back! Search every inch of this temple and don't stop until you find her!"

Lucy designated two new guards to stand watch in the foyer and sent the rest scurrying on what Willow hoped would be a wild-goose chase. She wasn't thrilled that Angel had abandoned her, but saving Buffy was more important, and not just to him. Nobody else could possibly stop the morning massacre.

Bleeding and disheveled, Lucy eyed Dem with guarded disdain as he cursed and fumed. Deluded into believing his word was law and his position secure, Dem didn't realize that the High Priestess would be glad to get rid of him. For now, though, she eased back into a posture of subservient deference. "Is there anything else—"

"No! Leave me alone."

As Lucy bowed out, Willow took the cue and walked briskly toward the door.

Dem pushed her back. "Where do you think you're going?"

"Out? I mean, if you want to be alone, that works for me. Really. Not a problem. I'll, uh—just find my own way." Smiling tightly, Willow tried to duck around him. Dem locked her in a clumsy embrace and tried to kiss her.

Willow went from trying-to-be-reasonable to no-way-in-hell in point-five seconds. Her knee connected with his groin, and the effectiveness of the instinctive defense stunned her almost as much as the unexpected pain stunned the boy. He released her, grabbed his crotch, and doubled over with a short, horrified wail.

Willow's dash for freedom was aborted by the guards stationed outside the door. With two spears aimed at her midsection, she raised her hands and fell back on her first line of defense. "He, uh, is just—*sick* over losing Buffy. So—maybe you should call 911! Or—or the medicine man or whoever you guys call in an emergency."

Dem straightened slowly and gathered the tatters of his dignity. "Take her back to the prisoner compound."

Willow swallowed a smile. Being released from harlot duty was a relief, if not a reprieve.

Dem glowered at her. "Tomorrow, you'll be first in line at the altar."

Buffy floundered, moving her arms and legs to escape the thick constricting tentacles and masses of stinging tendrils that swam in the river of blood. Swept through hellish caverns, she barely missed being rammed into rocks or impaled by long, shimmering stalactites that dripped fire as she streaked by. She twisted and kicked as something trapped her flailing arms, couldn't break free and choked on a shriek of angry terror as a cold hand clamped over her mouth—

"Buffy!"

The dreaded thing shook her, slapped her—

"Buffy!"

Angel! She froze.

"Come on, Buffy," he pleaded.

"Angel . . ." Buffy shook her head and sagged into his arms. The red river and burning stalactites faded, replaced by a stone tomb and a torch. "Where—"

"The bottom of the pyramid. Safe—for now." He folded her into his arms.

The strength of Angel's embrace anchored her, filled her with a torment she would never escape. She clung to him, but only for a moment, while she filtered out the lingering bizarre effects of Tezcatlipoca's mirror and grounded herself in an equally bizarre reality. Aztec temple . . . Black jaguar . . . Lucy and Dem. . . . Buffy pulled away to scan the cramped, humid chamber. They were alone.

"Where's Willow?"

Angle lowered his gaze. "There wasn't time—" He moved to stop her from racing through the narrow doorway. "You can't go back."

"I have to!"

"No." Angel stood firm in the heated indignation of her glare. "You can't do anything to stop Tezcatlipoca if you're a prisoner or dead. They're searching, but they don't know where we are."

"But—" Buffy's chest heaved with a resigned sigh. Angel was right. Too many lives depended on them staying alive and free to fight. Willow was on her own. "We'll have to hole up in here for the night. Preferably closer to the top."

"For the night?" Angel shifted between dismay and joy. "Why?"

Buffy quickly briefed him on the requirements for doing in Tezcatlipoca and preventing perpetual night. "But his smokiness has to be inside the mirror *before* it's broken or we might never track him down again."

"*Before?*" Angel frowned. "Guess that's what Giles wanted to tell me."

"You didn't—"

"Break it?" Angel shook his head. "Almost, but no, I didn't."

"Good, but there's another major glitch in the revised plan." Buffy hesitated to continue, but she couldn't avoid the disturbing problem. "If—*when* we stop the sacrifices, Tezcatlipoca will be too weak to kill the sun and he'll have to return to the mirror. So . . . we can't do anything until just before dawn."

Angel smiled and brushed a wisp of hair off her cheek. "You're worried about the dream."

"Angel, if you're caught in the open at sunrise—"

Buffy shuddered as his cold finger gently touched her lips.

"Buffy, I'd rather not exist than be in a demonic dark world without you. End of discussion."

Buffy didn't argue as she followed him through the twisting passageways, but her sadness deepened as they moved upward. She had tried to keep Angel out of danger and had failed, because what she saw in her dreams was inevitable.

Chapter 16

Giles awoke the instant the men entered the hut. He had slept fitfully, sitting up against the wall with Joyce's head cradled in his lap.

"Everybody up!" A surly, middle-aged man with a beard jostled Oz with his foot.

Oz swatted at the impertinent boot and rolled over with a groan. Willow poked him repeatedly in the shoulder until he opened his eyes and yawned.

"I'm up! I'm up!" Xander jumped to his feet, wide-eyed and disoriented.

"What?" Joyce raised her head. "What's happening?"

"They've come for us." Giles had explained everything to her last night with profuse apologies. Even though he could hardly be held accountable for Tezcatlipoca's activities and aspirations, he was responsible for miscalculating and leading everyone into the cult's trap yesterday. The feeling was compounded because Joyce and her artistic discovery, Juan, had inadvertently stumbled into the thick of things, too.

"Buffy?" Joyce sat up, her large eyes hopeful.

Giles shook his head. After Willow had returned to report Angel and Buffy's escape, he had thought they might attempt a rescue or try to contact him. They had not been seen. To Joyce's credit, she took heart rather than assuming the worst.

"Then she and Angel could be out there waiting for the right moment to strike, couldn't they?"

"Yes. Absolutely." Giles hoped that was the case, but he couldn't discount the possibility that the search parties had found and imprisoned them inside the temple. Or perhaps killed them, to insure that they wouldn't interfere with the morning's festivities.

"Hurry up!" The bearded man barked and jabbed his boot into Cordelia's leg. Juan leaped to her defense with a wild swing, then careened into the wall when the guard backhanded him across the mouth.

"Hey!" Cordelia stood and dusted herself off before checking to make sure her new and probably temporary champion-in-crisis was okay. The artist met all the revised romantic specifications she had adopted since the traumatic breakup with Xander. He was handsome, accomplished, not a teenager, available, and attracted to her.

When Giles caught the bearded boot looking his way, he urged Joyce to her feet. "Cooperation would be best for the time being."

"I have no intention of—"

"Joyce—" Giles looked at her pointedly. "We won't be able to take advantage of the right moment should one arise if we're drugged into a stupor or beaten unconscious."

"Do you have any idea how annoying it is that you're always right?" Smiling bravely, she slipped her high-heeled shoes back on and walked ahead as the guards herded everyone into the plaza.

Giles's eyes quickly adjusted to the erratic light of blazing torches.

The courtyard was a circus of celebration to herald the birth of Tezcatlipoca's regime. Humans drunk on the promise of power and immunity from the sacrificial knife formed a corridor to the temple steps. Black suggestions of evil entities frolicked in Giles's peripheral vision, and ghosts mingled with the living. Mr. Trick and a hungry horde of vampires boldly stood on the perimeter of the plaza.

On top of the temple, Dem sat on the stone throne holding his fan and arrows. Lucy stood by the rounded altar facing east with the black knife raised in defiance of the enemy sun. Four men waited behind the stone. The obsidian mirror rested in a recess in the wall of the rear structure, and the jaguar lounged on his perch above. The stage was set against a backdrop of pitch-black night. The hour before dawn was not any darker than midnight, Giles thought ruefully, but right now it damn well felt like it.

Quiet shrouded the group of intended sacrifices as the guards stopped them near the rack bearing the heads of previous victims. A dozen empty pikes had been added. Joyce stared at the grotesque display and felt some of the tension drain out of her. Buffy's head wasn't there.

Xander shoved his hands in his pockets as they were driven closer together and surrounded by the dark lord's army of guards and worshippers. "So—do we take a number or what?"

Oz tightened his protective hold on Willow. "Dem told Willow she'd be first, but I'll make them take me instead. Somehow."

"Good because I hate going first." Cordelia shivered and pressed closer to Juan.

"Oz, you can't." Willow nervously nibbled her lower lip and shrugged. "What difference does it make if I, uh, go first or second or third? I mean, I don't want to die and—and I won't because I have faith. In Buffy—"

Terrified squeals drew everyone's gaze as Sienna, Chance, Bart, and Kilya were pushed out of the crowd into the victim holding pen.

"Welcome to the menu." Xander scowled. "Now Tezcatlipoca can choose from columns A and B. Those who had a last meal and those who didn't."

Shock shattered Tezcatlipoca's influence over the teens. Chance absently tried to silence the hysterical Sienna. Bart hung his head and wept. Denial momentarily blinded Kilya to the realization that she had been duped.

"Hey! What's the big idea? We're on your side!" Kilya raged at the traitorous mob until Cordelia tapped her on the shoulder.

"I'll take that." Cordelia whipped the pith helmet off Kilya's head and put it on as she marched back to Juan. Speechless, Kilya just stared. No one was paying attention when four guards approached from the temple steps and seized Willow.

"Oz, no!" Heels dragging on pebbled stone, Willow struggled as two guards pulled her away. Her initial fear was not for herself but for Oz, who fought like a one-man pack of wolves to save her. He didn't stand a chance. The crowd had flowed around the others so they couldn't help, and Oz went down under three large men, kicking and screaming until they pounded him to silence. Xander, Cordelia, Joyce, and Juan finally managed to break through the crowd to pull the crazed men off him. He wobbled when he got to his feet, yet he still tried to run after her. Xander and Juan held him back, and his eyes filled with anguish as he met her gaze.

Giles lunged toward her, a hopeless act of chivalry that rewarded him with a spear driven into his thigh. She stopped fighting as he sank to his knees. One of the many things she had learned during her years as a Slayerette was that it was better to face death with dignity than to grovel in fear.

She almost believed it.

The crowd started to chant. "Tezcatlipoca, master of the depths, ruler of the dark, mercy to your humble servants."

Willow was petrified as she started up the steps with her head held high. Taking a dive off the pyramid was still an option, but the idea of turning to mush on hard stone had lost much of its appeal watching Dem pulp apples against the wall. So the least she could do was make the whole ugly, sacrifice business easier on the people who cared about her—as easy as watching a friend's heart get cut out and fed to a jaguar could be. Which was probably not possible. Letting Lucy carve her up like a holiday goose without screaming and making a fool of herself probably wasn't possible, either. So she just had to believe that it wasn't going to happen.

Which got harder the higher she climbed with no hint that Buffy and Angel were nearby. But then—they wouldn't spoil the element of surprise by dropping hints, would they? *Hey, bad guys! Here we are. Lying in wait to save the day.* Literally. Of course not.

Willow kept that thought in mind as the guards shoved her toward the altar. Her confidence fluttered under Dem's superior, hostile glare. When two men grabbed her wrists and pulled her back over the large, rounded butcher rock, she told herself it wasn't the last second just yet. Her eyes widened and a short cry escaped her throat as Lucy raised the knife and opened her hand.

When Angel and Buffy burst out of the wide doorway, Willow was slightly stoned on *yauhtli* powder and beyond worry.

Dem's excited euphoria evaporated in a frenzy of fang and fist. He cursed the search parties that had failed to find the fugitives as Angel barreled into one of the guards. He felt no sympathy as the man tumbled down the steps. The second guard panicked and tripped over a smoking brazier before fleeing after his partner. The incompetent coward deserved to be caught and drained of blood by the vampire that pursued him.

Dem's anger toward the guards abated when Buffy flattened the two altar attendants standing behind the stone. She had not fled as he had assumed, but had recklessly charged back into the dark lord's domain. Her audacious affront to Tezcatlipoca's honored *ixiptla* would be avenged.

Confronted by the Slayer, the two men holding Willow let go and ran. Buffy leaped over the stone and wrenched the knife from Lucy's hand as Willow slid to the floor.

"Get out of here, Willow." Fisting the knife, Buffy held the High Priestess off while Willow wobbled to her feet, using the stone for support.

"I knew you'd come, Buffy, but that was *tooooo*

close." Willow spoke slowly, her normal babbling speed reduced to a drawl. She shook her head, then frowned, bewildered by the effects of the Aztec drug. "I held my breath, but—guess *that* didn't work. But—I've still got my heart, huh?"

Lucy lunged for the knife. Buffy planted her foot on the woman's chest and shoved. As the High Priestess reeled backward and fell, Buffy stiffened and looked up into the glittering eyes of the jaguar.

The demon's rage flowed into Dem through the psychic bond, investing him with the ancient being's sense of invincibility and strength, and his overwhelming craving for Willow's heart and the Slayer's death.

Buffy spun and ducked as the jaguar sprang off the roof. She narrowly avoided being taken down, but the cat's claws ripped open her shoulder and she dropped the knife. Tezcatlipoca crouched as she backed away, focused on the beast, blood staining her shirt.

Dem's arrows and fan dropped from his hands as he ran toward Willow and slammed the drug-dazed girl back against the altar stone. "Get the knife, Lucy! Get the knife!"

Buffy watched the jaguar, trying to judge its next move, reminding herself that it wasn't a cat but a demon in feline fur with a vested interest in making sure she didn't live to cause any more trouble. At least Angel was no longer at the temple. He had gone to free Giles and the other prisoners and was currently drop-kicking guards and vampires around the lower plaza. As long as he stayed on the ground, his destruction on the temple steps as foretold in her dream couldn't happen.

One less worry, one less distraction—except that

Angel's salvation meant that other aspects of the prophetic vision might also change. A faint glow teased the eastern horizon, but the sun wasn't up . . . yet. And at the moment, Tezcatlipoca had the advantage.

The cat had advanced slowly after the first attack, pushing her back to the edge of the pyramid. Now it crouched, waiting, maliciously playing on her nerves before it sprang for the kill. The wound in her shoulder throbbed painfully and she was exhausted from dodging search parties most of the night. All of which was made ten times worse because Willow was still in danger and wasted on Aztec happy powder.

The jaguar's ears flicked back.

Buffy tensed, then almost lost her balance when Dem charged and flattened Willow against the altar stone. A rush of adrenaline drowned out his shouted words as she threw her weight forward to keep from falling off the pyramid. Grit bit into her palms as she hit stone on all fours and froze.

The jaguar snarled a warning, but it didn't charge. Its attention had shifted to the imminent slaughter of Willow Rosenberg.

Crazed with a lust for blood, Lucy scrambled forward and closed her fingers around the hilt of the knife. She stumbled to her feet and eased up behind Dem. The boy straddled Willow using both hands to pin her wrists to the stone. Lucy loomed over him and drew back the knife to strike, but Dem's body blocked a clear shot to Willow's heart.

Buffy gathered her feet under her.

"No!" Willow yelled. The sight of the black blade gleaming above had apparently dissipated some of her narcotic stupor.

Dem didn't move.

Buffy hesitated, poised to lunge.

"Let me go, Dem! Or—or you won't get out of here alive, either." Willow tried to pull free of Dem's hold and winced as he pressed down, grinding her wrists on the rough rock.

"Shut up!"

Buffy held her breath as the jaguar looked toward the altar and growled.

"Okay, but—but you *are* gonna die," Willow said breathlessly. "And . . . and if you don't believe me, well—just—just try to walk away, Dem. Go on. Try." Willow's chest heaved as she paused for air, her desperate gaze fastened on the knife.

"Move, Dem!" Lucy tried to shove him aside, but Dem stood fast. He flinched as he looked into Lucy's manic eyes.

The agitated jaguar twitched its tail and shifted position.

Buffy sensed Dem's uncertainty and waited, ready for anything. His link with Tezcatlipoca had been weakened but not broken, and the addictive properties of raw, unchallenged power were far more potent than any drug. Still, he wavered.

Lucy seemed to sense Dem's conviction slipping, too. Her gaze hardened and her hand flexed on the knife. Yet she hesitated until the jaguar roared, rejecting the *ixiptla* and releasing her to act. She drove the blade toward Dem's chest.

Dem released Willow to grab Lucy's wrist, but he couldn't stop the knife's downward thrust. Black stone honed to razor sharpness sliced his arm. He cried out but resisted the urge to cover the wound as Lucy jabbed at him again. His hand closed around her arm. He winced, tears welling in his eyes and blood oozing from his arm as he struggled to fend off the knife.

The jaguar leaped as Willow rolled sideways off the altar stone and collapsed, still groggy from the *yauhtli* powder. Buffy, anticipating the cat-god's savage response to losing its prey, was on her feet a few seconds before it became airborne. She threw herself at the beast, knocking him off his trajectory and almost knocking herself senseless. The screeching jaguar struck the rear wall, shaking the mirror in its alcove.

Tezcatlipoca's angry yowl snapped Lucy's attention away from Dem for a fleeting, crucial instant. In pain and weakened from the loss of blood, he rocked back just as Willow dragged herself upright. Willow swayed unsteadily and squinted at his blood-soaked arm.

"You're hurt, but—like Buffy says, it's a long way from your heart. Which in this case is a really good—" Willow grunted as Dem yanked her away from the stone.

Lucy hesitated.

The stunned jaguar staggered to its feet and shook its head, then glared at the couple lurching toward the steps. Its eyes blazed like hellfire, and the night shuddered with its frenzied, demonic shriek. Lucy's demented expression reflected the beast's frantic urgency. She whirled suddenly and raced after Dem and Willow, wielding the ritual knife.

Hearts, Buffy remembered suddenly. Without ritually removed hearts Tezcatlipoca would not regain the magical power he needed to hold back the sun. Her alert gaze shifted to the black mirror in the stone alcove, then to the east. The gray light of dawn flirted with the waning night, but sunrise was still several minutes away.

Tezcatlipoca was only a few feet away, between her and the mirror that was his haven from the light. The cat stared, silently intent, his gleaming fangs bared. He didn't need human hearts to maintain the jaguar's predatory strength.

Riddled with aches, bruises and bleeding slashes, Buffy fought a sudden dizziness and met the demon's glittering eyes.

In a few minutes, when he was forced back into the mirror, she could seize and break the dark glass—if she wasn't torn to shreds in the interim.

Chapter 17

Giles slammed his fist into the bearded boot's jaw. The guard crumpled to the ground as a rock zoomed by Giles's nose.

"Oops! Sorry, Giles!" Xander winced sheepishly, then staggered when a woman in shredded Aztec clothing rammed him in the back with her head.

Winded and in pain from the wound in his thigh, Giles couldn't spare a second to respond. The old man in the baseball cap charged with his trusty trowel drawn back like a knife. Giles caught Henry's thin wrist and disarmed him.

"Hey! That's mine!"

"You're in time out." Giles pushed the pouting senior citizen under the trophy-head rack where Joyce had taken refuge to catch her breath. He noted the darkening bruise under her eye without comment as he handed her the trowel. "If he moves—shovel him."

Joyce nodded and threatened the old man with her

mad-mom look. Henry folded his arms and slumped in surrender.

A flying body collided with Giles, throwing him onto the sidelines of the fray. Since Willow's seemingly interminable walk to the altar stone, the situation had quickly changed from tense waiting to brawling chaos, beginning with Angel's rampage down the pyramid steps. Confronted with a raging vampire, the cult faction had momentarily fallen back, allowing the prisoners to launch an offensive. The ensuing pandemonium had incited the starving vampires into joining the battle without concern for their victims' allegiance. As near as Giles could tell, only Tezcatlipoca's followers, untrained in the art of fighting the undead, had fallen to vampire fangs. It was difficult to keep the players straight in the capricious light of flaming torches.

Wresting a spear from a guard, Xander broke the shaft over his knee and impaled a vampire as it was about to bite Sienna. The girl shrieked and ran, frantically shaking undead dust out of her tangled hair. Xander threw up his hands in disgust. "I finally make a totally cool Slayer move and nobody notices!"

"I noticed." Angel growled and tossed another vampire into the side of the thatched hut. The impact dislodged a torch, setting the vamp on fire.

"Could I have a statement to that effect in writing?" Xander shouted as Angel drove two more vamps away.

Trapped in the thick of the melee, Cordelia, Juan, and Oz stood back to back, repelling wild-eyed cult members swinging at anyone within reach. A chubby woman crawled through the forest of legs, grabbed Cordelia's ankle and pulled. Cordelia bashed her over the head with the pith helmet, then gloated as she flipped the dented hat back onto her head.

"Nobody messes with me, lady. Nobody."

The flattened woman groaned and crept away.

Taking their cue from the Slayerettes, Bart and Kilya fought from a similar configuration a few feet away. Giles scanned for Chance and couldn't locate him, but his sweeping gaze caught sight of Mr. Trick in the shadows beyond the conflict.

"Willow!" Oz yelled and broke from his battle position.

Giles glanced at the temple as he cautiously moved toward the current leader of Sunnydale's vampire population. Dem and Willow stumbled down the steps with Lucy in pursuit. He didn't see Buffy, but the rear portion of the high platform was obscured by his low angle of sight. If she was in trouble, he couldn't help. However, he had a tactical ace that might tremendously improve matters at ground level.

"Mr. Giles." Mr. Trick smiled contemptuously. "Enjoying the party?"

Exhausted, hurting, and worried, Giles was not in the mood for casual barbed banter. "A bloody lot more than you will be in a few minutes, I dare say." To impress the point, he looked at the graying eastern sky, then over his shoulder as Dem and Willow reached the plaza several strides ahead of Lucy. Oz shoved Dem aside and gathered Willow into his arms. "I see Ms. Rosenberg still has custody of her heart."

Mr. Trick frowned, no doubt arriving at the same conclusion he had. Denied the hearts from the ritual sacrifices, Tezcatlipoca had already lost his war with the sun.

"I estimate dawn will officially commence in eight minutes, give or take a few seconds," Giles said calmly. "It would seem the party's over."

"So it would seem." Mr. Trick's face morphed instantly. "However, I'd hate to leave without sampling the refreshments."

Giles held the vampire's grotesque gaze. "Seven minutes and forty-five seconds."

"Another time, perhaps." Reverting to his human disguise, Mr. Trick nodded and flowed into the dark. His absence did not go unnoticed. All the undead vanished from the plaza to seek reliable cover, as Giles headed back toward the temple. But the situation was far from stabilized.

Juan and the teens had separated from the mob, and stood together near the head rack. Sienna ignored Chance when he emerged from under an overturned table and sidled up to Xander, who remained as disinterested and aloof as a worker bee that had just found the nectar mother lode.

"So like, how did you do that thingie with the stick, Xander? That was, like, way too cool. I mean, that creepy guy was gonna kill me and then he was, like, totally gone."

"Nothing to it really"—Xander pulled the spear stub from his back pocket and jabbed at the air—"for a veteran vampire killer. It's all in the wrist. And the *thwap!"* He jabbed again, stopping the motion abruptly. "The *thwap* is critical. I'm convinced. Absolutely."

While the Slayerettes seemed to have forgiven the four students Dem had maneuvered into the cult, Dem was *persona non grata.* Cordelia made their collective position caustically clear.

"Adios, Dem. And if you see me in school, pretend you didn't. I will."

Dem's slight nod before he moved away indicated an

acceptance of guilt, conviction, and punishment with a dignity he had not possessed prior to the ordeal.

With the vampire threat removed, the cult members milled about listlessly, too tired, battered, and disheartened to rally to Lucy's impassioned speech from the steps. Deprived of Willow and Dem, she darted to the severed-head display, grabbed Joyce and put the knife to her throat.

Joyce gripped Lucy's arm, but couldn't disengage herself.

"One heart and Tezcatlipoca can sustain the dark and beat the Slayer!"

Most of Tezcatlipoca's converts sat down to nurse their wounds or wandered away, perhaps snapped back to their senses by their near-death encounters with the vampires. When the jaguar roared, others gazed upward with the enthusiasm of slugs fenced in by salt.

"Buffy!" Angel raced out of his sanctuary in the thatched hut.

Giles swallowed hard as his gaze found Buffy. She stood precariously close to the front edge of the pyramid. The drop from her position to the left of the steps was almost vertical, and the jaguar was effectively blocking her attempts to move out of danger. He wondered why the cat didn't charge. It may have realized the Slayer could not be startled or bullied into taking a fatal misstep.

Or perhaps it was waiting, torn between escaping into the mirror and the possibility of consuming an empowering heart. One heart would buy enough additional darkness for Lucy to take another heart, and then another from the unsuspecting dig volunteers who had enabled events to progress this far. With each succeeding sacrifice, Tezcatlipoca's power would grow, until he was invincible.

Giles looked at the lightening sky as Angel ran past, but he didn't try to stop the vampire's headlong dash up the steps. Nothing could divert Angel from going to Buffy's aid, and Joyce's life was hanging by seconds.

Buffy's mother clung to Lucy's arm, but she didn't struggle. *Wise,* Giles thought, as he cautiously advanced. The High Priestess was psychotically obsessed, and he had no doubt that she would use the knife without provocation, whether to cut Joyce's throat or to cut out her heart.

Being engaged in a staring contest with the jaguar was just fine with Buffy, even though the cat had backed her to the edge of the landing again. Apparently, Tezcatlipoca needed a break, too, and the respite from an ongoing physical fight had boosted her depleted energies. Her shoulder ached, but the bleeding had stopped. She could probably repel another attack without taking the sky-dive express off the pyramid. Still, the prolonged waiting game was disconcerting. The battle noises below had ebbed, but she didn't dare let down her guard to look.

The cat forfeited, anxiously twitching its tail as its gaze darted toward the steps.

With her eye on the cat, Buffy risked taking a step forward, then another to the right toward the stairs. She stopped when the cat tensed suddenly, but she didn't realize it wasn't reacting to her movements until Angel bounded up the last few steps to the landing. A desperate panic seized her. The dawn she had fought so hard to save was imminent, and Angel was back on the pyramid.

"Angel—"

He raised a hand, warning her to stay back as he locked eyes with Tezcatlipoca. "Where's the mirror?"

"On that wall." Buffy nodded toward the squat rear structure.

Tension rippled through sleek black hide as the jaguar snarled.

"I'll get it," Angel said bluntly.

"No, I will! The sun—"

Angel was adamant. "As soon as Tezcatlipoca goes back into the glass, I'll take the mirror into the temple and break it."

Buffy faltered. Angel would be cutting it close, but daylight couldn't breach the interior of the pyramid. Even so, the jaguar remained a threat. It had been a long, exhausting night for Angel, too, and he had not come through his battle with the other vampires on the plaza unscathed. He was covered with cuts and bruises and looked as tired as she felt. If the cat injured or incapacitated him before he got to cover—

"Go on, Buffy. Your mom needs help."

Further protest stalled in Buffy's throat as she looked down and saw the knife hovering at her mother's neck. Giles was slowly moving toward Lucy. He hesitated suddenly. The insane woman was a loose canon with a short fuse and he was obviously afraid of provoking her.

"Okay. I'm going." She had no choice.

A curt nod and Angel's beautiful face was lost in the hideous distortions of the vampire. He taunted the cat with a menacing snarl, distracting it.

Buffy darted to the steps, tormented by the dream and the brightening horizon, driven by the fear that her mother would die before she reached the ground.

She was halfway down the steep stairway when the stone began to shake.

* * *

Angel felt the tremor just before the jaguar leaped. Feline claws raked his chest and arms as he threw his weight into the massive body. He staggered from the force of the collision, his strength drained, the fresh wounds in his cold flesh burning. The cat landed on its feet and crouched. Angel shook off the fatigue and glared into the cat's unblinking eyes. A black ear twitched, nostrils flared, muscles flexed—he braced for another charge.

The jaguar jumped straight up instead, yowling as a crack opened in the floor beneath it.

Angel faltered as another, stronger tremor rumbled through the pyramid, rattling a smoking metal brazier and toppling a stone idol. He reacted to the new danger with a single goal in mind—to stop the demon Tezcatlipoca permanently.

Spider cracks riddled the stone platform under Angel's feet as he dashed for the alcove and picked up the mirror. A shower of gritty mortar and pebbles flaked off the wall above him, and the supporting columns in the wide, temple doorway buckled. The structure's roof caved in as the columns collapsed, and tons of carved and painted stone crashed to the floor, sealing off his escape route.

Tezcatlipoca screeched and gave chase as Angel ran for the steps.

Giles felt the first vibration through the soles of his boots. His pulse quickened as Lucy's fingers tightened on the knife.

Joyce's eyes widened when the second, stronger tremor rumbled and rolled through the ground a moment later. A drop of blood appeared on her white skin where the blade nicked her.

"Whoa." Xander's gaze shot toward the ground. "The big bad magic-fingers monster is back."

Willow clutched Oz's arm. "Okay—this is an earthquake, right?"

"Feels like and sounds like," Oz said evenly.

Xander nodded. "Must be an earthquake. We've already got a temple."

"Ohmigod!" Sienna squealed. "I can't do an earthquake now!"

Giles suspected it wasn't an earthquake, a theory based on the layers of sediment that had covered the five-hundred-year-old Spanish campsite and the presence of a secondary fault line in the area. However, his worry about the imminent geological assault was overshadowed by Joyce's predicament. Lucy seemed to take the trembling in the earth as a signal from her demon master to kill.

Giles charged even as he realized he probably wouldn't reach the manic woman in time.

"Feel the wrath of Tezcatlipoca!" Lucy raised the knife, defying the rising sun.

Joyce instantly twisted out of her captor's restraining hold, but the High Priestess was stronger, quicker, driven by a soulless madness. And she wasn't wearing high heels. Lucy's leg shot out, tripping Joyce as she tried to bolt. Joyce fell, striking her head on the hard stone plaza. Lucy was upon her with the ferocity of a famished hyena, rolling the stunned woman over and sitting astride her. The ebony blade hovered over her shoulder, cocked back—

Clenching his teeth against the knifing pain in his thigh, Giles dove across the intervening space and fell short as the knife descended.

Juan, Oz, and Xander raced forward, but they, too, had reacted too late.

Focused on the black blade, Giles was unaware of Dem until he suddenly appeared behind Lucy. The boy wrenched the knife from her hand and quickly backed off. Screaming with outrage, Lucy leaped off Joyce and whirled. She lunged as the earth heaved with an ominous groan. Dem lost his footing and fell. Locked into the momentum of her forward thrust, Lucy dropped on top of him.

Giles saw the knife slide into her chest just before the world exploded.

The stone steps rocked, bringing Buffy to her knees as Dem Inglese saved her mother from Lucy's knife. Her relief was shelved to savor later. The pyramid was crumbling underneath her.

"Buffy! Keep going! Get down!"

Buffy looked up, stricken as Angel started down the stairs with the gold-framed obsidian mirror under his arm and the jaguar a few paces behind. The cat halted at the edge of the landing and her shouted warning was lost in its deafening roar. The savage shriek seemed to reverberate off air thick with destruction and doom, before it was consumed by a roiling thunder emanating from everywhere.

A golden sheen spread across the horizon as the sun began its ascent.

Tezcatlipoca railed against his ancient enemy with another shrill scream, his bid for dark supremacy lost in a barrage of photons. Buffy clung to the trembling steps as black fur shimmered and dissolved into smoke.

Angel saw Tezcatlipoca whip into the air and held up the mirror, daring the defeated dark lord to enter. Stone cracked and disintegrated as daylight touched him, but his stance was steady, his resolve unshakable. The plume snaked around him, mingling with the wisps of smoke rising off his scorched skin. He stood unwavering as the blue-gray smoke streaked away, turned and raced back to vanish in the sunless depths of the black glass.

An unearthly wail rose above the rumbling din as ghosts and demon beasties were absorbed back into the realm of the Hellmouth.

Angel drove his fist into the mirror, cracking the glass as the sun's orb cleared the horizon and bathed the pyramid in lethal light.

"Angel!" Buffy screamed as the image in her dream became immutable reality.

The earth split open, blasting dirt and rock into the morning sky.

And Angel disappeared in a flash of light.

Chapter 18

Buffy stared at the empty space where Angel had stood an eternal moment ago. Dazed with despair, she would have kept staring if not for her mother's terrified scream and the muddy rain that obscured the killing sun. Her eyes widened as she looked down.

The dig site was gone, buried under tons of mud and rock spewing from a volcanic cone near what had been the base of the hill. The cone expanded steadily, growing in height and width at a phenomenal rate. The lower third of the hill had already been devoured. The incomplete outer areas of the reconstructed Aztec city were collapsing and sinking into a deepening sea of muck.

People screamed, floundering as they tried to swim through the thick, swirling soup. Others clung to large boulders or were carried away by swift, raging currents. Rolf and Carrie clung to the window openings in the prisoner hut with the mud rising around them. The thatched roof was engulfed in flames that flared briefly when a barrage of flying boulders annihilated the building. The graduate students were blasted into oblivion along with it. Burning straw and smoking adobe sputtered and sizzled as pieces fell into the mire.

The old man hugged a solitary stone column, struggling against the undertow that tugged at his legs, his baseball cap still plastered to his head. Covered in brown ooze, Xander, Sienna, Willow, and Oz sat on an overturned, wooden table with enough buoyancy to float on the dense muck. Just before the old man sank, Xander snagged his arm and held on as the makeshift raft dipped and bobbed over swells and eddies. Clinging to the roof of Mr. Coltrane's half-submerged red Dodge Colt, Bart, Kilya, and Chance were whisked away on cascading brown-water rapids.

"Get clear of the temple!" Giles shouted. He stood on a stone island that had once been part of the temple's lower landing and frantically waved toward the west.

Dem sprawled at Giles's feet, hanging onto the edge of the rocking stone. He screamed when the rack of skewered heads popped to the surface in front of him.

"Juan! Over here!" Joyce huddled on another, isolated stone platform that was quickly falling apart beneath her. She had lost one of her shoes.

Buffy blinked, more astonished by the sight of Juan and Cordelia paddling a primitive canoe toward her desperate mom than she was by the cataclysmic annihilation of an ancient Aztec city that had not existed the day before.

She quickly snapped out of her grieving daze and scrambled backward on hands and knees as the steps above her collapsed with a domino effect. The wave rushed toward her trailing a wake of dust and debris. A huge boulder crashed into the stairway above her, and the stone under her right knee fell away. Digging in with her fingers, she narrowly averted a plunge into the gaping hole and slid the rest of the way on her stomach. She scurried on all fours to the edge of the broken landing as Juan pulled her mother into the canoe.

"Mom! This way!"

Juan and Cordelia paddled furiously, making little headway until the canoe was caught in a swift current that carried it within arm's reach of Buffy. The craft was swamped when Juan grabbed her hand. Drenched in mud, Cordelia and Joyce crawled onto the landing.

Cordelia wiped the gunk away from her eyes, muttering, "This is a good thing. Considering what some people pay for mud baths, my complexion should look dazzling tomorrow. If I live that long."

Juan smiled and bellyflopped onto the stone as the canoe vanished below the murky surface.

Buffy raised an eyebrow. "Okay, so where did you get a boat in an Aztec city?"

"Tenochtitlan was built on Lake Texcoco," Juan said. "I have done very many paintings of it. The Aztec fought Cortez's big warships from canoes. Unsuccessfully, of course."

"So," Cordelia added, "since this temple place was part of Tenochi—whatever, Juan went looking and found one. Good thing he's so smart, huh?"

"Good thing Tezcatlipoca was a stickler for detail and authenticity." Joyce tossed her remaining shoe into the roiling mud, then frowned as the landing bucked. She was, however, remarkably calm, considering her new designer dress was a filthy tattered ruin. "Now what?"

"We get out of here." Buffy crawled toward the western side of the platform, which was still connected to the pyramid. Although the center portion of the temple had caved in, most of the structure was still standing. For how long was anybody's guess. The strange volcano was still spitting out debris and dirt, and the rising mud was quickly consuming the complex. The mud level around Giles and Dem had risen above their ankles, and the separated segment of stone they stood on wobbled ominously.

"Giles!" Buffy paused opposite the librarian's position six feet away. "You've got to get over here! I know a way out!"

"It's too far to jump!" Giles looked at the raging mud flowing between them, judging the distance and shaking his head. If they fell in, the current would sweep them away or drag them under.

Buffy glanced at Juan and Cordelia. "Anyone willing to give up their pants?"

"Sure." Juan immediately began to strip off his soggy, mud-caked jeans.

"Juan!" Cordelia looked at him aghast, then shrugged. "Never mind. Better you than me."

"I have jogging shorts on! See?" Juan laughed and tossed the jeans to Buffy. His bright blue running shorts were instantly spattered with muddy drizzle. "I sometimes sketch all day from dawn to dusk. This way I'm prepared for the midday heat."

"I just adore intelligent men," Cordelia said.

Holding on to one pant leg, Buffy flipped the other to Giles. The librarian gave the end to Dem. Taking a deep breath, Dem clamped onto the denim life rope and jumped for the solid ledge. He landed with inches to spare.

Giles missed and was instantly caught in the current.

When the jeans reached their spread-eagled limit and snapped taut, he almost lost his grip. Buffy was yanked off her feet. Juan grabbed her legs before she was dragged into the churning muck and they slowly reeled in Giles.

"Thank you, although that hardly seems sufficient." Giles paused to still his pounding pulse and labored respiration rate. "Any sign of Willow and Xander? Oz?"

Buffy shook her head. "Last time I saw them they were table surfing."

"I see." Giles winced as he stood up, favoring his injured leg and struggling for balance on the shimmying stone. "Yes, well—I, uh—have some additional bad news. We won't be safe here much longer."

A boulder bombed a large, painted snake statue a few feet away, pulverizing the stone.

Point taken, Buffy thought ruefully.

"He's right, Buffy." Joyce shielded her eyes against the bits of grit and mud still raining from the sky. "The temple is surrounded by mud."

"Only on three sides," Buffy said, "if my guess is correct."

"You're thinking of the higher elevation on the southern side of the hill, behind the temple." Giles took off his glasses and reached for his shirttail to clean them, an ingrained habit whenever he was mulling over a problem. Realizing the wet, dirty material was useless he wiped the mud off the lenses with his finger.

"It's a *lot* higher. I know. I climbed it yesterday."

"Yes, but—" Giles glanced at the mud-streaked lenses and put the glasses in his mud-filled shirt pocket. "We can't get around the pyramid to reach it."

"Going around the pyramid isn't what I had in

mind," Buffy said. "I was thinking of going through it."

"Okay, let's figure out where we're at here." Xander glanced at the four pairs of eyes watching him intently. Now that the mud had started to dry, Willow, Oz, Sienna, and Henry looked like hybrids of the Swamp Thing and Desert Pete. "We abandoned the table because it was sinking and we didn't want to drown in mud."

"Right. And the point?" Oz asked.

"Yeah." Sienna frowned. "I mean, we like made it to dry land, didn't we?"

"The point is—" Xander glanced around their haven, which would be totally dark as soon as the last, barely burning torch died. "We took shelter in a huge stone pyramid that is about to come crashing down around us."

Everyone tensed as a rumbling tremor shook more mortar loose from the stones.

Willow sighed. "That is a good point . . . actually."

Oz nodded. "Except that there wasn't anywhere else to go."

Xander silently conceded. The flat, rectangular building at the front corner of the temple had been their only port when the U.S.S. Banquet Table had gone to her grave at the bottom of the deep brown sea. The room seemed to be connected to the main temple by a series of passageways, but he had voted against moving into them. The lone torch was about to burn out, and although it didn't matter if they were buried under a few tons of rock or thousands, they had access to the outside from their present location. At least until the small chamber began filling with mud.

"I don't know what I'm doin' here in the first place," Henry said, bewildered.

"You don't remember?" Xander squinted skeptically.

"Nope. One minute I'm scrapin' dirt off some old sword and the next thing I know, I'm hangin' onto a stone post in the middle of a mud storm. Strangest thing I ever saw. Raining mud and rocks—" Henry scratched his forehead under his hat, then patted his soaking, Aztec cape. "I lost my trowel. Can't dig without a trowel."

"If this temple is about to do the Jericho thing, I don't think a trowel will help much."

"Probably not." Buffy entered the chamber, followed by everyone else who was important in Xander's scheme of things. Even Dem, who had snapped out of his "I'm a god, you're not" attitude and saved Willow and Buffy's mom.

"Buffy!" Willow grinned. "Buffy's here. I feel better now."

"Is everyone okay?" Giles asked. "Any injuries?"

"I would have appreciated a flash-mud warning, but other than that, we're fine." Xander glanced at Henry. "Although Henry here doesn't remember much about recent events."

"I lost my trowel." Henry frowned.

"Yes, well—" Giles studied the old man, then glanced at Sienna. "What do you remember?"

"It was a great party and then, like—the world threw up."

"Couldn't have said it better myself." Xander noted Cordelia's less-than-spectacular appearance. Mud dripped off the brim of her pith helmet, which now sported a significant dent in the crown. Juan was hovering beside her, and didn't seem to care that she looked like the loser in a mud-wrestling match.

Sienna shrieked as a sizeable rock hit the roof, shaking loose grit and shifting stone.

Buffy lifted the sputtering torch out of its holder. "Time to move."

"Uh—" Xander hesitated as she stepped toward the narrow corridor leading into the temple. "Where to? I mean, I'm not high on having my remains displayed in an excavation exhibition a hundred years from now."

"Cool tabloid headline, though." Oz smiled. "Twenty-First-Century Teen Found in Aztec Ruins."

"There's an exit to the outside at the back of the pyramid. I know because I spent all night exploring these passageways with Ang—" Buffy turned abruptly and disappeared into the stone tunnel.

"It's the only way to get above the sinkhole," Giles said.

"What sinkhole?" Xander asked.

"The one that's going to swallow this pyramid." Taking Joyce's hand, Giles ducked under the low doorway into the corridor.

"Oh. *That* sinkhole." Xander grabbed Sienna and hauled her into the dark.

During her explorations the night before, Buffy had figured out that the maze was not built as haphazardly as it appeared. Now she moved through the corridors with confidence, bearing back to the right immediately after being forced to turn left. She kept the pace to a brisk walk until they acquired additional torches from the connecting chambers. The extra light made it possible to jog without getting disoriented. Getting lost, however, was not what worried her. The pyramid was going to fall, and she didn't want to be under it when it did.

"What was that?" Sienna clung to Xander when a significantly more violent tremor vibrated through the stone floor.

No one mentioned the obvious, as though silence would somehow prevent or delay the geological forces from undermining the massive structure.

"How much farther, Buff?" Xander asked.

She wasn't sure. "Not far."

She broke into a slow run.

Giles started to fall behind, hindered by the wound in his leg, which had started bleeding profusely again. Juan and Oz slipped under his arms. The support allowed him to move faster than he could have on his own.

Dem clasped his injured shoulder. Blood seeped through his fingers, but he bore the pain and discomfort without a whimper, and without losing ground.

The elderly Henry Stemp managed to keep up, and had finally stopped fretting about his missing trowel.

A stone block fell out of the ceiling and crashed to the floor behind them. The sounds of destruction, which had been muffled by layers of temple rock, suddenly grew louder and closer.

When Buffy spotted a glimpse of light at the end of a long, straight passageway, she felt hopeful for the first time since the ordeal had begun yesterday afternoon. They actually had a chance to get out of this Aztec hell alive.

Then the walls began to crumble.

"Run!" Grabbing her mother's wrist, Buffy bolted through a moving obstacle course of falling rock and blinding dust.

"Ow." Joyce stumbled and grabbed her bare foot. Blood flowed from a fresh cut in her heel.

Buffy stopped and jumped back as the ceiling caved in just ahead—at the spot where they would have been passing. She didn't stop to think about the close call or the bizarre bit of life-saving luck as the rubble settled, leaving a narrow crawl space at the top.

Buffy boosted her mother through first, then Willow, Cordelia, and Sienna. She started to balk when Giles ordered her to go next, then chose not to waste crucial seconds arguing. Once on the other side, she tackled the obstruction with single-minded determination, hurling rocks until the space was wide enough to accommodate the men's larger frames.

Xander wiggled through with a scowl. "Sticking around now won't help us move any faster. Go!"

Buffy ran, dodging and ducking chunks of stone, spurred on as the lighted opening expanded ahead. Her lungs begged for air when she finally raced into the open, and she paused to cough up the dust clogging her throat.

Joyce, Willow, Cordelia, and Sienna sprawled on the side of the hill, all of them choking and trying to catch their breath.

"Can't rest here," Buffy insisted. "Come on."

Sienna moaned. "I'm too tired to take another step."

"Your call, Sienna." Buffy shrugged. "Move or go down with the temple. Doesn't matter to me."

"Move, Sienna!" Willow's eyes flashed a warning. "Or—or I'll drag you up that hill by your hair. I mean it. I'm not gonna lose sleep because you gave up and I didn't do anything about it. Not gonna happen."

"I'd just love an excuse to vent my hostilities on someone," Cordelia said.

"All right, all right! I'm moving!" Sienna started to crawl. Cordelia yanked her to her feet and gave her a shove for motivation.

"Where's Giles?" Joyce glanced at the exit. A curtain of falling pebbles and dust covered the opening. "And the others?"

"They're coming." Buffy urged her mother up the incline toward the ridge and looked back as Xander, Dem, and Henry stumbled into the clear. Xander grabbed Henry when he stopped to pick up what must have been a particularly interesting rock and ordered him up the rocky slope. Henry adjusted his baseball cap and climbed—under protest.

Seconds passed, a minute—no sign of Giles, Juan, or Oz.

Buffy focused on climbing until she reached the summit. Ignoring Sienna's complaints, she herded everyone into a circular configuration of rock higher up on the western side, beyond the pyramid that loomed over the ridge. Then, unwilling to abandon the missing men, she turned to go back.

"There they are!" Willow grinned, then gritted her teeth as the stragglers finally staggered out of the temple and started their ascent.

Buffy was relieved to see them, but since the geological processes playing out underground weren't finished yet, the rear guard was still in danger. However, now that they were in the open, there wasn't anything she could do to help. Worried, she sought distraction in a survey of the devastation.

"Hey!" Cordelia used her last ounce of energy to jump for joy. "My car's still there!"

Several people who had managed to escape the mud and falling rocks were running for their cars. Miraculously, the parking lot had survived relatively untouched. A pickup truck had been flattened by a boulder bomb, and another car was overturned. The rest were just covered in mud like everything else within a mile of the volcanic cone.

The reason for the destruction discrepancy between locations was easy to determine from Buffy's high point of view. The volcano had blown the supporting rock under the hill away in the initial blast, leaving the slope vulnerable to erosion from underneath. The hillside terrain had sunk lower than the parking area, and gravity had drawn the mud into the lowered elevation. Rock and debris were no longer shooting out of the cone, and the entire area from the dig site to the temple was awash in mud.

"Uh-oh." Willow started as the earth's incessant grumbling intensified. "I think I've got a really bad feeling about this."

"Down!" Buffy yelled. "Get down!"

"What's happening?" Joyce dropped to the ground and flattened.

Buffy didn't answer. She couldn't be heard over the thunderous roar as rock moved against rock along the fault line. The pyramid shuddered and groaned as she crawled forward to peer down the slope.

Xander and Dem scrambled the last few feet and tumbled into the protection of the rocky depression. Henry took his time completing the ascent, not because he was hurt or tired, but because he kept pausing to sightsee. Juan and Oz were only halfway up with Giles braced between them.

"Great! Ringside seats for the grand finale." Xander squatted beside Sienna. She didn't smile. "That was a joke."

"I'm, like, way too scared to laugh." Sienna buried her head in the hollow of his shoulder.

Cordelia eyed the girl askance. "Not exactly Slayerette material, is she?"

"No," Xander said pointedly, "but then I wasn't thinking of asking her to patrol the cemetery on our first date."

"Probably not a good idea," Willow said sincerely. "No offense, but—taking Sienna to the cemetery would be like, well—like putting out vampire bait. You know, like the way they use chopped up fish stuff to, uh—troll for sharks."

"Thanks for that analogy, Will. From now on, every time I look at Sienna I'll see fish heads."

"I went shark fishing once." Henry scratched his unshaven chin. "When I went down to visit my sister in Florida a few years back. Didn't catch one."

"That's a shame." Xander glanced back at Dem, who sat by himself on the far side of the enclosure. "How's the shoulder, Dem?"

"It's okay. Thanks." Dem locked his gaze on the pyramid as large sections of the tiered sides began to break off.

"How's Oz doing, Buffy?" Willow asked. "I can't look."

"They're almost here." Buffy watched Giles' slow and painful progress and fought an impulse to scramble down the slope. The ground quakes were growing more violent and she'd only make things worse if she fell. A major tremor rattled her teeth and sent a cascade of small rocks tumbling down the steep grade. The climbers tucked their heads but couldn't avoid being pelted by the rocky deluge. Juan swayed when a large stone struck his head, but he kept his footing.

Her mother moved up beside her and whispered earnestly, "Get your butt up here, Giles."

Buffy smiled, wondering—not for the first time—if her mom's feelings for the sometimes dashing, always charming, mostly proper librarian went deeper than she let on. As Giles pulled himself onto the ledge and rolled down into Joyce's arms, she decided—as usual—that she really didn't want to know.

A sharp crack louder than a sonic boom applauded Juan and Oz as they clambered into the dubious safety of the rock bowl.

Buffy thought she was beyond sheer astonishment after all she had seen in the past few years, but she gawked as the back of the huge pyramid split down the middle. The fissure widened, revealing the Coyote Rock formation imbedded within the stone. The side tiers separated from the building and crashed into the mud rising like a berserk tide around the base. The force of the impact vibrated through the hill. Aware that their high refuge could just as easily break away and fall, no one moved or spoke as the massive temple imploded.

The sacrificial stone rolled down the canted upper platform and into the center maw. The broken remains of the two small structures plunged straight down as the perimeter walls caved in. A cloud of dust and debris rose and hovered as the ruins began to sink. Brown mire swirled, dragging tons of stone into a voracious vortex.

Silence prevailed among the witnesses until the last remnants of the temple disappeared and the roiling whirlpool settled into a calm lake of thick mud.

"That was interesting." Xander casually folded his arms and peered down.

"Damn right about that, son." Henry nodded.

"Is it over?" Sienna whined.

Oz glanced over the edge. "I'd say so."

"No! It's not!" Willow gasped. "The mirror! What happened to the obsidian mirror and Tezcatlipoca and—"

"Tezcatlipoca's history." Buffy spoke more sharply than she had intended and softened her tone as she continued. "For good this time. Angel broke the mirror after the jaguar smoked back into it."

"You're sure?" Giles asked.

"Positive," Buffy said. "The sun is safe—until it goes nova a few billion years down the line."

"I'm thrilled." Xander smiled.

"But what—I mean, where—" Willow hemmed and hawed with more anxious uncertainty than usual. "So, uh, where's Angel?"

"Angel's gone." Buffy met her mother's concerned gaze for a fleeting moment, then looked away.

"Gone like see-ya-later gone or—" Xander hesitated, his question answered by the empty look in Buffy's eyes.

Gone like ashes to ashes. . . .

Gone.

Chapter 19

Buffy paused on the school steps as the sun dipped lower in the western sky. She felt warmed knowing it would rise again tomorrow, but chilled because she had paid such a great price for that assurance.

Angel was dead.

Forever this time.

She had mourned him before, and she had mourned him alone. Neither Giles nor her friends had known that Willow's spell had restored his soul a moment before she'd shoved the sword into his body and sent him to hell with Acathla. It wouldn't have mattered. His crimes against them as Angeles could not have been forgiven then. She hoped they could be forgiven now.

That was the only thing that would make the loss tolerable—that and the thought that he may have redeemed himself with his selfless act.

Ironically, his legacy was the sun that had killed him.

The sound of her bootheels on the corridor floor drew her out of her numb reverie. No sad faces allowed. Never again would Tezcatlipoca stalk the earth plotting to bring about eternal night. A celebration was in order. Nobody had to know the depth of her sorrow.

"I think we should call it Tezcatlipoca's revenge." Xander lounged on the steps to the upper tier.

"What?" Buffy asked as she strode smiling into the library.

"The mud volcano." Willow looked up from the computer.

"So it really was a volcano." Buffy sat in the only vacant chair beside Cordelia. "But was it a normal, natural phenomenon or something Tezcatlipoca cooked up to get back at us?"

"Natural, yes," Oz said. "Not so normal."

"Mud volcanoes are somewhat rare, actually. Hello, Buffy." Giles hobbled out of his office and set an open book on the table. "How are you?"

"Fine." Buffy smiled tightly as everyone looked away or shifted uncomfortably. "What about you? And Dem? How'd you make out at the hospital?"

"We'll both recover with minor scars. They're keeping Dem overnight for observation, however."

"Complications?" Buffy looked around for the doughnuts, didn't see any, and sat back.

"Emotional trauma mostly." Giles took off his glasses and used a handkerchief to clean them. "Unlike the mass converts, Dem and Lucy experienced Tezcatlipoca's personality through a direct link. They were not totally responsible for their actions."

"That's no excuse," Cordelia scoffed.

"Perhaps not." Giles replaced his glasses and began pacing. "However, we should remember that Dem was the *ixiptla*. Tezcatlipoca literally integrated himself with Dem's emotional and mental processes. The fact that Dem broke the connection by the force of his own will is, quite honestly, astounding."

"I suppose." Willow frowned thoughtfully. "I guess I'm willing to give him another chance—to be friends. He did save me from Lucy at the last minute, even though he almost, well—you know, almost—"

"We know." Oz patted her hand.

"I doubt Buffy's mother would be alive if he hadn't intervened." Giles placed a hand on Buffy's shoulder and removed it quickly when she winced. "Did you see a doctor?"

"It's just a scratch. Jaguar. Nothing to worry about." Buffy's pointed gaze demanded that no one worry.

Xander took the hint. "So none of the others remember anything that happened?"

"Most of those that survived have no recollection. Others seem to remember certain aspects of the events that are part of their usual routine. Sienna remembering the party, for instance." Giles smiled, amused. "And Henry finally recalled what became of his trowel."

"Too bad." Cordelia rolled her eyes. "One more jab and I would have shoved that little shovel through his stupid baseball cap."

"What did happen to it?" Xander asked. "Just for the record."

"I confiscated it, and Joyce lost it when the volcano erupted." Giles perched on the end of the table and folded his arms. "I've, uh—promised to buy him a new one. Strictly for use in his garden."

"Speaking of Sienna—" Buffy cast a mischievous glance at Xander. "Do you have a hot date tonight?"

"Actually, no. I've developed a mysterious allergy to the word 'like' and an aversion to dating vampire bait."

Xander paused awkwardly. "And because Sienna decided to give Chance another chance."

Buffy perked up. "Chance made it out alive? What about Kilya and Bart?"

"All in one piece, and all of them quitting the History Club." Xander sat up, brightening. "So since we're the only members left, we can meet here in the library as usual, but get *credit* for being in the History Club!"

"Works for me," Buffy said. "We do cover a lot of history, even though most of it isn't part of the approved curriculum. Right, Giles?"

"Yes, well—" Giles frowned uncertainly. "I suppose we could function under the guise of the History Club . . . at least until Mr. Snyder assigns a permanent faculty advisor."

"Whoa!" Willow tapped a few keys on the computer, her fascinated gaze on the monitor. "The Piparo mud volcano in Trinidad has a long history of eruptions."

"There you go." Xander settled back in a relaxed sprawl on the short stairway.

"It's going to blow up again?" Cordelia scowled. "It took me three hours to wash all that mud out of my hair!"

"Probably not in the near future. Perhaps not for a few centuries." Giles flipped through the book on the table. "Mud volcanoes can form under several different sets of geological conditions. In this case, I believe large quantities of water from the torrential rains that uncovered the archaeological site were trapped in the underlying stratified rock. Movement along the fault line no doubt triggered the eruption this morning. In fact, I think it's entirely possible the same mud volcano buried the Spanish campsite five hundred years ago."

A lull developed following Giles's discourse. Buffy sighed, trying to work up the nerve to ask about Angel. It hadn't escaped her attention that no one had mentioned him. She just didn't know if it was out of deference to her grief or because they were secretly glad he was gone.

Unable to stand prolonged lapses in any conversation, Xander closed the window of silence. "So—what's everyone doing tonight?"

Cordelia grinned. "I'm going to Juan's reception at the gallery. As his date."

"I thought the reception was last night," Xander said.

Giles explained. "Seeing as how the hostess and the guest of honor were unable to attend last night, Joyce is holding the affair again."

"And I've got to get ready." Cordelia jumped up and looked at Willow. "Let me know as soon as you hear back, okay?"

Willow looked stressed. "Okay, I'll e-mail the company and ask, but—I'm pretty sure the guarantee doesn't cover combat damage."

"For a hundred and fifty dollars, it better! I can't hang a dirty, dented pith helmet in a dorm room at Stanford." Cordelia turned to Giles with a frown. "Are we still going to get credit for participating in an archaeological dig? Because I really need that notation on my transcript, even if we didn't actually dig up anything."

Giles nodded. "Yes, I'm quite comfortable giving credit for your intensive exposure to Aztec culture."

"Great!" Cordelia beamed. "See you at the gallery, Giles."

Willow sighed with exasperated resignation as Cordelia hurried out the door. "If Cordy tackles Stanford the way she tackles pith helmets, she'll graduate *magna cum laude.*"

"So will you, Willow," Oz said. "The question is whether you'll graduate *magna cum laude* from M.I.T."

"Well, my acceptance letter came today. They, uh—apologized because the one they sent before I wrote got lost in the mail, apparently." Willow shrugged. "But I—well, I don't know if I want to live in Massachusetts."

Buffy stared at the wood grain in the table. One of the results of Angel's sudden demise was a decision to take serious action regarding her future, including college. Giles would help her write query letters to appropriate schools. She just didn't want to deal with it today.

"Will you be going to the gallery tonight, Buffy?" Giles asked. "I'm afraid I don't mingle well with Sunnydale's social elite."

"Uh—no." Buffy shook her head. "I don't think so. I'm kind of tired."

This time Xander didn't break the strained silence. Oz took the plunge.

"Okay. I'm gonna go out on a limb here." Oz took a deep breath and leaned toward her. "Did you actually *see* Angel burn?"

"Well, uh—" The blunt question was unnerving and Buffy stammered. "Well, yes—I did. There was a flash, and he—"

Oz pressed. "I mean burst into flames and roast. Sorry, Buffy, but it could be important."

Buffy frowned as she replayed the event in her head. "No. A little smoke and charred skin, but no flames. Why?"

Oz had everyone's undivided attention.

"Well, because if there's any chance the sun *didn't* fry him, then he's buried in the mud. And since when is being buried all day a problem for a vampire?"

Xander jumped up. "Who's driving?"

Giles was the first one to the door.

* * *

Buffy shouldered her shovel and scanned the wide brown plain. The only evidence that Coyote Rock Hill had ever existed was the long, high ridge to the south, where they had taken refuge during the pyramid's final collapse.

"This isn't normal." Xander leaned on a large pickaxe, one of many tools he had packed in Oz's van for the camping trip that was essential to the current operation.

"No, quite the contrary." Confounded, Giles took a hesitant step onto the cracked, dry mud flat. The surface held his weight. They had expected to find a lake of muddy ooze.

"Maybe all the water just—well, drained away," Willow suggested. "Super fast . . . for some reason."

"Some weird effect of the Hellmouth?" Oz looked at Giles for confirmation.

"Possibly. I certainly don't have a scientific explanation." Giles glanced toward the west, suddenly nervous as the sun's orb touched the horizon. "If Angel is here, we must find him quickly and leave immediately at sundown. Before the other vampires that went underground dig out."

"They ran," Xander said.

"Yes, but they didn't have time to get far. This whole area will be overrun shortly after dark." Giles glanced at Buffy. "Can you locate him?"

Buffy exhaled. Her Slayer ability to sense the presence of vampires would locate any undead within range. She had a rough idea of where Angel was buried—if he was buried and not cinders.

"If there's a vamp out there, I'll know. I just won't know if it's Angel until he surfaces." She pulled a stake from her back pocket. "Just in case."

Giles nodded and motioned her to lead the way.

Buffy walked toward the ridge with a lighter heart. She

desperately wanted to believe Angel had survived, but in the event that he had not she had the comfort of knowing her friends had forgiven him. They hadn't said so in words, and might not even be consciously aware of it, but their genuine concern and actions were proof enough.

Buffy stopped fifty yards from the rock wall, where she estimated the pyramid steps had been, and closed her eyes. She felt the tension in the others as the sun slipped below the horizon, and she sensed a presence. "Over there."

"Let's get to it, then, shall we?" Giles drove his shovel into the ground.

They dug without speaking, as daylight segued into twilight and darkness slowly encroached.

Oz heard the scrabbling sounds of digging below ground first. "Somebody's down there."

"What if it's not Angel?" Willow asked uneasily.

"It better be Angel." Dirt flew off Xander's shovel as he dug faster. "I did this totally cool Slayer thing with a spear, and he's my only witness."

"Maybe we should stand back." Buffy fisted her stake and stared at the hole, her nerves so taut she could hardly breathe. The others stepped away and shifted their grips on the tools, to use them as weapons. She prayed it wouldn't be necessary.

When a hand broke through the dirt, Buffy's spirits plummeted. The skin was smooth, not charred. "This one's not burned."

"Vampires heal quickly, Buffy," Giles said calmly. "And the mud may have facilitated the process."

Buffy knew that, but she didn't dare let her hopes cloud her judgment or dull her reflexes. If the vamp wasn't Angel, the crushing disappointment might hinder her ability to react quickly to the threat.

"Here he comes." Willow covered her eyes with her hand and peeked through her fingers.

Buffy planted her feet farther apart, her hand flexing on the stake.

When the vampire burst upward with its distorted face covered in sticky mud, Xander cocked his pickaxe back.

Buffy recognized Angel instantly. She dropped her stake, jumped into the hole and threw her arms around him, so delirious with joy she forgot how dangerous intimate contact could be.

"Buffy—" Assuming his human countenance, Angel held her tightly and gently kissed her hair.

"So Buffy's dream did come true." Willow grinned, then frowned. "Only it didn't."

"More or less." Oz draped his arm over her shoulder and started back toward the parking lot.

"I do hate to break up the happy reunion, but we really must vacate the area." Giles didn't wait.

"The other vamps," Buffy explained as she and Angel climbed out of the hole. She retrieved her stake and shoved it back into her pocket with an apologetic shrug. Xander picked up her shovel and hurried to catch up to Giles.

Angel and Buffy lagged a little behind, together yet forever separated by the love that bound them. There were times when Buffy wished she had never met him, touched him, or known him. But this wasn't one of those times . . . tonight she allowed herself to be ecstatically happy that Angel was still in her world.

He glanced over his shoulder. "What happened to the temple?"

Buffy smiled. "The earth ate it."

About the Author

Diana G. Gallagher lives in Florida with her husband, Marty Burke, three dogs, three cats, and a cranky parrot. A Hugo Award–winning artist, she is best known for her series *Woof: The House Dragon.* Dedicated to the development of the solar system's resources, she has contributed to this effort by writing and recording songs that promote and encourage humanity's movement into space.

Her first adult novel, *The Alien Dark,* appeared in 1990. She and Marty coauthored *The Chance Factor,* a STARFLEET ACADEMY VOYAGER book. In addition to other STAR TREK novels for intermediate readers, Diana has written many books in other series published by Minstrel Books, *including The Secret World of Alex Mack, Are You Afraid of the Dark, and The Journey of Allen Strange.* She is currently working on original young adult novels for the Archway paperback series, *Sabrina, the Teenage Witch.*